Goodnight,
CINDERELLA

Goodnight,
CINDERELLA

RICHARD POSNER

M. EVANS & COMPANY, INC.   NEW YORK

Library of Congress Cataloging-in-Publication Data

Posner, Richard.
Goodnight, Cinderella.

Summary: Relates how a poor but hard-working seventeen-year-old girl wins her prince at the Senior Prom.
[1. Interpersonal relations—Fiction. 2. High schools
—Fiction. 3. Schools—Fiction.] I. Title.
PZ7.P8384Go 1989 [Fic] 89-17091

ISBN 0-87131-587-4

Illustrations by Laurie Zacarese

M. Evans and Company, Inc.
216 East 49 Street
New York, New York 10017

Manufactured in the United States of America

9 8 7 6 5 4 3 2 1

Chapter One

This is the story of a poor but hard-working girl who wins her prince at the Senior Prom. It's a fairy-tale romance for all young people who believe in true love and happy endings.

Once upon a time, a seventeen-year-old girl named Kimber lived with her father and brother in a distant kingdom called Long Island, in a town called Westfield. Kimber was small-boned and exuberant, with cascades of glossy hair, and chocolate eyes in a delicate face. Even though she worked in the Young Miss Shop in the mall, she couldn't afford fashionable clothes. Money was tight.

But Kimber never lost her energy, and her smile never faded. She kept up her grades in school, held down her job, and did all the cooking and cleaning at home. Smiling was tough sometimes, when she had to come home late, finish her homework, and drop to her knees to scrub the kitchen floor . . .

"Nice head! Like I'd really drop to my knees!"

Who said that?

"I did."

Kimber? You're a fictional character! You're not supposed to break into the narrative.

"Well, it was getting a little silly, no? I liked the part about being small-boned—nice way of saying I have no chest—but scrubbing the *floor*? Yeah, dressed in rags, with a babushka tied around my head . . ."

I was coming to that.

"No! What are you *telling* people? I wash the kitchen floor about once a month. And I vacuum the stuff Corey spills all over the place. But I don't even do *that* too often because the head fell off the electric broom and we can't afford a new one.

"Sure, I do the cooking and the cleaning, but not exactly with gusto. I run around with my spray can and my dust cloth, and I put the dishes into the dishwasher and a few thousand other chores which I really don't want to get into. It's bad enough, without dropping to my *knees*.

"And I don't wear rags. I wear a big Geneseo sweatshirt—which is probably where I'm going next year—and dungarees and old canvas shoes. Got the picture?"

Are you finished?

"*You* screwed up the facts. Some Omniscient Author you are. You could use a research assistant."

You know your literary terms.

"I took *notes* in English last year. I got accepted to Wesleyan, but I'm not going because they won't give me a scholarship. Anyway, go back to the story."

Maybe *you* want to tell it.

"No way. I do essays the period before, in the cafeteria. I'm the editor of the literary magazine, but that's because nobody else wanted to do it, and I needed a club so I wouldn't be kicked out of the Honor Society. Anyway, I'm not into lengthy narratives."

Well I am. So you don't mind if I go back to *this* one.

"Go ahead."

You're all heart. Anyway, Kimber Del Rey was counting the days . . .

"Who?"

I nearly finished a sentence that time.

"Sorry, but I was choking on my cola there. *What* was that name?"

Kimber Del Rey. I know I changed . . .

"Delaney! Kimber *Delaney.* It's Irish. Well, my Dad is Irish. My Mom is Hungarian. Where did you get Del Rey from?"

It sounded better for a fairy-tale romance. I'm the author, remember? I can rename you.

"I can't *wait* for the rest of this. How come if you're changing things, I don't get to have honey blonde hair and green eyes flecked with amber? And call me Tasha. I'd rather be Tasha than Kimber Delaney with chocolate eyes (do they come with almonds?)."

This is crazy. I made you up and you're offended.

"I don't get offended. It's like you said, I bounce right back. 'You're always so *perky*,' everyone says. Deena breaks into tears if I'm cranky. And Lou gets *extremely* frustrated. You want to read about *that* scenario?"

I know about that scenario. But it doesn't come this early in the . . .

"Okay, I'm in the cafeteria, about eight in the morning. It's early April, and it's cold out. I got to sleep at one because I had to study for a Calculus test which I'm going to bomb.

"But here I am at the table, with the Calc book open on my lap and a container of orange juice and a buttered bagel on a Styrofoam tray. I am totally grogged out. My hair is matted and I haven't put on makeup yet.

"Deena's right next to me, kind of sitting sideways. She has short blonde hair and *immense* aquamarine eyes that *roll* up toward you, begging for affection. She's telling me how Brett hasn't called yet. Brett is her true love who she's supposedly going to the Prom with, and he broke up with her a month ago.

"And Martha is across from me, looking like turd. I love Martha more than anyone on earth. She has carrot red hair that explodes all around her face, and she's got major freckles. She's wearing a stonewashed denim jacket with ten thousand buttons on it, and ripped jeans. She's crabbing because her mother is on her case for getting a bad interim report. Which is not surprising since Martha has cut about eighty percent of her classes in the last month and a half.

"Now it's *frigid* in the cafeteria because they don't turn on the heat right away in the morning. My whole body is in pain. The math symbols are doing the herky-jerky on the page, and it's like Ack! Oof! I'm dead.

"Enter Lou.

"Lou is *dressed up*. He comes *bounding* over, in a yellow sweater, black jeans, and black Adidas. Dressed for success. He glares at Deena and Martha like he wishes they'd leave, and he's like, 'Hi. Are we getting together about the limo after eighth?'

"He says this without moving his lips, like a ventriloquist. He's leaning down, one hand on the back of the chair, one hand on the table. I feel avenged because there is slime on the table.

"Meanwhile I'm pissed off about taking Calculus when I shouldn't have taken it, and he wants to know if we're having this summit conference about who's going in the limo. Like do I care at this moment? Does the cosmos revolve around this issue?

"But at the same time, I'm scared. I can feel my chest pulling in. My fingers are crushing the orange juice container. I hate myself because I let him do this to me.

"So I say, 'Yeah, I guess so.'

"He gives me a hard look, like he's peeling off layers of my skin. 'What's wrong?'

"Nothing's wrong. What'd I say?'

" 'You're in a lousy mood.'

"He points this out to me, like *I don't know*! So I go, 'I'm not in a lousy mood,' which I *am*, but I've got to deny it.

" 'You're *acting* like you're in a lousy mood.'

" 'Well, I've got a major Calc test next period which I'm going to fail, and I got four hours of sleep last night. I'm not exactly chipper.'

"There is a drop or two of acid in my voice now, and this tells Lou it's not a great idea to keep arguing. So he goes to Plan B, which is to say, 'Well, I'll wake you up.'

" 'Not now.'

" 'Come on,' he says. 'I haven't gotten my morning smile yet.'

"I have no choice now. Everyone shows up to see Kimber smile, so they can have a nice day. What I want to do now is scream.

"But I smile. Right at that moment, I hate Lou. His fingers press into my shoulder, and it makes me sick.

" 'See you third?' he says.

" 'Sure.'

"He says 'Bye,' to the girls and strides back to the caf door where his friends are waiting. I'm shivering now, looking hard out the window at cars and dead trees. My eyes are wet, so I blink like crazy. And what *started* all this?"

You were saying how you bounce right back.

"Oh, boy. Well, I guess I sort of wandered again. I do that all the time. I spill out my whole life two minutes after I meet somebody. Sorry if I screwed up your story."

You *are* the story.

"Well, it was a pretty short one."

This story is about you finding your prince and going to the ball.

"*Finding* my prince? I'd like to *lose* him. But yeah, we went to the ball. But it wasn't a terrific fairy tale. Anyway, I'll shut up. Just get the name right and don't do stuff like putting me on my knees, okay?"

Sure.

"Thanks."

Does this happen to other writers? Well, I've got a deadline and the electric bill to pay, so let's try:

Kimber Delaney fell into bed each night after midnight, and woke up at five-thirty in the morning, too tired to feel the shower on her skin. She took the bus to school, and smiled for her teachers and sometimes let her head drop to the desk.

But exhaustion couldn't make her forget that this was her senior year, and that May was the Westfield Senior Prom, the magical dress-up night when seniors said good-bye . . .

"Wrong."

Now who's here?

"I heard Kimber talking and I didn't see anyone, but Kimber talking to herself is no big deal. Then I heard that bull about the Prom."

You must be Martha.

"How do you know?"

You're my character. I invented you.

"Well, I didn't mean to be rude. Only it *is* bull."

I bet you're going to tell me why.

"Well, if you're writing about Westfield, get it straight."

What's straight?

"First of all, there's about eight hundred kids going to the Prom, but only about four hundred seniors. The rest are juniors and out of district. That's because most of the senior girls wouldn't even spit at the Westfield guys. Second, the Prom is the *least* part of the weekend. Nobody says good-bye at the Prom. You have your picture taken and then you get the hell out and party on the beach or in the city. You say good-bye on Sunday night if you can see straight."

That certainly sets a romantic mood.

"Yeah, romantic. When you finish with Kimber, I'll tell you *my* romance story. It's juicy—a hot foreign guy, a hotel room, and lots of humiliation."

You sound bitter.

"No psychoanalysis, thanks."

I didn't mean it that way.

"Nobody means it. Anyway, if you're going to b.s. about the Prom, I'm splitting. Time for the deli. Oops. I'm supposed to go to French. They'll put me on academic probation this time, and down the tubes goes Martha, but heck, they always knew I was no good. Bye."

Fortunately, I can fix all of this in rewrites. I'll give it one more shot and then I take a break:

Kimber Delaney had been going out with Lou Ross since the end of her junior year. She met him on the bus going to the Junior Banquet, and was charmed by his serious eyes, good looks, and intelligence. Lou had never known an impulsive girl like Kimber. Opposites attracted that night, and they slow-danced as colored lights spun overhead.

Lou was the unofficial prince of Westfield High School. His father was a successful orthodontist and his mother ran a greeting card business. That made the Rosses one of the richest families in the school district. Lou drove a black Camaro, and excelled at lacrosse. He planned a brilliant career.

This made Lou a little uptight, though. He—gee, I haven't been interrupted yet. Come on, Lou, don't you want to contradict anything?

"What?"

Don't you want to set the record straight?

"Uh . . . no, not at the moment. I'd rather not say anything without some time to think."

Oh. That's right. You had professional help with your college application, didn't you?

"This is not going to be published, is it?"

Sure. Any changes?

"I'll have to look into it."

Better consult your attorney. This could lower your class rank.

"You don't worry me. I'll be able to buy and sell you in a few years."

You're probably right. But I'll risk it. To go on:
Lou unwound only with his pals, which meant some fairly heavy drinking. Lou's friends wondered why he'd gotten mixed up with Kimber Delaney, who was poor, and a flake. Kimber's friends wondered why *she* put up with *Lou*, who, as Martha liked to say, had his thumb up his butt.

"I put up with him because I needed him, okay?"

Kimber. I missed you.

"Why do you *think* I went for Lou? He was hot. He had money. Most guys his age are immature hormone cases. He acted like twenty-five, you know? All his words came out just right. He knew how to give me a neck massage without breaking my spine. He took my breath away."

You sound like you're still in love.

"Sometimes I am. And sometimes he's like fingernails on a blackboard. I don't know what I feel anymore. But I know why I went for him. Why he went for *me* you'll have to ask him."

Lou? Any answers?

"I really wish you wouldn't keep interviewing me. Kimber is really sweet, but sometimes she makes a big thing out of . . ."

"Out of what, Lou? Out of nothing?"

"I didn't say that."

"What was I, a liability? Were the scouts from the big corporations looking at you? I guess I was pretty embarrassing."

"Could we not argue here?"

"I'm not arguing. But you never said anything nice about me in public. In private, you were great. You gave me poems, and roses, and earrings, and you made me feel beautiful. At least you did for a while. But you never *acted* like you loved me."

"Hey, screw this."

Hold it! Kimber, you aren't supposed to have a fight.

"You need two people for a fight, and Lou always runs. It's not your fault, anyway."

At this rate, I'm never going to get the story *started*.

"This *is* the story. Don't you get it? Maybe you should just leave us alone."

Then whose love story do I tell? I don't have any other leading men for you, Kimber. Maybe your friend Jason Goldman . . .

"*Yes! My* story! The love saga of Jason and Kimber!"

I was *kidding!*

"I'm not! Listen, it's a natural. Jason Goldman: suave, witty, irresistible. He conquered the women of Westfield, but his heart was consumed by passion for the girl he couldn't possess."

Jason, you're a minor character.

"I know. But I figured since everybody else was saying something, I'd say something, too. Kimber, fight for my right to more dialogue."

"Jason, get away. You're the last person I need right now."

"Oh, yeah? How come you're smiling?"

"Because you're funny."

Listen, I don't even have any background notes on this guy. I just threw him in.

"Oh, Jason's on the literary magazine with me. He's very brilliant and very hilarious, but he doesn't know when to shut up."

"Also mention that I'm compact and darkly attractive."

"Yeah. He's short and skinny and his mouth and ears are too big for his face."

"And an exciting dancer."

"He *is* a good dancer. And he plays rock songs on the violin. Nobody else does that, right, Jase?"

"Not with my ability."

"Okay, I'm laughing. Now I'm going to English class which I'm ten minutes late for. I'd like to forget this whole day."

Jason, if you were really in love with Kimber, why didn't you make a play for her?

"Because my mother won't let me date non-Jewish girls and because she was totally dominated by Lou."

I'm losing my grip on all this. Kimber was unhappy with Lou, but she stayed with him. You liked Kimber, but you didn't tell her because she was with Lou. Lou was tired of Kimber but he held onto her. Whatever happened to *dating*?

"Take too long to explain."

What do I do with all my work? This was supposed to be a story about a teenage girl finding true love. Obviously, she's *found* it, and nobody's thrilled.

"We're all jaded by too much television. Anyway, if you ever find out how the story ends, don't let me know. See you around."

Alone at last. With a touching story about a poor girl who found her prince at the Senior Prom. Except the girl *has* her prince and they're on the rocks, and the Prom is no big deal. End of story.

"No, just the wrong story."

Martha? I thought you went to the deli.

"I'm back. See? Fried egg on roll."

So what do I do, Martha? Scrap this fairy tale?

"No, don't give up on Kimber. She needs a happy ending."

Well, obviously, I can't tell it right.

"So let *us* tell it."

Let *who* tell it?

"Me. Jason. Deena. We know what went on. Just keep us from wandering too much."

Kimber said she wasn't into lengthy narratives. How about you? Do you scrawl your homework the period before?

"I don't do it at all. But I'll stick with this."

Go ahead. I've sure hit a brick wall. Just remember, it's supposed to be a *love* story.

"Hey, that's what our lives are—love stories. Anyway, you want to hear about the Westfield Senior Prom, right? The magic night of nights."

Without heavy sarcasm, if possible.

"Straight from the heart."

Your blank page, kids.

Chapter Two

Okay, this is Kimber. I'm not thrilled about this, but Martha said it was important. I don't know what's so important. If some guy wants to write a phony teenage love story, so what? There's a million of them on a rack down at Genovese. My neighbor's thirteen-year-old Jeanine reads that stuff. She belongs to this book club—"For Girls Only" or something like that. She gets two of them a month.

Okay, okay, I'll get to the story.

Let me tell you about Deena first because she falls in love more than any of us. And about two months before the Prom, she fell in love with Phil.

Wait. Even better, let me tell you about Deena breaking up with Brett. I know that sounds like beginning at the end, but you have to know about Brett anyway so you can understand what went on with Phil.

Sorry. I'm losing it.

(Deep breath)

Anyway, Deena breaking up. This is a great lesson in teenage love. Deena knew it was over, but Brett never told her or anything. He just stopped calling her, and when she called *him,* he'd kind of breathe and sound annoyed. She'd say, "Brett, what's wrong?" and he'd go, "Nothing's wrong. Every time you talk to me, you ask me what's wrong!"

Whenever a guy talks like that, he's saying, "It's over," and you *know* that's what he's saying. But as long as he isn't *saying* it, you can make believe he's not and keep on torturing yourself.

Which is what Deena kept doing. She'd have one of those phone conversations where she'd listen to him breathe and scratch off her nail polish, and then hang up and cry. You can use up a whole night crying, usually when you've got three hours of homework. Then the next day your teachers give you a hard time and you get to feel *double* misery because your boyfriend is blowing you off *and* you're flunking.

We tried to talk to her. One day in April, we walked to the Deli on Post Road and had a talk. This is a kind of ritual: the HTHT (heart-to-heart talk). It always goes the same way.

I remember it was pretty cold, and my boots crunched on the gravel. Deena was crying, and Martha was at her right side, by the road, and I was on her left side, *schlepping* over people's front lawns. I remember feeling so bad for Deena. She was a wreck. Her face was the color of skim milk, and her eyes were sunken in.

"Deena, he's making an ass out of you," Martha said.

"I know."

"Well, if you *know,* then get rid of him."

"How?"

Martha gave this disgusted sigh. "What do you mean, how? Tell him you're not going out with him anymore."

"I can't."

"Why?"

"I *can't.*"

I said, "Did he threaten you?"

Deena shook her head, and shuddered pathetically.

"So why can't you tell him? You're a mess, Deena. It's not worth it."

She didn't say anything, and we all ran across the road. The Deli was on the corner, in the middle of a big dirt parking lot. There were millions of other Westfield kids around.

We went in and I liked the blast of warm air. I have this fragile little body, remember, and I get *cold*. We bought Combos and Yoo-Hoos and stuff and hung out for a while with kids we knew, and then we started back. The sun was splitting up the clouds and I could see this jaggy crack of blue in the middle of all the dark gray. Really neat.

So now the HTHT continues. Deena goes, "Why is he doing this?"

"He's a creep," Martha said.

"He used to put a white rose in my locker every Tuesday. We met on a Tuesday."

Martha gave her a savage look, with one eyebrow up. "You gave him your *combination*?"

Deena just shrugged.

"You're a total jerk," Martha said. "When was the last time you got a white rose?"

Deena shrugged again.

"Case closed."

My chest was filling up now with frustration. "Look," I said, "it doesn't matter if he's not giving her roses any more. Are you still in love with him?"

Deena had her chin tucked way down against her jacket. "Yeah."

I traded a pitying look with Martha. I said, "Is he cheating on you?"

"No!"

"Okay, don't get hyper. I had to ask."

Deena trembled with sorrow. "I don't know what I'm doing wrong."

Martha flung herself to the side. "Oh for God's sake! Why don't you just lie down and let him drive over you a few times until he feels better?"

"Easy, girl," I said.

"Come *on*! Deena, what about what *he's* doing wrong? He's not calling you, he's not taking you out, he's ignoring you in school, he's making you sick, and he's having a great old time using you like a yo-yo! Give it up! He's a loser."

"I know," Deena sniffled.

"So lose him."

"I know."

She knows. Got that? She *agrees*. So we walked along the chain link fence by the school parking lot and hooked a right through the gate. We crossed the parking lot, heading for the door to the Art Wing. And Deena said:

"I just don't know what to do."

Bingo. Back to square one. The whole conversation is useless. By that time, we heard the bell ring inside and we had to hustle our butts to get to our lockers. That's why we didn't throw Deena to the ground and jump on her face.

But that's typical, you know? And this can go on for *months,* usually until the guy gets caught cheating and then the girl can go gunning for him and have a major scene with the girl running down the hall and the guy screaming "DON'T WALK AWAY FROM ME!" and other fun stuff.

Which, fortunately, didn't happen with Deena and Brett. First of all, Brett was such a nerd that he wouldn't ever yell at her, and second of all, Deena found Phil.

Now the way *that* happened was at this family party . . .

STOP!!!

"What was *that*?"

Jason tickled me.

"I can see where this is going to degenerate pretty quickly."

No, I think he wants to say something. Is that okay?

"Handle this any way you want. I'm on my lunch break."

Well, I hope he doesn't get obscene or anything. Anyway, I'm going to skip a line and then it's Jason talking. And I'm going to leave out all those quotation marks except when the author talks to us, okay? Here's Jason:

Hi. I wasn't going to jump in here now, but *somebody* has to save this story. Your first major mistake was letting three girls take over the narrative. I mean, have you ever *heard* three girls tell a story? You could farm the north forty before they get to the point. They're babbling away about Deena breaking up with Brett and all *you* wanted to do was tell the story of a poor, funny-looking kid who goes to the Prom with a rich, handsome jock . . .

Funny-looking? You creep!

I meant that with affection.

How about if I ram my car into you with affection?

Oooh. Kinky but *nice.*

Total brain damage. It's very sad.

I know. But let me have the floor for a while. You can have the walls. Just leave me the floor.
Anyway, let's get back to rejected love. Like the day I asked Kimber to the Prom.

Get *away*! You *never* asked me to the Prom.

May my pectorals increase if I'm lying. Just listen, Kimber. It'll come back to you. Martha and Deena were there, too. It was at the emergency oh-my-God-*Expressions*-is-going-to-die meeting.

Wait. Nobody out there knows what I'm talking about. Kimber's the editor of the Westfield High Literary Magazine, *Expressions*. I was going to do it, but I was already involved with the History Club and the Chamber Orchestra and the newspaper.

But Kimber was there. So I joined the publicity staff because nobody ever did anything on it. Kimber is not a natural leader. She only became editor because nobody else could read and Mr. Alterson, the advisor, was desperate. I shouldn't put down the magazine, though. It's pretty decent. And I admit it's pretty amazing to see your name in print. It's even better to see *my* name in print.

You have some nerve accusing *me* of getting off the point! Nobody even knows what you're *saying*!

Ah! Kimber, thou hast pierced me to my heart. But thy words are true. I have digressed. I promise, from now on I'll gress.

So this was an emergency meeting in the middle of March. Picture if you will a gray, cold day with little flurries torn from the menacing clouds. In Room 28, in an average suburban high school, the radiator clanks ominously. A fluorescent light buzzes. There's a feeling of dread in the air. All of us could feel the dread. It felt soft and fuzzy . . .

Oh my God, I don't believe him.

ALL RIGHT! I'll be serious.

We had this meeting because we had to get the magazine to the printer, and half the poems had disappeared and half the artwork hadn't been done. This happens every year. So Mr. Alterson was pulling out his remaining hair. Mr. A's a cool guy. He gets totally stressed out and has fits.

It was three-thirty on a dark and stormy afternoon, and Kimber and Martha and Deena and I were in Room 28. Deena was drawing vines and flowers. That's Deena's specialty. You give her drawing paper and a black Flair pen and you say, "Deena! Draw vines and flowers!" And she just cranks them out by the yard.

Kimber and Martha were flipping through piles of original submissions, looking for the lost poems. Mr. Alterson was freaking. He'd go to the file cabinet by the windows and rifle through all the files, and then he'd go back to his desk and move all the books and papers around, and then he'd go to the storage closet and *talk to the shelves.*

What was *I* doing, you ask? I was proofreading some of the accepted poems because Mr. Alterson was backed up with work. Actually, I wasn't proofreading. I was looking at Kimber. My chest hurt from being in love with her. She wore a soft, fringed dress. She was framed against the window. It was perfect. I was suicidal.

"Not to interrupt, Jason, but I thought you didn't want Kimber to know how you felt?"

Well, if we're all telling our own stories, why not? Anyway, this all happened already, so there's not much risk.

"Kimber, how do you feel, hearing all this?"

How do I feel? I feel that Jason's being unfair and cruel. But as long as he thinks he's hilarious, that's fine.

"Jason? Want to go on?"

Oh, sure. She's really nuts about me. She just likes to cover it up. And anyway, right after this I'm going to commit suicide by listening to old Wayne Newton albums.

And besides, I'm part of the story. I was *there,* in Room 28, wishing I had the guts to ask Kimber to the Prom. I knew she'd say no because she was with Lou. I knew she wouldn't even take me seriously. But I wanted to ask her.

I mean, it was un-American. Lou had no competition. He was Macy's and I was just a little Mom and Pop store in the neighborhood.

At that moment, she was looking at poems and calling out names while Martha checked them off a computerized list. I could tell she was happy. She kept flipping back her hair and humming. That's what she does when she's happy. Mr. Alterson kept coming over and looking at the girls with this haunted face. He'd say witty things like, "How's it going?" and Kimber would say, "Stunningly," and he'd rub her shoulders and look relieved.

It was really *quiet* in the room, with rain hitting the windows, and the radiator hissing, and cars swishing by out on Post Road. And then fate threw the dice.

I looked down and there, in my sweaty hands, was a poem they were looking for. I recognized the title from the names Martha was calling out. There were butterflies in my stomach. Actually, I was just *starting* to feel nervous, so they were still caterpillars. I thumbed through the rest of the pages I was proofreading. YES! They were ALL there! *I had found the LOST POEMS!!!*

"Hey!" I said.

Kimber turned around. "What?"

I milked the moment. S-l-o-w-l-y I said, "Does the name 'Last Summer' ring a bell?"

Kimber's eyes widened. It was a reward just to watch that. She glanced back at Martha and then at me. "That's one of the missing poems! You *have* it?"

I held up the page, nonchalantly. I used to do things chalantly but I've become more mature.

"Oh my *God*!" she yelled. "Jason, I love you!"

I know she didn't mean it, but I let the words slither around inside me like warm mercury. I got up and handed her the page. She grabbed it and I watched her eyes go click-click-click across the page. Her whole face broke into a smile, like the sun coming out after the rain.

She turned and gave the page to Martha. Martha ran her finger down the list. "Yup," Martha said. "That's one of 'em."

By this time, Mr. Alterson was leaning over Martha's shoulder. "All right," he said. "Now we need ten more."

Kimber deflated a little. "I know."

I let all three of them suffer just a moment longer. Then I did an exaggerated yawn and said, "Oh, you mean the ten poems over there by my desk?"

Kimber *exploded* out of the seat and shrieked, *"WHAT??"* and barrelled past me. I was spun around like Wile E. Coyote being sideswiped by Road Runner. Kimber ravaged the poems, her lips moving as she whispered each title.

She stuffed all ten poems into her delicious little hands and brought them back to Martha and Mr. Alterson. The three of them looked at the computerized list and babbled excitedly. "Excitedly, excitedly, excitedly . . ." they babbled.

Now there was electricity in the room. There used to be gas, but they modernized. ALL RIGHT! SORRY! Here's Kimber and Martha and Mr. Alterson, pointing and chattering. I'm trying to keep my heart from jumping out of my chest. My throat is closing. My hair falls out and scales cover my body.

Kimber peels off from the group and turns around to find her pen on the desk. She's facing me. I look at her. She smiles and says, "Jason! Thank you! You're beautiful!"

"I'm only reflecting *your* beauty," is my answer. I swear to God, I said that.

Kimber laughs, this tripping little laugh. She flings out her arms—

I'm switching tenses here. Let me switch back so this is coherent:

Kimber laughed, this tripping little laugh. She flung out her arms, and I took two steps and hugged her. She hugged me back. I shut my eyes and focused every ounce of consciousness on the pressure of her body against mine. I memorized each soft parabola and I even felt her heart beating. And that is no joke.

I opened my eyes and she was still hugging me. I could feel her fingertips against my neck. I could smell her hair. *My* face was twelve millimeters from *her* face. My Id screamed for me to kiss her, to force her lips apart, to take her with brutal savagery. Brutal Savagery wasn't there at the time, so I refrained.

I can't help it. I'm compensating.

But it was a major moment. I was sweating on the *inside*. Her head darted forward and she kissed my jaw. I think she wanted my cheek but it's tough to aim at times like these. Her lips were cool and dry. Which is more than I can say for myself.

"Thanks," she said again. "You saved our lives."

Cleverness eluded me. My brain had turned to green slime. And that's when I said, for no reason, "Kimber, ditch Lou and go to the Prom with me."

I can't *swear* I said that. I *think* that's what I said. Looking back, it's entirely possible that I said, "Homina homina homina homina," with a lot of drool in between the words. Maybe it just *sounded* like "Kimber, ditch Lou and go to the Prom with me."

Anyway, Kimber said, "You're crazy," which is a clue that I may have really said what I thought I said. Then again, she would have said "You're crazy," even if I'd said "Homina homina homina homina," so there's no proof. But I still believe that at that insane moment, I asked Kimber Delaney to the Prom.

Speaking of tragedy, as Kimber broke the embrace, I looked around and there was Lou, looking through the little square window on the door. My teenage lust turned to fear of injury. How much had he seen? How much time did I have to live?

He opened the door and came in. You could see Mr. Alterson tighten up because he knew that if Lou was here, Kimber was gone. Lou never came to *see* Kimber, he came to *fetch* her.

He strode over to her. He had on his Members Only jacket, and his Westfield gym bag over his shoulder. His hair was wet because he'd been outside. He looked dark and dangerous and romantic. I wanted to carve scenes from the Old Testament onto his nose.

Kimber looked up and gave him a sweet smile, but her eyes rolled over and died. "Hi," she said.

He talked very low, the way he always did to her. I stood far away from them, ready to run if he turned on me, so I may not be remembering all the words right, but he said something like, "You said you'd be finished at two-thirty."

"Sorry," she said. "I have to log in these poems and Deena has to finish drawing."

She gestured to Deena, who was still drawing vines. Mr. Alterson said, "I just need to keep her for a few more minutes. This should have been at the printer already."

Lou looked at Mr. Alterson like he was a toad and then looked back at Kimber. This time I really *couldn't* hear what he said, but I could see his cheeks tensing. Her hands started rolling up the piece of paper she was holding.

I thought of leaping on him and wrestling him to the ground. I thought of shouting to Kimber, "Tell him you can't go! Tell him he doesn't own you! Tell him you're going to have my baby!" I didn't do any of this because I'm a snivelling coward.

Kimber said something back to Lou, and Lou walked back to the door. Mr. Alterson's eyes got hopeful. But Kimber said, "Mr. Alterson, I have to go, okay?"

Mr. Alterson was hurt. He said, "If you have to go, then go."

Kimber said to Martha, "Can you stay and help?"

"Yeah, until the three-thirty bus," she said. You could see that Martha was pissed off at Kimber for crumbling. I got worried because Martha really *would* start carving scenes from the Old Testament on Lou's nose.

But Kimber is hard not to love, even when you're feeling murderous. "Thanks," she said to Martha. She gathered up her books and cradled them to her chest. She shook her head to clear the hair from her eyes and then she stopped and looked at me. What I wanted to do was throw a tantrum. But I stood bravely. She smiled and said, "Thanks again, Jase. You're amazing."

"That's why you're giving up your family and career to run away with me to Tahiti."

She laughed and kissed me right on my stunned lips. And it made me feel like fly doo-doo. Because I realized that even if Lou *had* seen Kimber hug me, it didn't *bother* him. Just like it didn't bother him now when she kissed me. Because I was no threat. You know what it feels like to be a male and no threat?

So I could be forgiven for suddenly screaming in animal rage and flinging a desk through the window. Of course, I didn't *do* that, but I could be *forgiven* for it.

Kimber said "Bye!" to Mr. Alterson, and then she looked at Deena and said, "Bye, Deena! Thanks!"

Deena looked up and waved, and then looked at the clock. "Oh no!" she said. "I have to get the bus!"

Mr. Alterson's whole universe was crumbling at this point, so naturally Martha said, "I have to make the bus, too. Sorry."

"Okay, I'll finish up," Mr. Alterson said. The man had nothing left in life but his lesson plans. I knew I'd stay awhile and help but I didn't want to say it. I wanted Alterson to suffer along with me.

I looked out the window at the rain. I was *glad* it was raining. It was Hemingwayesque. I heard Kimber's locker clanging out in the hallway, and I thought about Lou waiting for her and how she would hurry up so he wouldn't be mad. I wondered if he beat her up. I wondered if they'd go to his house and make love. I wondered what Mom made for dinner.

Anyway, there it is. You want to talk about being in love and being stupid? At least Deena *knew* she was being stupid. And *I* knew I was being stupid. But that was a crucial moment in the story because Kimber could have said yes to me, and then she wouldn't have kept going out with Lou and none of the other disasters would have happened.

Now we're back on track. Personally, I'm exhausted. I'm going to lie down and put a cold compress on my gonads. Thank you for listening, and send all contributions to the Jason Goldman Fund.

Okay, Kimber. Your turn again.

Thanks, Jason. That was wonderful. I'm sure everyone got a big laugh out of it. As long as you made me look like a total dishrag.

Don't be sore, Kimber. The clown must entertain in his own way.

Well, it wasn't entertaining. It was stupid and obnoxious. I'm not a complete jerk. I always knew you were my friend, or at least I thought you were. Instead of playing head games, you could have just talked to me.

About what, Kimber? About how I was crazy for you and would you go out with me? Come on. You know the rules of teenage love. One guy. Even if he makes you cry all the time. No trying anyone else unless you do a formal breakup and agree to see other people. And you weren't about to break up and Lou wasn't about to surrender his little love slave.

Shut *up*! Who do you think you are, you twerp!

I don't know. I never met this part of me before.

(Sigh) Okay, Jason. Sorry I blew up. I never meant to hurt you, babe. I just didn't know. I didn't know a lot of things.

Well, that's what we're here for. There are eight million stories in the naked high school, and this is one of them. So do go on. And on, and on, and on . . .

Get out of here, slimeface. It's not fair that you make me smile when I want to hate you.

Chapter Three

I *didn't* mean to get upset with Jason. He just gets a little out of hand sometimes. But I do love him. Not the way he wants, but I can't help that. Martha and Deena understand what I mean. They're like my sisters.

Want to know when I met Martha? Would you believe seventh grade? Westfield has this summer program for honors kids, with courses like Backpacking and Astronomy. It's kind of like day camp except it only costs three dollars. That's why I went. My friends were *really* going to camp, but Mom and Dad couldn't afford it, so I signed up for the Theater Arts course.

That's where I met Martha. She was a *real* honors student, in the Gifted and Talented Program. I remember this pudgy little thing with a mass of red hair and freckles. She wore glitter on her face, and plastic junk jewelry on every finger. At the end of the course, she made a rubber band chain for the teacher.

And she was *deep.* She showed me this story she was working on, an outer space epic that was about twenty pages long. I couldn't even understand it. But it was *professional,* you know? I know Martha said she couldn't tell stories, but Martha lies a lot.

Anyway, we became friends right away. I was even littler than

I am now, and we both thought we were ugly as scabs. I was actually the quiet one back then. I sat in the front of the room and kept my head down and never talked back to the teacher. Martha spent half her life in the principal's office. Even at thirteen, she was smarter than half her teachers, and she let them know it. Teachers don't get off on looking stupid.

But I thought she was hot stuff. She'd already gotten her period, and she'd already made out with guys, and it was like instant older sister. We spent the whole four weeks writing notes to each other. I made her describe every second of what it was like to kiss a guy. And she wanted to know all about my parents' fights and if I was going to be a child of divorce. It was heavy stuff.

That September, we wound up in English and Sequential I together, and we took up where we left off. We laughed hysterically most of the time. I got a reputation for being a troublemaker, and my parents got called up for a conference with *all my teachers*. It was awesome. My dad went to the conference, because Mom didn't want anything to do with me anymore. He was so sad when he sat me down at the kitchen table. He said all my teachers loved me and thought I was so smart, and it was a shame I let Martha lead me astray.

Dad told me he wouldn't forbid me to see Martha because he knew I'd just sneak around and see her anyway. But he gave me this long talk about independence and being my own person, and maybe influencing *Martha* to act better. He was so sweet. Of course, he was dreaming. Nobody influences Martha. But I told her I was in major trouble, and we kind of cooled it for a while. Or maybe the teachers got used to us. But I don't remember any more conferences.

I remember Hostess cupcakes, though. We were both crazy about Hostess cupcakes. We bought boxes of them and always carried two or three around when we went out.

I remember the two of us strutting through the streets of my neighborhood, eating Hostess cupcakes. What a sight! Martha had her hair permed and it looked like an explosion in a Brillo factory! I was wearing this spiky hairdo and I'd had my hair lightened but it came out green. I can still see the two of us in these *ensembles* of sweatshirts and T-shirts and ripped shorts and fluorescent sneakers, with our lumpy little bodies and both of us in braces. We thought we were two elegant ladies. We'd stroll around, giggling and yakking, and always watching for hot guys to notice us. But the best part was the chocolate all over our teeth. God, somebody should have videotaped it.

Oh, wow. This was *not* on the agenda. Why didn't anyone stop me?

"Because it's worth hearing, Kimber."

Gee, thanks. From you, that's a major compliment.

I don't know about my life history being important, though. In fact, I used to make up a *different* life history. In eighth grade, we had to write our autobiographies. So I wrote how I was born in Singapore, because my dad was an exporter, and how we lived in France for a while, in a villa in the country and I learned how to ride horses and grow wine. It was a neat story. I had the teacher going for a while, too.

The horse part I put in because I was so jealous of all the girls who *did* ride horses. On Long Island, most girls take dancing lessons or horseback riding lessons. When I was six, I got ballet lessons. I remember going to this studio in a dirty little shopping center. It was always cold, and there were sleazy dancers rehearsing their routines to really loud records.

I never got to ride horses. That was way too expensive. I remember other girls chattering about their beloved horses, which they *owned*. I used to dream of going to a stable and grooming my own horse. It sounded so exciting when they talked about it. I'd turn away and draw horse pictures.

It was always like that. The other kids would come back to school with their Trapper Keepers and I'd come in with my

Cheap John's notebook. They'd have all these cunning fashions from boutiques and I'd have knockoffs from McCrory's. They'd buy lasagna from the lunch lady and I'd have a peanut butter sandwich in a My Little Pony lunchbox. It's mean to grow up that way. I crawled into my own little world because I was so ashamed; of course all the other kids called me stuck-up.

I'm not blaming Dad. He's just one of those people who's always in the wrong place at the wrong time. He started out as a salesman for Revlon, but he's scared to go talk to people and he developed an ulcer the *first* year on the job! He was unemployed for five years and Mom worked and they had to take out loans. Dad could never find a job that paid off.

Then Corey came along and it got worse. He was hyperactive, and they had to get Ritalin to calm him down. He was a terror. He'd run around the house screaming or stand and bang on the stairs. At night he kept smashing his head into the wall. Didn't do a lot for my nerves. He's not hyper now, just obnoxious.

Anyway, the whole point is that I was really alone, and when Martha came along, it was like a gift from heaven. She saved my life in a way.

If you're wondering why I'm giving Martha such a big buildup, it has to do with the whole mess on the Senior Weekend, which led to her suspension from the Prom, and to her cheating with Lou, so I wanted to make sure you understood—

"Wait! Run that in reverse for a minute. *Cheated with Lou?*"

Oh, yeah. I guess nobody mentioned that. But hang in, I'm not ready to talk about that yet. First you have to know about Martha and Rob, and why she started to go out with him, and the fight in school. And about the Senior Weekend.

In fact . . . Martha, maybe you want to tell about all of this.

You said *you* were dying to tell it.

I was kidding. But seriously, I didn't see the fight, so maybe you'll be more accurate?

I didn't see it, either. But I want to say something about me and Rob.

Kimber's right, I was pretty loose back in the seventh grade. But by the time I got to be a senior, I didn't have much of a romantic life. I was all screwed up with hating the system and reading Hermann Hesse and listening to head-banging music. Not exactly catnip for the average Westfield guy.

So when the Senior Banquet came around, I went stag because Kimber and Deena were going. I made a lot of jokes about the Banquet being stupid and all the bimbettes running around pulling up their strapless gowns. Meanwhile, I bought a strapless dress. And I went to the beauty salon and got my hair curled, and I spent two hours in the bathroom, putting on makeup.

So at the Banquet, I'm hanging out with Kimber and Lou, and Deena and Brett (she was still with Brett back in December). The scene is the Island Manor House. All our purses are on the table with the rolls and glasses of ice water, and the DJ machine is pumping bubbles and blasting party music. I feel so stupid I want to take poison.

I meet Rob while we're on line for the buffet. A hundred dressed-up teenagers are standing on this line, trying to look suave and not spill spaghetti on their clothes. Kimber and Lou are in front of me, and Rob is behind me with his friends, except, of course, I don't know him. So, feeling stupid as I do, I grab an apple and stick it in my cleavage and start belly dancing. Kimber and Deena go hysterical, and even Lou is smiling.

Then I hear this guy say, "Could I get some fruit?"

I turn around and this guy is looking at me with a snide grin. He's a little shorter than I am, and built, with ashy hair and blue eyes. He's wearing a neat pearl gray suit and his face is attractive, except he put on too much zit cream. There are a couple of guys behind him on line, snickering. Obviously his friends.

And here I am, with an apple in my cleavage. "Sorry," I say. "No problem."

I move up, and let him get to the fruit. My face burns and I pray that I get off this line fast and that he's sitting on the other side of the room.

I keep my head down and I slouch over and I point to stuff in the chafing dishes. The girls who are serving give me strange looks. The blood is pounding in my head as I become more and more embarrassed. Finally, I'm at the end of the buffet table. I can feel his eyes like two drills in my back. And my back is now in a major sweat.

I start to walk away and he goes, "Aren't you going to take out the apple?"

His friends crack up. I'm holding a plate spilling over with food, which I have to balance with both hands. And the apple is still in my dress. I went down the *whole food line* with this apple.

So I say . . . well, it's a word I won't repeat, but I say it loud. He cracks up. I walk away as fast as I can with an apple in my dress and a plate of food in my hands. I have to walk about a mile and a half in between tables to get back to where I'm sitting. I feel everyone looking at me. It's one of the low points of my life.

I finally take the apple out of my dress. Kimber and Deena laugh for about forty minutes, and make bad jokes. "Why not watermelons?" and humor like that. I remember eating but I don't remember tasting anything.

Before I'm finished mopping up sauce with a roll, Rob comes over to the table. He's very careful where his eyes are looking. He says, "I was trying to find you."

"Why?"

"I didn't mean to laugh at you. But you were pretty funny."

"Thanks. My agent will be happy."

"Huh?"

Whoops. I realize that he's not that swift. But he's cute. I become aware of my dress and my hair, and my sweat.

"Nothing," I say. "It's okay."

He looks confused, but he recovers. "Anyway, I'm Rob Trainor."

For a minute, I don't know what to say. Everyone at the table is looking at me. *They* realize he's hitting on me, but I don't. This is not usual. If a guy wants to get to know a girl, he asks a friend who knows her to set up an introduction. He doesn't just wander over and say hello. Rob's friends must have *dared* him to do this.

So I'm not ready for his approach. I sit there and go, "Uh . . . uh . . ."

Deena punches me in the arm, very subtle. My brain kicks in, and I say, "Hi, I'm Martha Sullivan."

"Hi."

"Hi."

This threatens to become a dead end. But Lou says, very smoothly, "I'm Lou and this is Kimber, and that's Deena and Brett and . . ." and he goes around the table.

Rob says, "Hi," to everybody and everybody says, "Hi," to Rob. Rob is now pretty flustered, but he looks me in the eye and says, "So you want to dance?"

I say, "Huh?"

Deena rolls her eyes. Kimber makes a whimpering noise in my ear. And my brain says, Oh! He asked you to dance! He asked you to *dance*! He asked *YOU* to *DANCE*!

Now the sweat is rolling down my ribs and I don't dare pick up my arms. But I manage to say, "Sure," and to get up without pulling off the tablecloth or knocking over any glasses.

I follow Rob back to the dance floor, bumping into people, wondering what the hell I'm going to talk to him about or how long I should dance with him, or what I do after we're finished dancing. Finally, we get to the dance floor, except you can't see it because there are hundreds of bodies jammed together, boogying down. Rob leads me through the mob to a space he likes, then he turns and starts moving. I start moving, too.

He's not really a dancer, which makes me grateful because I don't know what I'm doing myself. But I get into it, and of course every few minutes I discreetly yank up my dress. He's having a pretty good time, smiling at me. And at that moment, the music gets to me, and I begin to get infatuated.

Of course, I don't know anything about the kid. Maybe I'm compensating for being embarrassed. Maybe I'm just too lonely. But that's how it starts, right? Timing. I needed to be asked to dance more than I needed anything else in the world.

So we dance for about a half hour, and then we walk out into the lobby. This is a second floor lobby, carpeted, with couches and mirrors and potted plants. Kids are on the couches, sometimes couples, sometimes friends. One boy and girl are having THE TALK—you know, where he looks deep into her eyes and touches her shoulder and she looks down and nods every once in a while. I love when guys do THE TALK. They get so intense. Usually it's because they've done something retarded and they're desperate.

Rob and I find a loveseat near a railing and we sit down. I slump back and kick off my shoes because my ankles are swollen. I realize Rob has a great view of large feet inside pantyhose. I'm nervous because I don't know what to say.

He sits next to me and we're both quiet. I wish I was with Kimber and Deena, comfortable and secure.

Rob says, "So what classes do you have?"

Good opener. Let him know right away that I'm a dexter. I tell him the whole lineup: Advanced Placement English, Regents Physics, Advanced Placement Calculus, Advanced Placement European History, Creative Writing. Might as well chase him away now.

He says, "No wonder I don't see you."

"It's a big school."

"I don't take advanced courses. I just want to get out."

"I don't cover myself with glory," I reassure him. "I'm about to get dropped from two of them for cutting."

He says, "Oh, yeah?"

"Yeah. It hasn't been a wonderful year."

There's more silence. This is not an unusual opening conversation when you meet someone. Unless you're like lab partners or work in the same place and have a lot to talk about, you grope.

But by then, I kind of sensed that Rob wanted to go out with me, and I kind of wanted to go out with Rob. I knew he was an average guy, probably pretty nice, but nobody I could ever talk to about who I was and what I felt. That was okay. I was pretty desperate for somebody to be with.

That's the tough thing. You have to *be* with somebody. Every song tells you that. Nothing's worse than being alone. And if you don't have somebody, you start looking for all the things that are wrong with you.

"So," Rob says. "Did you ever eat the apple?"

I smile. "Nope. You want it?"

"Yeah, sure."

"I'll have it wrapped up for you."

He's stretched his arm along the back of the couch and now I feel his fingers softly touch the nape of my neck. My hair is so stiff it makes scratching sounds. I let him go ahead and I even wriggle a little to make it easier.

"Do you like basketball?"

"I guess."

"I'm on the team."

"I'm impressed."

"Ever go to a varsity game?"

"No."

"There's a scrimmage on Friday. Maybe you could show up, and we'll do something after. Go to McDonald's or something."

I'd been asked out. Scrimmage and Mickey D's. I actually feel my heart turn over. My pulse is racing. I suddenly realize, in a rush, how much I need this. I suddenly want to kiss Rob.

So I do. Which is also unusual. Generally, you go on a test date first and then spend time with a guy so you can both decide if you want to get involved. Kissing and other things happen after a while (unless you meet at a party and get wasted). But Rob and

I are ready. We talk some more and his hand gets to my shoulder. I turn to him and look hard into his eyes. He bends toward me. I shut my eyes and we kiss.

Rob kisses excellently. I can feel that he's pretty tight and muscular. That's what I want.

And you've got to *know* that because of what happened later. The Martha Sullivan who said yes to Rob Trainor was a different persona. Not the real Martha Sullivan. Not the one who destroyed herself on the Senior Weekend or got suspended from the Prom.

Poor Rob didn't know that girl when he asked me out. He got to know her pretty soon, though.

Okay, Kimber, you can tell the story now.

Chapter Four

Okay. The hallway fight. This came a couple of weeks after the Senior Weekend. It was the end of April, and the Prom was the only thing the seniors were talking about.

I was pretty excited. *And* pretty depressed. Not just because Lou and I were sour. Because I knew I'd have to settle for a cheap dress. Since I was a little girl I'd dreamed about going to all the boutiques in Manhattan and getting fitted for the most gorgeous, romantic Prom dress in the world. It would be strapless and lacy and I'd wear elbow-length white gloves and baby's breath in my hair and everyone would look at me and whisper.

Well, I knew I wasn't going to any Manhattan boutiques. Maybe not even the mall. And I was pissed off about it. Actually, I was pissed off about Lou, and about going to Geneseo instead of Wesleyan. And I was guilty about Dad and Corey.

Maybe you're wondering what was so terrible about Corey, since I keep bringing him up. I told you he was a hyper kid. Well, he was also smart. Maybe smarter than I am. When he was six, he was reading newspapers and stuff. Corey's one of those kids who can never take notes and still ace the test.

But that isn't the whole story. It's his attitude and what it does to Dad, and to me. Like the night of the Sumpfest.

See, there's a sump at the end of Cindy Lane. It's a party place for a lot of kids from Westfield School District. When I say party, I mean about four or five hundred kids. This was a night at the end of April, and it was muggy and hazy, the kind of weather that makes you feel like stabbing someone.

I was loading up the dishwasher from dinner. We don't have dinner together very often. Dad works all these jobs and Corey and I are never home at the same time. But tonight we had meat loaf because I felt like cooking. Corey wasn't too thrilled about it. He hunkered over the table with this sullen look and kind of sucked up the food. He finished in about four minutes and then mumbled, "I'm goin' out."

"You're through already?" I said.

"Yeah."

"No dessert?"

"I'll have somethin' later."

"No way. Once I clean up, the kitchen's closed."

He made a sarcastic face. "Yeah."

"I *mean* it. Daddy?"

Dad looked tiredly at Corey. "Kimber's in charge of the kitchen."

"Give it up," Corey said under his breath. Then he kind of unravelled from his chair—he's about six feet tall and he's all limbs.

He said, "See ya," and he was gone. I heard the screen door slam. Then I heard Corey bellow, "Yo! *Greg!*" to his friend.

While I loaded the dishwasher, I thought about my homework and shopping for a Prom dress and how Lou hadn't called me and about Martha's mess (I'll get to it!) and I started to cry.

Dad stayed at the kitchen table. He's a pretty decent-looking guy, about five-ten, kind of slender. He has receding hair and a bald spot in the back of his head. He buttered a piece of bread and ate it while he stared at the microwave. It was like he was waiting for a show to come on!

It's hard for me to talk to Dad about what he's going through. I was twelve when Mom walked out and I knew that she'd been cheating on Dad with some college professor. But Dad never showed his emotions. So I was doing dishes and he was staring.

The phone rang, which broke the tension. Right away I knew it was bad news: "Can I speak to Mr. Delaney? This is George DePaul, Corey's math teacher."

I wanted to tell him, "My dad is tired. Flush Corey down the toilet and do us all a favor."

But I gave Dad the phone and I went back to the sink. I saw Dad's face get a little more waxy. He mumbled stuff like "Okay. We'll get on it." I put the water on harder. I couldn't stand it. I wanted to smash Corey's head against the wall. He was playing games. He *knew* if he screwed up the teacher would call. He also knew Dad wouldn't nail him.

Dad held out the phone and said, "Would you hang this up for me?"

I hung up the phone. "What did the jerk do now?"

"Failed a test with a thirty-three."

"Is that all?"

Dad got up and walked out of the kitchen. While he was upstairs, I heard shouts outside. Then I saw a red glow in the foyer.

Cops.

My heart was in my throat right away. I went to the front door and looked out through the screen. At first I couldn't see anything. It was a dark night, and the air was thick and heavy.

So I opened the screen door and went out. I saw hundreds of kids all over the street and all over the DeMarcos' front lawn. The DeMarcos live in the house right by the woods and their front lawn is a hill.

A cop car with its roof light on was parked by the DeMarcos'. The kids were swirling all around the car. Other cars idled on the street, with headlights on. I knew what was happening before anyone told me. The cops had probably chased these kids out of the sump and they'd wandered up here.

The screen door slammed and Dad came out. I heard his shoes crunching on the driveway. "What's happening?"

"I think the cops are chasing them out of the woods."

I could feel Dad stiffen up. Joan and Marty Reese were on their driveway next door, and the Burkes, two houses down, were outside, too. It was like everybody had to protect their houses. Dad and I walked over to the Reeses and watched while the cops got the kids moving.

"Who called the police?" Dad asked.

"Not me," Joan Reese said. She's this petite blonde and she wore a housecoat and slippers.

"I didn't know anything was going on," Marty said.

The two Reese girls were running around the wet lawn and screaming in their pajamas. Millions of little kids were around. It was like a party. Joan said, "There must be four hundred kids in there. Where did they come from?"

"Sumpfest," I said.

"Who?"

"They probably got chased out of the sump."

Marty said, "What were they doing in the sump?"

"Spring party. First warm night of the year."

Dad had his hands jammed in his pants pockets. "Why did they have to discover *us*?"

"We have the woods," I said.

I watched all the movement, and I shivered. I saw these kids all the time in school, but out here they were dangerous. When these kids got trashed, they got out of hand.

One of the cops went over to the Angelos' and was talking to Joe Angelo at his front door. Meanwhile, the kids were tramping out of the woods, shouting, belching, and singing. Cars kept roaring up the street and stopping. They were filled with other kids looking for the party. When they saw the cops, they moved on.

The kids were streaming past our houses now, headed aimlessly down the block. The night smelled like rain and grass. I could see a yellow moon and smeary black clouds.

Suddenly Dad cursed and took a few steps toward the edge of the Reese driveway. I saw Corey right away. Corey sticks out in a crowd. He was up near the DeMarcos' front lawn, with a bunch of kids.

"Corey!" Dad shouted. Dad must have been upset because he doesn't go around yelling in the street.

He called a couple more times, and finally Corey turned. He waved at us and yelled, "I'm with Greg and Scott!"

"Get over here!" Dad yelled.

Corey came strutting back. He looked goofy in his sweats and his unlaced hightops. At one point, his head disappeared among the branches of a maple tree. He batted at the leaves and bopped over to Dad. "Yeah?"

Joan Reese said, "My God, he's taller than he was five minutes ago."

Marty said, "He's growing up."

I walked away. I let the darkness slide over me as I stood between houses and watched the exodus of the kids. I knew it would go on for a couple of hours, and that unless the cops stuck around, the kids would all come back.

Joan Reese asked Corey, "What's going on at the Angelos'?" and Corey said with a smile, "Some of the kids pissed on his lawn." Everyone laughed about that.

Then Dad started lacing it into Corey for hanging around the kids from the woods. Corey was rolling his eyes and going on about how he was with Greg and Scott and not with the kids from the woods. Dad said Corey would be hauled in by the cops just for being there and Corey said no he wouldn't.

Dad said "Maybe you'd like to stay in the house right *now*." And Corey said, "I'm not going to get in trouble, okay?"

"I don't want you up there," Dad said.

"I'm goin' to be with my friends," Corey said.

"Not up there."

"Dad, give it *up*!" Corey said.

"End of discussion."

"NO! I want to be with my friends."

"Sorry."

Corey hooked up over Dad like a big question mark. "I'm goin' with my *friends*!"

Dad turned away and walked back toward the Reeses, who were leaning on their Toronado. Marty Reese is a contractor and makes all kinds of money, which makes Dad feel low.

Corey wasn't going to let it alone. If he didn't go back up to where the cops were, he'd look wimpy in front of his buddies. So he went after Dad and yelled, "I'm goin' with my friends, *okay*?"

Dad looked furiously at Corey and said, "Don't shout at me."

"I'm goin' with my friends."

"Not up there."

Corey yelled so loud I thought the cops would come down. "I AM GOIN' WITH MY FRIENDS!"

He flung his body around and started clomping up the driveway. That's when I snapped. I stormed up the sidewalk and I yelled, "STOP!"

Corey turned around and glared at me. "What do *you* want?"

"Daddy told you not to go!"

"Get out of my face."

"Don't tell me to get out of your face. I'll *slap* your face in a minute."

"Oh, yeah. I'm really worried."

I was a little scared because he's pretty big. But I was so mad I didn't care. "You *better* be worried," I said. "You're a total waste. Your math teacher called tonight because you flunked another test."

"Shut up," he said.

"No. You are so smart and you just let it rot. You're going down the tubes. You don't want to get a job, you don't want to read, you don't want to join a club, you don't want to do *anything*. And now you make a jerk out of Daddy."

His jaw twitched a little and I could tell he didn't like hearing it. But he gave me this huffy expression and said, "Leave me alone, Kimber. You're not my mother."

"I'm as close as you've got."

"Yeah, well you're *nowhere* near."

He turned around and stomped up the block to where his friends were. Now I *knew* he'd come back in two minutes because he still wasn't ready to defy his father totally. But he's only fourteen. The next time he'd stay up with his friends longer. And pretty soon he wouldn't listen at all.

I leaned hard against a maple tree and looked at the cop car. I was so mixed up. I knew I wasn't just yelling at Corey. I was yelling at Lou, even though Lou is the opposite of Corey when it comes to using his brain. But he's really the same. Obnoxious to people who care about him.

So I was letting out a lot of frustration. I had this overwhelming need to break up with Lou. But I was afraid of being alone and I hated myself for being a coward.

Oh, *man.*

"What's wrong?"

You said you'd keep us on track. I was supposed to talk about the fight Rob had in the hall over Martha. Not about me and Corey.

"It's okay, Kimber. You're on track."

No way. This is supposed to be about teenage love.

"It is."

What did any of this have to do with love?

"Think about it, Kimber. It'll come to you. But maybe we'd

better hold off on that hallway fight for a while, and move on to another part of the story."

Okay. Anyway, I realize Deena's sitting here and she hasn't said *anything* yet, so maybe she should have a chance.

"Fine, if she wants to."

And I'm *sorry* about hogging all this space with my own troubles. It's really selfish. Go ahead, Deena. Tape my mouth if you have to.

Chapter Five

Well, I don't know if I want to say anything. You made me look like a fool before.

Come on, Deena. We're all being honest here.

Well, you're so bitter about everything. My mom and dad are still in love, after twenty-two years. On their twentieth anniversary, he had a limo pick her up and drive her to the Waldorf in Manhattan. But he didn't let her know what was going on. He gave her little clues in rhyme. It was so beautiful.

Okay, it's great that your mom and dad are romantic. *My* mom ran out so I wouldn't know.

See what I mean? I'm sorry you have a lousy life, but it doesn't mean love doesn't exist.

So tell us about you and Phil. True love.

It *was* true love. You can put us down, but it doesn't change anything.

So tell us how it began. But don't leave out the night of passion at your house.

Forget it!

Well, *we* get to tell your story then, and we have to call it the way we see it.

No way. You'll make me sound like a slut. I'll tell it, but you'd better not add *anything*.

You got it.

Yeah, I got it, all right. But you know what? I'm not really angry. I feel sorry for you, the way you went out with Lou and hated him. But I *don't* feel sorry for myself. At least I gave my heart freely. You're afraid to do that.

Here:

I drew a rose for you, because I love you, and I wish you the eyes to see and the soul to feel, so you'll know when love comes.

Everyone says I forgot about Brett as soon as I saw Phil. I didn't forget about Brett. You don't just turn someone off like a faucet, you know? And I don't think he really turned *me* off that fast. I think his friends influenced him.

So I was upset for a while, but I could still see all the beautiful things about him. I didn't forget the roses he gave me, or the night he put the gold chain around my neck and whispered, "This isn't a chain I'm giving you; it's my heart."

So I kept the necklace. What was I supposed to do, melt it down? The necklace is a *symbol* of love. I *knew* Brett was gone. But the chain reminded me of when he was here:

"Love grows in the spring and dies in the winter. . . .
But its seed lives on, to grow again."

I met Phil at my Aunt Jenna's house up in Westchester. You go through this old run-down area and then you get to a hidden section with huge old houses on acres of land. This was in March and the trees were bare.

It was Uncle Mike's fortieth birthday, and they were having family and friends. I didn't know a lot of people there, and I was kind of uncomfortable. Aunt Jenna pumped me about my love life and I had to go to the bathroom to cry!

I was in a sun parlor when I saw Phil. We were sitting around and having fish. Joseph—that's their servant!—came around with the fish and we all took some. I was getting a headache sitting there and listening to these people talk in *low* tones, you know the way upper-class people talk? They were talking about invest-ments, like quarter *million* dollar investments. I mean, Mom and Dad take fifty dollars out of their paychecks to put into this fund, but these guys were heavy hitters.

I didn't understand most of it, even though I passed Econom-ics, so I was looking out the glass walls at the way the clouds looked against the landscaping. It was all kind of gray and pale yellow. And I saw Phil.

He was playing wiffle ball with some nieces and nephews. They were all dressed up, but they were running around and screaming at the top of their lungs. Phil was batting wiffle balls out to them and they were running after them. It wasn't too orga-nized, and it made me laugh.

I could tell that Phil was in college or in business. I liked watch-ing him. He had this lanky way of moving, but easy and natural. He had a gorgeous smile, and I could tell he loved children. He was so patient with them. So I got up and went outside.

It was pretty cold. I could feel the wind cutting through my blouse, but I didn't want to put on my coat. Maybe because *he* wasn't wearing a coat. I stuffed my hands into my jumper pockets because my knuckles were getting dry and blue, and I kind of stood around while he batted wiffle balls. He said, "Hi. I'm Phil Pizer."

"I'm Deena Russo."

His face looked pinched and cold. He said, "Are we related?"

"I don't know. Aunt Jenna's my aunt. My Mom's sister."

He thought for a minute. "Well, my Dad's sister is married to Mike's brother. So I don't think we're blood relatives."

"Doesn't look like it."

The little kids were yelling for him to keep hitting the ball. He hit another one out and they scrambled for it. He said to me, "Where are you from?"

"Long Island," I said. "Westfield. Nobody knows where that is."

"I know where it is," he said. "I live in Smithtown."

That's when I started to feel something. Maybe it was just the coincidence, but I got a little chill in my stomach.

"That's wild," I said. "Do you go to school or anything?"

"I go to Stony Brook," he said.

Fantastic. I gulped, and said, "I go to Westfield High. I'm a senior."

I just said it right out. I was terrified but I couldn't lie to him. He smiled at me and said, "I graduated from Westfield."

"No *way!*" I felt myself smile. "That's amazing."

"Yeah, *I* thought it was pretty amazing."

The little kids were jumping around now, pulling at his sleeves and whining for him to play. He gave them a smile and said, "Hey, listen, I want to talk to Deena for awhile. You guys choose up sides."

They groaned, but he handed one of them the yellow plastic bat and he came over to me. "Want to take a walk?"

I nodded. "Sure."

So we walked around the property. It was so easy to talk to him. I could feel the pain lifting off my chest.

And then he said, "Are you going out with anybody?"

I couldn't look him in the eye. I kept my head down and I kind of mumbled, "No."

"But you *were.*"

"You're pretty observant."

"Well, you have beautiful eyes, but there's a lot of crying in them."

I nearly fell down. I mean, how many guys talk that way? He was so incredibly sensitive. This was magic. Him being there, just when I needed somebody. And being the way he was. Part of it was that he was in college, and more mature. But he was so gentle and honest. That's something that's inside you.

I couldn't think of anything to say to him. My face was burning and I knew it was bright pink. I stepped on pine cones to make them crack. Then he bent down and picked up something and said, "Here. For you."

It was a piece of evergreen branch, like this:

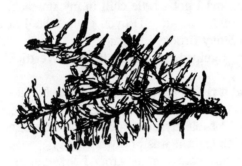

And he said, "The evergreen isn't beautiful, but it can take the weight of the snow and it will never die."

I held that piece of evergreen in my palm and trembled. Then I closed my fist around it and I looked right into Phil's eyes and I said, "Thanks."

He looked at me with so much feeling that I nearly fainted. His eyes are deep deep gray—well, you know what his eyes look like. He reached out and his fingers stroked my cheek. He said, "Come on. You're freezing to death out here."

So we walked back to the house and my whole day was different. Just when I needed to be cared for and touched, Phil came along. He is such a beautiful man, and I emphasize the word *man*. The way he knew what was in my heart, and the way he played with those children—I could imagine him as a father and a husband.

We spent the whole afternoon together, just talking. I kissed him good-bye, and I gave him my phone number. And he called me the next day. That's how I met him, and it proves that there's such a thing as true love and that you can find the right guy, sometimes when you're not even looking.

How's that, Kimber?

Pretty emotional, Deena. Are you going to tell the other part of it?

What other part?

The night in your house?

You're really pushing that, huh? Why? You think it proves something? Or do you just want to make me look stupid?

I just want to have the *whole* story.

Okay. I'm not afraid to tell it. It wasn't anything that major anyway. Only *you* make a big deal out of it.

The whole thing was silly. Phil and I went out together a few times and it was totally wonderful. It was so easy to talk to him. I told him all about my drawing and my dreams. He listened and held my hand and kept telling me I was beautiful. I needed to hear that.

And he never hit on me like some crude high school guy. He let everything take its natural course. You can call me anything you want, but when love is there . . .

Deena, nobody's calling you anything. That isn't the point, anyway.

I think it is. But I know when I'm right and when I'm wrong. I was wrong to go against Mom and Dad, I know that now. But it wasn't wrong to be with Phil.

It just kind of happened that Mom and Dad were going away for the weekend, on this cruise to nowhere. They always do stuff like that. It's really great the way they're so into each other. Mom asked me if I minded, and I said of course not. Why should I mind?

Uh, didn't you have that art exhibition that weekend, Deena?

Oh, give me a break, Kimber. I love when you try to concoct

things. Yes, I had the art exhibition, but I wasn't mad at Mom and Dad. They've seen my paintings plenty of times. Dad was lucky to get these tickets at the last minute, so I wasn't going to pout about it. In fact, I immediately asked Phil if he'd come see my artwork, and he said he'd love to, which made up for Mom and Dad not being there.

In fact, that's how he got to be at the house. I called him up and asked him if he wanted to go to the exhibition and we started talking and I said look, Mom will freak out if people try to call and don't get through. So why don't you come over? We can play Pictionary or watch a movie.

So he came over and we played some games and I made peanut butter cookies and we had wine coolers. We weren't trying to sneak around behind anyone's back. It was really innocent.

But it started to sleet and we'd gotten a little bit wasted, and I was afraid to let Phil drive home. So I said why don't you stay? He was really concerned about it. He kept asking me if my parents would get mad. I told him no, which wasn't exactly the truth.

And that was the whole thing. I know it was wrong, but it was late, and one thing led to another. I didn't feel guilty, except about doing that to Mom and Dad.

So if it means that much to you for me to tell it, there it is.

Deena! Come on, *all* of it!

Why are you so hot on this, Kimber? Are you jealous or something?

Yes. I admit it. I'm burning with jealousy.

All right, anything to get you off my back. Here it is, the big major incredible REVELATION!!!!

The next morning, I was making french toast. Phil came up behind me and he started to nuzzle the back of my neck. I squirmed and said, "Cut it out, I'll set the kitchen on fire." And he put his arms around my waist and kept nuzzling.

And then—wow, here it comes, you'd better lie down, folks!—his lips brushed against my gold chain . . .

Which gold chain, Deena?

The gold chain Brett gave me!! What are you, *psycho* or something? I was wearing Brett's chain. I *explained* it to you! It wasn't that I was still in love with Brett, but it represented the *memory* of our love. Why doesn't anyone understand?

We understand, Deena. But Phil didn't.

That's what you really want me to tell, right?

Okay, fine. Phil kind of stiffened up and held the chain between his thumb and forefinger and said, "What's this?"

"A chain," I said.

"Gift from your parents?" he asked, but I knew he'd already figured out that it wasn't.

I shook my head and kept turning the french toast with a fork. Outside, it was cold and sleety. My heart was racing like mad.

He stepped back. "Were you wearing that *last night*?"

I kept turning the french toast.

"Deena, were you wearing that last night?"

I nodded.

"Who gave it to you?"

"Nobody," I mumbled.

He didn't say anything for a minute and I died inside. I couldn't believe I'd been so stupid. I turned around and said, "Phil, don't make anything out of it because it's nothing. It's stupid. It's a mistake . . ."

I'm not even sure that's what I said. He looked at me like I'd turned into a lizard. His eyes froze over. He said, "You little slut!" in this low, awful voice, and then he spun around and ran out of the kitchen.

I remember that I left the french toast and it started to smoke and burn. The whole kitchen filled up with smoke and the smoke detector went off. I ran after Phil, totally panicked. He'd put on his shirt and his coat and he was headed for the front door.

"Let me explain," I yelled at him. "Phil, don't do this, *please* . . ."

I kept begging him to stay but he opened the door and slammed it behind him so hard that the knickknacks on the hall table rattled. I stood in the foyer crying hysterically, with the house filling up with smoke and the alarm going off. The neighbors were out because they heard the smoke detector and they saw Phil get in his car and drive away, which is how I got nailed.

And anyway, I ruined the frying pan so I had to explain that, too.

So I spent the day in my room crying and smashing things. I wasn't nonchalant about it, which is what everybody thinks. I *hated* myself. Is that what you want to hear?

Yeah, actually. It's kind of reassuring, Deena. And it shows that too much true love can be pretty dangerous.

It doesn't show anything except that I was stupid once.

Once? None of us were stupid only once.

Well, you can talk about anything you want. I've told you how I met Phil and how I almost lost him. But you *do* recall that we got back together, right?

For a while. Before your course of true love ran right through mine and made a huge mess. But I think you've been pretty brave to own up to all of this, and I think you're pretty super for giving me a rose, and I still love you, okay?

Okay. I just wish you'd understand me a little more.

We'll try. But *after* we tell the whole story!

Chapter Six

"Hi, this is your friendly author. I think all of you are doing a terrific job, and I'm impressed with your honesty. It takes a lot of courage to admit some of the things you're admitting."

Okay, what's the catch?

"No catch, Kimber. But you *did* say that I should keep you from wandering, right?"

Are we wandering?

"Well, I'd say you were *avoiding*. Nobody wants to talk about what happened after the Senior Weekend."

You're right. None of us wants to talk about how dumb we were.

"And I don't blame you. So I thought I might steal a chapter or two for that hallway fight. Do you mind?"

No. I think we were kind of hoping you'd help us out.

Okay. (I don't need the quotes now, Kimber.) Let's be brave and set the scene for the catastrophes:

It was April in Westfield, just after the Senior Weekend in Washington, D.C. Spring wasn't exactly in the air. Northwest winds blew cold rain and pewter skies over Westfield day after day. But the seniors could smell graduation. Huddled in their winter coats, they counted the days. And they struggled with love.

April was a critical time for love. Old romances soured, and new ones bloomed. Breakups left girls sobbing in the bathroom. Fights brought teachers running.

For our six swains, the fuse was especially short. The Senior Weekend had been a nightmare. Six hundred seniors, armed with boom boxes and junk food, had descended on the nation's capital with liquor and mischief:

Two football players were sent home for climbing to the hotel roof and rappelling into their girlfriends' room.

Eight seniors were barred from the Saturday night dance because they had a water-gun brawl in the lobby of the National Archives.

An entire wing of the hotel was suspended from Sunday's trip to Great Adventure because they staged an ice cube war.

And three girls were reprimanded for drinking with four Swedish boys. Rumor said that one of the girls spent the night with one of the guys, but there was no evidence—yet. For the purposes of *this* story, we're not concerned with the forty-seven seniors who were disciplined. We're interested in that alleged party with the Swedish boys. Because the girl in the rumor was Martha.

But for the moment, we'll skip to a few days after the weekend. On this particular Tuesday, at 10:03 A.M., the halls seethed with students, passing from third period to fourth period. Rain pattered dismally against windows. Let's locate our players in this scene:

Martha was coming from the Music Suite, where she'd finished

Concert Band. As she edged around a corner, she was caught up in the swirling tide of students in the gym lobby. Meanwhile, Rob was heading toward the central hallway from the "A" wing, which is on the opposite side of the building. He'd just gotten out of Mystery and Magic, his senior English class. He figured to meet with his buddies by the stairway and talk about what they were doing later. Rob's hair was damp from walking outside. His eyes looked like windows into hell. He hadn't gone on the Senior Weekend, because his boss at the garage wouldn't give him Saturday off, and he needed the money. So he'd *heard* about Martha but hadn't been there.

Now, between the "A" Wing and the Music Wing is the Social Studies Wing. Out of one of those rooms came Greg Fratelli and John Brody. They were jocks, but not the cream of the team. They were best known for massive parties that ended up on front lawns with cops making arrests. They were also the two guys who got sent home from the Senior Weekend for mountaineering on the roof.

They were ticked off at getting caught, and they were even more ticked off that Martha had slept with this Swedish guy and only got reprimanded. So they were not going to miss any opportunity to terrorize Martha and her boyfriend.

Meanwhile, Kimber was walking Lou to his Calculus class on the second floor. She did this even though it always made her late for Physics. But Lou *expected* to be escorted by Kimber. She remembered when she'd *flown* to his classroom, with heart hammering and palms sweating. She remembered the pride that threatened to burst her smiling face as she and Lou walked together.

Now she waited with impatience, and self-hatred. The Senior Weekend had been soggy and miserable. Lou had complained the whole time, and he and his buddies had played cards during the Saturday night dance. So on this morning, Kimber was sore. She and Lou walked without touching, each waiting for the other to talk.

Deena didn't take part in the melee that was only four minutes away, but it's important to know that she'd gotten back together with Phil. She'd cried her heart out for three days after he walked out, and then he called again. They met at El Torito and talked. Then they held hands across the table and looked into each other's eyes. She promised him that she would never wear Brett's chain again.

Deena, at this moment in the story, was walking into her art class which was opposite the Music Suite. She looked forward to the class because she was working on a pastel portrait of Phil. She was going to give it to him for his birthday.

That places all of the participants. In the next few seconds, Martha squeezed from the gym lobby into the Social Studies wing, and . . .

Hey! What am *I*? Chopped liver?

Jason! Oh. I guess I *did* exclude you. But this scene has to do with the main characters and the hallway fight after the Senior Weekend.

I went on the Senior Weekend. I went on Lightning Loops. I went on Rolling Thunder backwards. I shut my eyes a lot but I survived.

Well, okay, but this dramatic moment involves couples, and you're not part of a couple. . . .

So I'm not worth talking about.

Don't be defensive.

Sorry. But you see? You considered me *nada* because I didn't have a girlfriend. That's exactly what drives people like Kimber and Martha into stinko relationships. Individual hominids *can* be useful citizens. One can function for a time without a romantic companion, *¿si?*

I guess you have a point.

Leave my appendages out of this. But place me in the scene. I was, at the moment of the donnybrook, in the school store, to ask Mr. Carman if *Expressions* could sell magazines there. So I was only ten yards from the arena.

All right. Let's place Jason Goldman in the school store.
Now, within the next few seconds, Martha squeezed from the gym lobby into the Social Studies wing. Greg Fratelli and John Brody met between two classroom doors and laughed to each other as they scanned the passing bodies. Rob shuffled behind a logjam of students feeding into the central hallway. On the second floor, Kimber and Lou passed the main stairway, about to turn left to head for Lou's classroom.
At 10:04:23, Greg Fratelli pointed and said to John Brody, "Hey, look!"
It wasn't hard for Greg to distinguish Martha in the crowd. Her frizzed mane of carrot hair was a flag. Greg edged along the row of lockers to get into position. At six feet, four inches, Greg was powerfully muscled. Black hair hung in a lick over his forehead. John Brody wore clipped, white-blonde hair and was lankier. They *leaked* strength.
When Martha was opposite their doorway, Greg thundered, "HEY! SULLIVAN!"
This was not thunder you could ignore. Heads swivelled, and the stream backed up. Martha knew Greg was calling to her. She tightened her lips and looked down.
"YO! DON'T KEEP WALKING, BABE!"
Martha flushed, trying to escape. But John had already maneuvered into the hallway and blocked her. She stopped short of his monolithic form and looked into his eyes.

"Don't walk away," he said.

"Suck ice," Martha told him.

"Where's Robbie?" John said. "Or is it Sven?"

Greg bulled his way to where John stood. They created a blockade that forced everyone to flow around them.

Greg said, "Do Swedish guys yodel when they do it?" He and John snickered.

"What the hell is wrong with you?" Martha said.

"Nothin's wrong with *us*," Greg answered. "Something's wrong with *you*. Right?"

"Could you let me get to class?"

"You won't get in trouble. Just show your Honor Society Pass, no sweat."

Martha's jaw worked with impotent rage. She felt her eyes grow wet. "Get the hell away from me."

"No way," Greg said. "You can hang with us, babe."

John said, "I have Swedish blood, Sullivan. Want to taste some?"

"Cretin."

She was painfully aware of eyes, stabbing her like hot pins. She knew if she tried to sidestep her tormentors, they'd block her again. They were determined to make her late for class. Getting her in trouble was a payback. Making her look like a slut in front of strangers was a double payback.

At this moment, Rob was leaning against the brick wall by the central stairway. He checked his watch, scanned faces, and sighed. The kids were moving faster, like red blood cells through a vein.

"Damn," Rob murmured. The guys had gotten hung up, probably at the Deli. He blew out a breath, and headed down the Social Studies hallway.

He didn't become aware of the obstruction until he was almost on top of it. When his eyes registered the two jocks, he automatically adjusted his path to go around them. Even though he was a jock himself, he didn't think much of these boys. There were guys who played sports for fun, and there were guys who played to inflict pain.

As he slithered between John Brody and a trio of gum-cracking girls, Rob realized that everybody was looking at the jocks. He looked, too. He saw Martha.

Martha said, "Rob!"

Rob saw that she was crying, and his stomach tightened. But his brain was sending conflicting messages.

"What's going on?" he asked.

"Hey, Rob!" John Brody rolled his shoulders menacingly.

Greg said, "Don't sweat it, Robbie. We're just getting a piece."

Rob didn't need this. The whole damned hallway was watching him. He levelled his gaze at Martha. "You want to walk with me?"

She nodded.

But the boys weren't going to let it go. John Brody stepped between Rob and Martha. "Stay loose, Robbie."

"Hang it up. I'm not in the mood."

"No? I hear Martha's *always* in the mood."

Rob's head throbbed. He knew he'd get his jaw broken if he fought with these guys, and he couldn't afford to get laid up now. Worse, he didn't feel *mad* enough to fight. He was sore at *Martha* for putting him in this position.

John crowded Rob, daring him to make a move. Rob clenched his fists. "Get out of my face, Brody."

"You want to go somewhere?"

Martha stared at Rob. The surrounding kids were beginning to thicken, forming a ring around Martha. They smelled a fight. For Martha, a fight meant the principal's office and suspension, and as it was, she had to appear in Mr. Sachs's office next Tuesday about the Senior Weekend.

Rob knew the stakes. If Martha was a normal girlfriend, no problem. He'd be whaling on these guys right now, getting his face kicked in. But if he fought for *Martha*, he'd look like a fool.

His friends *expected* him to dump her. She'd shown him up. Everyone in this hallway understood that Martha deserved what she got.

So Rob said, "I don't have time for this."

With his face afire, he turned away. He'd done it. He'd dumped Martha with those words, and she knew it.

John Brody perceived that Rob was throwing in the towel. Part of him respected Rob for having the guts to wash his hands of Martha. But part of him was already pumped for violence. He felt a rush of disappointment at being deprived. His body ached for a fight.

So he gave Rob a light two-handed shove. "Get lost," he said.

Rob countered with a shove back. "Keep off."

The smell of battle charged the heavy air. On the second floor, Lou and Kimber were passing the staircase when someone said, "There's a fight in the hall."

Kimber felt her throat pull taut. She couldn't deal with fights. Lou's eyes flickered down the stairs and caught a boy charging into the hallway.

"Hey!" Lou called. "What's going on?"

Kimber sighed angrily. The call of the wild! The kid downstairs yelled up, "It's that girl from the weekend! Some guys fighting over her!"

Kimber felt her blood freeze. "Oh, God. Martha."

Lou uttered a brief obscenity. Then he stunned Kimber by wrenching away and hurling himself at the stairs. Kimber said, "Where are you *going*?" and followed him. She slid her hand along the railing and then swung herself into the turn. But Lou had already disappeared down the corridor.

Kimber saw and heard the commotion as she emerged into the hallway, but she was bumped by a burly Phys. Ed. teacher. She tried to make headway, but the corridor had gridlocked. How had Lou gotten through?

Lou had simply cannonballed his way along the lockers, flinging aside anyone who stood in his way. Blindly, he shoved and grunted until he found the ring of spectators. He arrived just as John Brody shoved Rob for the second time. This shove spun Rob hard against the lockers.

Lou stared at Rob, and then saw Martha. She looked at him, dumbfounded.

But that was nothing to her astonishment when he held out his hand and yelled, "Come on!"

John Brody, who had been awaiting Rob's charge, turned at this unexpected noise. He couldn't comprehend what was happening, since his entire mind and body were primed for combat. Greg Fratelli had been watching dispassionately.

"Butt out," Greg warned.

Lou gave Greg a stare of such contempt that Greg was taken aback. Then Lou renewed his offer to Martha. "Come on, let's go."

Martha reached out to take his hand. "I'm with you."

But Greg Fratelli got there first. His hand came down like an attacking hawk. "HEY! ARE YOU *STUPID?*"

Lou was lean and of average height. Greg expected to flick this insect aside. But Lou was not going to be flicked. His fury, fueled by a secret that not even Kimber knew at the moment, was backed by strength from playing lacrosse. He jabbed Greg in the kidneys hard enough to stun Greg into letting go. Then he pushed hard, against Greg's chest. Greg pitched backwards into the crowd, taking down a few bystanders.

John Brody plucked Lou from the center of the hallway and spun him around. But his intended jawbreaker never landed. John was bearhugged from the rear by the Phys. Ed. teacher, Mr. Eduardo.

"That's it!" Mr. Eduardo grunted, straining to hold John. Lou felt himself yanked backwards and knew instinctively that these were faculty hands.

"Okay," Lou panted. "No sweat. I won't do anything."

Lou had been captured by Mr. Albanese, a paunchy assistant

principal. Mr. Eduardo was still wrestling John, who was cursing and spitting like a trapped wolverine. Lou looked for Greg Fratelli, who was gone! No honor among jocks.

Rob was gone, too. Martha looked at Lou with curiosity. "Are you okay?"

Lou nodded. He was still confused. Martha kept staring at Lou. She knew what his secret was, but she hadn't totally connected it to his sudden appearance.

Kimber finally broke through the mob. She looked with incoherence at her hard-breathing, flushed boyfriend, who stood guarded by the AP. She also saw Martha looking at Lou, and figured out that Lou had rescued Martha. The realization made her feel ice cold and empty.

"Lou?" she said. "What is going *on*?"

He shook his head. "Nothing. Go to class."

"Don't play games!" she cried. "Since when do you get into brawls in the hallway?"

Martha said, "He was trying to help me." She said it a little defensively.

"What was happening?"

Martha put a helpless hand to her face. "These jerks were hassling me."

John Brody had finally ceased his struggles and stood sullenly inside a classroom. Mr. Eduardo guarded the door. Dimly, Kimber heard the late bell sound.

"Great," she said. "Now what do I do? They'll send me outside and I'll be ten minutes late."

Lou glared at her. "Kimber, we're in a little trouble here, you know? The biggest problem in the western world is not your lateness to class!"

Mr. Albanese raised his eyebrows at the outburst. "Calm down," he ordered. To Kimber, he said, "We told the hallway duty people to let you go to class from this corridor. Just don't stop anywhere."

"Thanks," Kimber said. But the news didn't make her happy.

She knew Lou was right; she'd been selfish just now. No. She'd been *jealous*. Jealous of what?

And now she *had* to get going. Angrily, she said, "I'll see you after eighth."

"Yeah, sure," Lou said, pushing back his hair.

"Call me later," Martha said.

"Okay."

Kimber turned, with a frustrated backward glance, and stalked up the corridor wondering how it happened that *her* boyfriend was under house arrest with Martha Sullivan. It didn't make sense. At least, it *shouldn't* have made sense. If it did, she'd be *really* upset.

Mr. Albanese checked the now-deserted hallway for stragglers. Then he muttered something into the walkie-talkie, which crackled a return message. "Over and out," he said, which made Martha giggle.

"Okay," he said. "Main office. Let's go."

Martha looked searchingly at Lou. "Where did you come from? Krypton?"

"Upstairs."

"Thanks. I don't know what to say. I didn't expect you to fight for me."

"It's okay."

She licked her lips and wiped half-dried tears from her cheeks. "Rob got here first, but he *didn't* fight for me."

"Are you surprised?"

She shook her head, then lowered it as fresh, unexpected crying came. She sniffed, angry at her weakness.

Lou embraced her. She shuddered in his arms, once, and then stiffened. He let her go and she took a deep breath and smiled. "Thanks."

"No problem."

She looked terrible. Her mascara, which she didn't put on too well in the first place, had run in teary rivulets down her freckled face. But her smile was like the sun rising over an Adirondack lake. That's what Lou thought of, anyway, since he loved to go speedboating on Adirondack lakes. He hadn't thought about Adirondack lakes with Kimber, not in a long time.

But right now, Lou was not rational. Adrenaline made him high. He glanced at John Brody in the classroom and shuddered. He imagined his jaw wired shut for six weeks. He'd been a horse's rear end. The excitement of it made him intoxicated.

Meanwhile, Kimber returned the nod of the English teacher guarding the central stairway and continued down the wide corridor past the school store and the library. Windows on the opposite wall showed breaks in the clouds.

She was growing more agitated each second. She glanced at the window of the school store and saw Jason inside, talking to Mr. Carman. Jason turned and saw her. He waved wildly and blew kisses. She laughed silently and waved back. He raised a finger to tell her to wait.

She leaned against a showcase window and watched Jason. Mr. Carman got a wrapped brownie from a shelf and gave it to him. Jason slipped the brownie into his shirt pocket and came out into the corridor.

"Hi," he said. He went up to Kimber and scrutinized her face. "You are in major pain, sweetie. What happened?"

Startled, Kimber felt her eyes fill. She clenched her hands and bit her lip, hard.

"Uh oh," Jason said. "*Bad* news." He gently hugged her and she hugged him back, sobbing idiotically.

"I'm sorry," she said into his bony shoulder.

"I have this effect on women," Jason said. He rubbed her back. "Let it go. Just try not to get mucous on my shirt."

She laughed and pulled back slowly. She gripped his hands tightly. "Thanks, babe. I needed a hug."

"*I* need exotic sex," Jason said.

"Stop," she admonished. "Don't joke. I just need a friend."

"No joke," he said. He dug the brownie from his shirt pocket.

It had gotten pretty mashed. "I bought you a present. Hugged brownie."

She laughed, half crying again, and took it. "Thank you." She kissed his cheek.

"I'll never wash my face," he said. Then he cringed. "Whoops. I promised no jokes."

"Walk me to class, okay?"

"Sure. What *did* happen?"

She shook her head. "There was a fight down the hall. Some jocks were harassing Martha, and Lou jumped in."

"*Lou* jumped in?" Jason's eyes glimmered shrewdly. "Interesting."

He hooked his arm through hers and walked with her past windows filled with stormy sky. Kimber appreciated the warmth of Jason's affection because she was very cold and lonely right now. She kept her confusion to herself because she wanted to sort it out. She was too stubborn to throw the problem into someone else's lap.

Jason swallowed yet another poison pill, and contented himself with being near Kimber as her confidant. He hadn't seen Lou, looking dangerous and sexy in the corridor, but he could imagine. He knew the way Kimber and Martha must have looked at him, and he knew it was a look he would never in his life know from a woman.

So, as John, Martha, and Lou were escorted by Mr. Albanese to the Main Office, Kimber and Jason walked the empty hallways. The fight had only lasted for thirty seconds, but not one of them was in the same romantic situation.

Chapter Seven

Yikes. That is *weird*, seeing myself like that (this is Kimber, by the way). The memories are *not* thrilling. I had all these conflicting feelings inside me. I was scared and jealous and angry and who knows what else?

See, that's the problem. Somebody *declared* that you have to get *engaged* the minute you go out with a guy. You're supposed to be in love, and totally committed to each other. It's tough. My Mom and Dad were married for fourteen *years* and it fell apart. And we've got all these other pressures—getting into college, getting a license, getting jobs—so handling commitments is not easy.

Take getting together, for instance. Way back about a million pages ago, you said that Lou and I met at the Junior Banquet and fell in love while we were dancing. Not exactly. Yeah, Martha and Rob got together like that, but only because Rob was wasted. Lou and I followed the *Law*.

"What's the Law?"

I'll tell you. Now stay with this. It ain't easy:

I was a gung-ho junior, jumping up and down all the time, joining everything in school. You know, like my smiling face is in *every club photo in the yearbook*! I mean, if there was a meeting somewhere, I went to it.

You should have known me then. Boy, I was bouncy. No, I was *obnoxious*. I used to flutter around going "Yippee, we're going to build a float, yippee, we're going to sell cookies, yippee, we're going on a field trip!" I wore all these cutesy-poo outfits to school and I sat *right in front* in every classroom.

I was compensating, of course. I was blown away by Mom running off and I couldn't handle it. Corey became a dirtbag, but I went the other way. I had to have a million friends and every teacher had to love me and I had to win awards. *You* know.

So Lou became aware of me, and he was interested. His friends thought he was nuts because I was this geek running around singing in the hallways, but Lou was tired of being the All American scholar/athlete. Anyway, he thought I was cute. I won't argue.

So now he had to find someone who knew me to let me know he was interested. That's how it works. A guy cannot just walk over and say, "Hi, I noticed you running around singing in the hallways, and I wondered if you wanted to go to the movies Friday night." I *know* that would be logical. But it's not *done*. You have to be introduced.

Fortunately, Lou's friend Joe knew Brett, who was going out with Deena at the time, and Deena and Brett knew *me*. So Joe caught hold of Brett and told him that Lou was interested in me. Brett told Deena. That Friday night, Deena and Martha and I went to the mall to hang out. As we're wandering around eating ice cream cones and looking at jewelry, Deena says that Brett told *her* that Lou was interested in *me*, and was *I* interested in *Lou*?

I was kind of dumbfounded because Lou was the *star* of Westfield High. He was rich, he was hot, and he was brilliant. So I told Deena she was crazy, but she said *Brett* said *Joe* said it was true. So I figured what the heck, if it was a joke, I'd find out soon enough. I said yeah, sure I was interested.

Which meant we got to Step Two. Lou and I had to get together. It so happened the Junior Banquet was coming up. Now I was good friends with Courtney Rothstein, who was Junior Class President. This kid Fred McKinley was doing all the bus lists for the banquet on the computer, and Courtney got him to put my table and Lou's table on the same bus. That is, the *people* at our tables, not the tables themselves.

Oh God. I'm starting to sound like Jason.

Anyway, comes the night of the Junior Banquet, and Lou and I are on the same bus, and of course so is Brett and Deena and everyone else. So now Brett can introduce me and Lou. It's okay, because I know that *Lou* is interested and Lou knows that *I'm* interested. That means we can see if either one of us is interested in going further than being interested. Got this so far?

We started off, with Deena and Brett, and Martha, and me, and Lou, and some other people dancing in a group, so the unattached kids wouldn't feel left out. The fast dancing was every man for himself, but by the time we got to the slow dancing, it was okay for Lou to give me the eye, and for me to dance with him.

And yeah, I fell in love while the colored lights spun. How could I *not* fall in love? He looked totally mint, and I'd gone a long, long time without a boyfriend. Flat, funny Kimber was now scooped up in the muscular arms of the most beautiful boy in school. Talk about teenage fairy tales! I rested my cheek against his neck and shut my eyes and went delirious. This was major romance.

But I couldn't tell Lou how I felt because this was just getting together. Oh, yeah, we went out into the lobby and talked for a while. I learned how he hated all the pressure on him to be the best and how he loved sloppy joes and how he liked to paint watercolor pictures when he was a kid but his Dad wouldn't let him because it was wimpy. I kept pushing back a lick of his hair and gazing moistly into his eyes and getting sicker and sicker with love.

We even kissed a few times, on the dance floor, and on the bus, while everyone looked discreetly the other way. But we were *not* going out yet.

First we had to find out if we *really* got along. To do that, Lou had to call me. If Lou didn't call me, I'd know he wasn't interested. So I went home to bed, clutching my battered white teddy bear and praying.

But YAY! Lou called the next MORNING!!! We set it up to go to the beach one night (which is *not* a date!). Now I *know* what you're thinking. THE BEACH AT NIGHT!!!! O-o-o-o-o-h-h! but that's not what happens (well, not usually). You go to the beach, or to his house, or to your house, to get to know each other alone, to decide if you want to go further. And that's what we did. It was cold because it was March. There were patches of icy snow on the dunes. We sat on hard, freezing sand, all bundled up in coats, and we talked. Yeah, we made out a little. I would have made out a lot, to tell the truth, except it was too cold to take off anything. And it got late and he had to drop me off at my house.

But I knew I was crazy for him. And now we were ready to discuss the terms of our relationship.

Terms, you repeat? Is this a *contract*?

Not written (teens don't write much), but yeah, it's a kind of contract. Lou and I (*if* he called me again) had to decide if we were both ready for a commitment, which meant we'd be *going out* with each other, which meant an exclusive relationship. Or maybe we *weren't* ready for a commitment, which meant we could *see* each other, which meant we could see other people, too. But that never really works out, because if you're seeing other people, you're basically going through the same process with some other guy and pretty soon you're going to get a commitment.

To make a long story short, Lou called me again, and we both decided we wanted a commitment. Once we agreed on that, we had our first date. I remember hanging up the phone when we decided to go out with each other, and doing a cartwheel in my room! I knocked the stereo off its shelf. I was irrational, man.

And by the end of the summer, he was tired of *me,* and I was pissed off at *him,* and he was taking me for granted, and I hated him for being a user, and it wasn't much fun. But it's not that easy to break up after going through that whole routine. You feel so *guilty.* You don't want to be the one to end it. Besides, it's socially convenient—maybe even necessary—to have a boyfriend, for all the banquets and stuff. You get more afraid of being solo than being miserable.

And the worst part is you get jealous if you think he's looking at another girl or even if another girl is *interested,* and you're jealous even if you can't stand him any more. Which brings me back to when I saw Martha looking at Lou like he was naked. Half of me had been wishing he'd break up with me, and now I was spitting because he looked interested in my best friend.

Talk about screwed up.

"Well, I don't know about screwed up, but I don't think I've seen such rigid rules since the eighteenth century! You mean you can't just meet someone, feel attracted, and start dating?"

I guess you *can,* but it's unusual. You're just expected to go through the procedures.

"So if Lou was really interested in Martha after that hallway fight, he'd have to go to someone who knew Martha and get introduced, even though he already *knew* her?"

No. Because then he's hitting on his girlfriend's best friend, which is cheating, which is a whole other story.

"It wouldn't be part of *this* story, would it?"

(Sigh) Yes, it would. Let me build up to it, though.

A couple of days after that hallway fight, I was down in the Music Suite. I had to go to work at four, and I just didn't feel like going home. The sun was warm and the sky was soft. It was spring, and I was sick of homework and tests and teachers.

I was also sick of listening to Martha's complaints and Deena's complaints and everyone else's complaints. So I went into the band room, which is this cavernous room with peeling yellow walls and steam pipes running along the ceiling. I flung my jacket over a chair and sat at the beat-up piano and started to play. I took lessons starting when I was eight and I stopped when I was thirteen. I can play pretty well, except I'm rusty.

I was doing fragments of Clementi and Chopin and anything else that popped into my head. I got more and more frustrated as I played because I didn't see anything working out for me. I sat there crying, and wished for some fairy godmother to wave her wand and solve my problems.

The door opened, and Jason walked in.

I *heard* the door but didn't look for a minute. I had this silly fantasy that it was some terrific guy, and he'd listen to me play and fall in love with me and change my life. But you can sort of *feel* who's around, even without seeing, and I knew it wasn't my fantasy.

So I looked over and said, "Hi, Jason."

"Heard you playing," he said. "Sounds pretty good."

I said, "Thanks, I'm just fooling around."

"I could get into that."

I smiled. "How come you're here?"

"We were supposed to have a newspaper meeting, but Mrs. Gibbs never showed up."

"Oh," I said.

"How come *you're* here?"

I told him. I kind of knew that Jason had really come in because he wanted to be with me. I *hope* that doesn't sound conceited. You know the feeling, right? When you know someone likes you?

Pretty soon, we got into talking about me. Jason is very good at drawing someone out. He asked why I was so down and I talked about Martha and Deena and Corey. Eventually, I talked about how I had to go to a State school because there was no money, and that led to talking about the Prom and how I was miserable because I couldn't get the dress I wanted.

Jason was sitting in a folding chair, facing the piano. "So you need cash, huh?"

"Yeah."

"Get another job."

I laughed. "Right. In my spare time."

"You could always go into business."

"Doing what? Selling my body?"

"Hey!"

"Shut up."

I smiled, but suddenly I got a hairy surge of anger. I slammed both hands on the keyboard, making a crashing chord. Then I slumped back. Jason got up and leaned on the piano. "Why don't you have a fund raiser?"

I laughed. "I could start my own club and have a candy sale."

"That's exactly what I mean."

"What's exactly what you mean?"

"Buy a bunch of candy and sell it. You could make a bundle. *Expressions* made a thousand bucks on its candy sale."

I wasn't sure if he was serious or not. "Jason, there's one little catch. I'm not a club."

"So? The ravenous students of Westfield couldn't care less. They'll buy candy from anybody."

I exhaled tiredly and shook my head. "Sometimes you're more weird than usual."

"Okay, don't listen to me." He looked up at the ceiling and his lips moved in silent calculation. "Let's see, if you paid thirty-three cents each for the candy and you sold them for fifty cents each, that's seventeen cents profit. Figure twenty items to a bag is a total of six dollars and sixty cents, and you make ten dollars, which leaves three dollars and forty cents profit. So if you sell fifty bags, that's a hundred and seventy dollars right there! Pretty easy money."

I stared at him. *"Jason!* I can't *do* it. The school doesn't allow you to sell candy for your own profit, remember? It's got to be a club activity."

"So if anybody asks, tell them you're selling for *Expressions.*"

"Sure. And then everyone will come to me and ask where they can pick up candy to sell."

"So give them the candy and then pocket the money."

"Get *away!*" I stood up, suddenly restless. A warm wind was blowing the tree branches, which were just starting to bud out.

Jason said, "I was kidding about the last part. You just say that you don't know what club it is. Nobody's going to ask anyway."

I looked at him over the top of the piano. "Why are you so into this, Jason? Are you on drugs?"

"Yes," he said. "Tylenol. Actifed. Kaopectate. I have a five-Flintstones-a-day habit."

I rolled my eyes and went to the window. I looked out at the empty parking lot and the tree shadows on Post Road and the cars going by. I said, "Sometimes your jokes are really cruel."

"What did I do wrong?" he said. "I was trying to help."

"You just make it worse."

Jason came over to where I stood. He looked almost like an old man in his blue polo shirt and jeans. The sun caught his face and emphasized how pale he was. But his eyes were so piercing that they scared me.

"Kimber, I wasn't kidding about selling candy."

"It's *illegal,* Jason!"

"Yeah, but it's exciting."

"You're loony."

"And you're beautiful."

I sighed angrily, but somehow, insanely, he was getting to me. "Where am I supposed to get all this candy?" I asked. "I can't call up a fundraising company and order it."

"Cheap John's," Jason said. "Three candy bars for a buck. As much as you want. Fifty bags times twenty pieces is a thousand pieces . . ."

"Is three hundred and thirty dollars!" I said. "If I had three hundred and thirty dollars, I wouldn't need extra money!"

"Okay, okay," he said. "So start small. Start with ten bags. Ten bags times twenty pieces is sixty-six bucks."

"I don't *have* sixty-six bucks."

"I can lay out forty," he said. "Can you put in twenty-six? It's an investment, Kimber. Guaranteed return. And I won't take profit, just my forty back."

He stood there with his eyes gleaming. I looked out the windows again and then at him. "I don't believe I'm even discussing this. I have to be at work in an hour."

"So let's go to Cheap John's and see what they have. We can make a decision there."

"Jason, I'm not going to do it."

He took a step closer to me. "Why not, Kimber? You're graduating in two months. End of high school. End of childhood. And you never did anything stupid or unsafe or wrong." He grabbed both my arms and stood close to me. "Just one time, be crazy. Get some cash, buy a dress that'll melt Lou's underwear. Feel terrific. You deserve it, Kimber. More than anybody else."

I started to shiver, and my eyes got wet. Usually, Jason just hugged me and said warm things. But now he was causing pain.

But I was turned-on. All at once I *wanted* to sell candy. I realized—now get this—that I was jealous of Martha for being in trouble! Somewhere inside my twisted brain, I thought that Lou found her irresistible because of what she'd done on the Senior Weekend! *I* wanted to be irresistible!

This all flashed through my mind in about a nanosecond. But the spring sun was warm on the side of my face and Jason was hypnotizing me. So I said, "Okay, let's go to Cheap John's and *look* at the candy. But I'm *not* going to do this."

He smiled at me. "Ah, you're weakening. Soon, soon, you will be mine forever. HA HA HA HA HA HA!"

He did a diabolical laugh and I laughed, too. Then he grabbed me close and made a big thing out of kissing my hand and my lips, exaggerated and humorous, you know? But it still sent a little electric shock through me.

"Come on," I said to Jason. "Your car or mine?"

"Mine's got an oil leak," he said.

I nodded and we gave each other a high five. He smiled at me with the closest thing to real love I ever saw in a smile, and I smiled back. *Boy,* did I feel great at that moment.

And boy, did things go downhill.

Chapter Eight

Not to keep you in suspense, I *did* go to Cheap John's with Jason and we bought a bunch of candy. It was fantastic, walking up and down the aisle, picking out Milky Ways and peanut butter cups and throwing it all into shopping baskets. I hadn't felt this way for at least six months. It was the way I *used* to feel, when I was into all those clubs.

We stood on line, and I kept thinking that detectives were going to come up and arrest me. The cashier gave us this bizarre look when we put all the candy on the counter. Jason had like eighty dollars on him, and I gave *him* a look. I think he must have planned this. So he paid for the candy and the cashier put it in four big plastic bags. I was laughing hysterically by the time we got out to the parking lot.

"This is insane," I said. "And where am I going to get bags for this? It's got to look like the bags the clubs use."

"We've still got a bunch of them left from the *Expressions* candy sale, remember?"

"We do?"

"Yup. Locked in Mr. Alterson's closet. I'll ask him for the bags tomorrow morning and we can have it all ready to sell by tomorrow afternoon."

The sky turned brighter and the sun reflected off millions of pieces of broken glass in the parking lot. "How are you going to get him to give you the bags?"

"I'll tell him I have to organize my munitions collection."

He smiled and I shook my head. I would have hugged him but we were each lugging two bags. We got to my car and I put the bags down to unlock the door. "I can't believe I'm doing this. I'm going to get suspended."

"An acceptable risk."

"Sure." We loaded the car with the bags of candy and I stood by the open door, looking at Jason's hair blowing in the wind. "Thanks for doing all this for me."

"Hey, you're giving me your body, so it's no big deal."

I laughed, and drove Jason back to school, by which time the whole car smelled like a chocolate factory. And of course, on the way, I had a Snickers and Jason ate two packages of peanut butter cups. We gossiped about kids we knew, and ranked on teachers we hated, and for a few minutes, everything was okay.

Maybe this criminal activity led to the weird talk I had with Daddy that night. It isn't even part of this saga, but let me tell you about it anyway.

Like I told you, we didn't talk much. He'd come home beat, and make phone calls and write out his reports until about eleven at night, and then he'd have a snack in the kitchen and go up to bed. I'd listen to him trudging around downstairs and I'd watch lights go on and off and think about how lonely he had to be. When he turned off the lamp in his bedroom, and the house got dark and quiet enough to hear the refrigerator humming, I'd sometimes cry for him.

The night after I bought the candy, I came home from work and he was sitting in the family room watching TV! Wow, I thought, this was pretty unusual. I said, "Hi," while I hung up my coat in the hall closet.

"Hi," he said.

I came into the family room and he was sitting in this battered old chair with a torn brown slipcover on it. We'd gotten the chair from my Aunt May before I was even born. Mom and Dad could never afford to buy a new one. Dad was watching a Mel Brooks movie on the VCR.

I perched on the arm of the chair and kissed his head. "How come you're relaxing?"

"I'm exhausted," he said.

"Good reason. Did you have dinner?"

He said yes. That's when I noticed the glass on the coaster next to him. It was one of the tumblers from the bar and it was half filled with a kind of brown/orange liquid and ice cubes. That was Daddy's favorite drink: rum and orange juice.

But Daddy was *not* a drinker, except at parties and then he only drank one or two. Of course, he hadn't had many parties lately.

He knew I saw the glass. I didn't say anything, but it kind of dropped the floor from under me.

I went in and made myself supper and I snuck a look at *Moby Dick* while I ate. I couldn't deal with it, even though we were having a major test on it in two days. I kept thinking about the four bags of candy in the car. My stomach clutched. Suddenly it was the most loony idea in the world.

That's when I went in to Daddy. I thought about asking his opinion of this venture. I think I hoped he'd forbid me to do it. I also wanted to see if he looked really sloshed.

So I plopped down on the couch and stared at him. Not exactly subtle. Daddy aimed the remote control and zapped Mel Brooks. Suddenly the set was a gray square of glass and the family room jumped back into focus. Daddy said, "What's up, Kimber? You look like something's on your mind."

I shrugged. We'd never had long talks. Daddy's shy and

even when I was a little kid, he ducked away from one-on-one.

"Nothing much," I said. "I didn't mean for you to turn off the set."

"No problem. When I turn it on again, the tape will be in the same place. Magic of technology."

"What did people do before VCRs?" I asked.

And that's what started the weird conversation. It went something like this (I'll write it like a play because we didn't do anything while we were talking except sit there, so there's nothing much to describe):

DADDY: We learned to be disappointed. That's something you kids don't know. If we missed a TV show, it was gone. Especially way back in the early days when everything was live.

KIMBER: I know about being disappointed.

DADDY: Yeah? *When?* Any show on TV can be taped, and there are thirty-seven channels, and if you don't like what's on, you go rent a movie. I remember we had one movie theater in town, and the picture changed on Wednesday. Once you saw it, you had to wait until next Wednesday to see a new one.

KIMBER: Well, I notice *you* embrace the new technology.

DADDY: Sure I do. But I worry about *you* guys. You don't learn how to discover yourselves.

KIMBER: I've discovered myself, don't worry.

There was a long silence. I could hear the refrigerator humming in the kitchen. Daddy looked at me really hard, the way he used to when I was little and got in trouble in school and he *knew* it. Then he picked up the drink and had some.

DADDY: Are you upset about the drink?

KIMBER: (I shrugged.) No.

DADDY: Yes you are.

KIMBER: I'm really not upset. I'm just surprised because you never drink alone.

DADDY: I've done it a few times. Usually, I just get sleepy and it's no fun.

KIMBER: So how come tonight?

DADDY: Now and then it gets really rough. Sometimes I can't go downstairs and face the work or deal with the debts or think about most of my life being over.

KIMBER: Come on! You're young!

DADDY: My genetics give me ten or twenty more years at the outside. (He smiled.) I know I'm being morbid. I don't want to scare you, princess. I haven't turned alky yet.

KIMBER: Good. I know life stinks, Daddy. But you have to keep fighting.

DADDY: Well, I'm glad you believe in me. (He took another swig and leaned way back, his eyes half shut.) So. Anything else to discuss?

I was about to say no. I really was. I knew he wanted to put the movie back on and be alone with his thoughts. But I was scared he was going to commit suicide, so I didn't want to leave him alone. That's one reason I came up with my question. The other reason is that, seeing him drunk, I thought of Lou, and the words tumbled out. "Daddy," I said, "How did you *know* you were in love when you got engaged?"

DADDY: What?

KIMBER: When you met Mommy and decided to get engaged. How did you know you were going to stay in love forever?

DADDY: (Looking just a mite embarrassed!!) Well, we *didn't* stay in love forever.

KIMBER: I know. What made you think you *would*?

DADDY: Why are you asking this now? Are you getting engaged?

KIMBER: No. I'm just interested.

He leaned back and his eyes half closed again. "It isn't that interesting," he said. "I was never *in* love with your mother."

His voice was steady and very calm. He'd thought about saying this to me. He wanted me to know. But I wasn't exactly ready.

KIMBER: Come on!

DADDY: If you want to hear the truth, that's the truth.

KIMBER: You were *never* in love??

DADDY: I didn't say that. I've been in love. The worst was a girl named Lauren. I met her when we were both camp counselors upstate. She had a boyfriend back home, but I fell in love anyway. I gave her my favorite record albums and wrote long hopeless letters. She enjoyed the attention. She didn't even flinch when she told me the guy was coming home from the Air Force.

KIMBER: I never knew.

DADDY: It wasn't a classic love story. I met your mother when I was already twenty-five. We were made for each other. She put guys off because she liked to be in control, and I put *girls* off because I was boring. We both needed company.

KIMBER: It sounds real exciting.

DADDY: We had some fun dates. I think I *wanted* to get married, just to get out of the rat race of finding girlfriends. So I bought her a ring and gave it to her in the car, in the parking lot—

KIMBER:—behind Waldbaum's, I know. And you had the ring in a paper bag and you dropped it in the car. I've heard the story a million times. But it always sounded romantic.

DADDY: Well, it *was* romantic. We just weren't in love. I don't think I ever loved her. I got used to being married, and there wasn't enough money coming in for me to think about getting out.

KIMBER: You would have stayed married to Mom *forever* if she didn't leave?

DADDY: Probably.

KIMBER: (I was wiped out by now.) I can't believe this. I always blamed Mom for walking out on you. But you were probably happy as a clam that she left!!

DADDY: Not most of the time. Getting used to somebody is pretty close to being in love once the infatuation wears off.

KIMBER: *No.* Being in love is being sensitive and caring and being there for each other. It's not *hating* each other.

DADDY: I never hated her, except when I learned that she was cheating on me. (He paused for a minute, like he was going to cry or something, but he composed himself and went on.) I don't know why I was going through the mug of change she used to keep by the kitchen sink. I never touched that mug. But I needed money for something, and I figured I'd steal a couple of bucks worth. And of course I felt the ankle bracelet and got it out and read the engraving on it. She'd always wanted an ankle bracelet because she never got one when she was a teenager. Why she put this one in the mug with the change I don't know. I sure as hell never went through her jewelry box. Anyway, once I saw the ankle bracelet, I knew what was happening.

KIMBER: Didn't you *feel* anything, Daddy? When you found the ankle bracelet? Didn't you cry or care?

DADDY: I didn't go after the guy and have a fist fight with him, if that's what you mean. I knew the guy, anyway.

KIMBER: That's not the point. I just thought you loved her. I never *dreamed* about getting married to someone you don't love.

DADDY: Kimber, I wish I could still have your vantage point on love. It's all promise for you. All dreams. You feel infatuated and you think it's that way all the time.

KIMBER: That's not true. I know infatuation wears off. But *love* doesn't wear off. Not real love. And people stay in love, all their lives. I've seen them.

DADDY: (He finally put down the glass.) I know. And I wish I'd known that kind of love. I didn't get married cynically. Believe me, Kimber, I don't want you to follow in my footsteps.

KIMBER: What about now? You have another chance.

DADDY: (He gave me a sharp look.) That's not something we should be discussing.

KIMBER: Daddy, I *want* you to fall in love. I'm not jealous.

DADDY: No, you're not. You're an exceptional girl, Kimber. I don't know why I said all this. Don't take it too hard. There's no doubt in the world that I love *you*. Right now, I need a refill.

KIMBER: Don't!

DADDY: (He stood up with difficulty.) I won't pass out. And I won't finish the bottle. I just need to be very very crocked tonight.

That ended the conversation because I was crying. Daddy went to the bar and slowly mixed another drink. I watched him bring the drink back and sit down. His whole body seemed to sigh.

I went over and knelt down by the chair and hugged Daddy and he hugged me about as tight as I ever remember. He smelled sweet and perspired. Then he patted my back and tousled my hair and told me to go finish my homework. He quickly put the movie back on and I went upstairs to my room.

Forget sleeping that night. I tossed around in the dark, watching moon patterns on my ceiling. I was so confused and troubled. Daddy was like . . . well, you know, the adult generation. I was supposed to learn from his experience. He was the wise old sage who could tell me what love felt like and how you made it work and how everything would turn out all right. I was all screwed up about Lou and I guess I wanted some guidance. Even a lecture about "when I was your age!"

Instead, I got this thunderbolt and it tore down my world. I mean, if Daddy had said he had three other wives somewhere, I would have handled it better. I knew how mixed-up I was about Lou and now Daddy said you could *marry* someone feeling like that. It was the worst thing an adult could ever tell me.

I hated my father that night. I vowed to phone Mom and apologize and ask to live with her. I vowed to see a lawyer and get Corey out of this house. I punched my pillow and cursed him and cried.

Of course, a lot later I knew how much Daddy hurt, and how shattered his life was. Meanwhile, Daddy and I still talked to each other, but it was cold as snowballs. And the angrier I got, the more I vowed to make things work between me and Lou, to prove to Daddy that love was real.

Which was exactly the wrong way to feel then because of what was going on with Martha. And with Deena.

"Deena? I thought she was just looking for a motel room to share with Phil."

Oh, yeah, she was. Deena the hopeless romantic. But remember what got Deena in trouble with Phil the *first* time.

"Being a helpless romantic."

You got it. So now, Deena had been back with Phil for a few months, except Phil was in college and too busy to dance around her, and Deena's hormones were getting restless. Then came the party at Brandie's house, and a little more TNT was added to the mixture.

"What party was this?"

Deena has to tell you about it because Martha and I weren't there. Willing to spill the beans, Deena?

Yes. I intend to narrate *everything* that pertains to me, just for my own self-protection. Not that I'm angry. I feel total sympathy for you, Kimber. Going through what you went through, you have every reason to be sarcastic.

Uh, Deena, just stick to your own story and don't analyze me or my dad, okay?

Wow. Testy, aren't we? Sure, Kimber. But don't *you* go interrupting, the way you usually do.

Chapter Nine

I'm *happy* to talk about that party because I didn't do anything wrong. It was just luck that Lou happened to be driving by.

First of all, my *hormones* weren't acting up. I was in love with Phil. Yes, I missed him. He was loaded up with tests and papers, and even though he was only fifteen minutes away, he might as well have been in Europe. We called each other whenever we could, but we couldn't be together that much. I moped around my room, going crazy without him.

Then my friend Cindy told me there was a party at her friend

Brandie's house on Saturday night because Brandie's parents were away for the weekend.

"Is this an open house party?" I asked, because I know what goes on and I didn't feel like getting involved.

"No, just people she's inviting," Cindy said.

So I said okay, I'd come. Maybe I was stupid to believe that it would stay a closed party, but I don't think the worst of people right away. And I needed a lift. I figured I'd try to forget about missing Phil.

On Saturday night, Cindy picked me up and drove me to Brandie's house. My dad's Accord was being fixed and he needed to take my car so he and Mom could go out. That's why I couldn't drive myself home. I want you to see how innocent this is, how it just *happened*.

Brandie lives in a fancier part of Westfield called Westfield Park. It's got big Colonial houses with brick fronts, and huge lawns and winding streets with old-fashioned street lights. I was wearing this jumpsuit with my hair loose around my shoulders. I felt pretty.

There were about twenty people at the party when I got there. It was kind of quiet. The tape player was going, and Brandie had big bowls of chips and pretzels and M&M's, and soda and beer and wine coolers. She'd locked up the bar because she said her father measured how much was in each bottle.

But some kids had brought their own, and there was Jack Daniels and vodka. Still, things were peaceful. I felt miserable as soon as I got there because it all made me miss Phil. Cindy right away scoped the hot guys, and she went into her flirting stance with her hip against a doorway and a brew in her hand. She had on a turquoise shirt unbuttoned most of the way. You see? I get the reputation because I give my love to one man, but people like Cindy get away with acting like tramps.

I took a wine cooler and sat on the sofa and let the music swirl around in my head. Every time a song played that was special for me and Phil, my eyes filled up. Brandie had on a leather outfit and her hair was totally wild. Her boyfriend Steve was there. He's got long hair down to his shoulders and very sensitive lips. But he dresses like a total scrub, so Brandie's folks are on her back to dump him.

Maybe that's why she was a little outrageous that night. She strutted around, singing along with the tape and chugging down one drink after another. She polished off about four beers and then started on vodka and grapefruit juice. I would say she was pretty polluted after an hour. Steve hung out by the tape player, hunched in a chair and shaking his head up and down to the music. It was weird.

The trouble started about ten-thirty. There was a knock at the door and it was Bill, who used to be Cindy's boyfriend. Bill is total scum, and we were so happy when she finally broke up with him. He was deep into drugs, and he spent half his time suspended from school. The hard-to-believe part was she really loved him, and she wouldn't listen to reason. But her parents said they'd ground her for the rest of high school.

So we knew there was going to be trouble now. Someone told Cindy that Bill was at the door, and Cindy said, "I don't want to see him."

"He won't go away," they said.

Cindy said okay, she'd talk to him (I think she wanted to talk to him anyway). She stood in the doorway whispering. Then a car pulled up and suddenly there were a bunch of guys at the door.

"What's happening?" someone asked.

"I think it's his friends."

"Uh oh."

Uh oh is right. Bill's friends are major dirtbags. You see them every night behind the 7-Eleven, dealing drugs and sprawled all over cars. They are as scuzzy as you can imagine. It sounded like Bill was arguing with them to leave because he wanted to talk to Cindy. Cindy sounded pissed off, too.

The next thing we knew, Bill and his friends were *inside* the house. Brandie went over to them and started telling them to get out. They kind of placated her, you know, like "Don't worry, it's no sweat, we're not gonna do anything." Except they didn't leave.

Then Steve got up—you remember, Brandie's boyfriend—and s-l-o-w-l-y walked over to where the dirtbags were hanging out. I sat rigid on the sofa, staring at the china closet or the carpeting or anything else I could find.

Steve said to Brandie, "You want these guys out of here?" He didn't say "guys" but I can't put down what he *did* say. In fact, I've changed a *lot* of words in what comes next.

One of the dirtbags said, "Stay loose, man."

Steve said, "Don't tell me to stay loose. Get the hell out."

"To hell with you."

Oh, forget it. It just doesn't sound right. They cursed back and forth to each other, and they started shoving, the way guys do. Then Brandie said, "Forget it, Steve. They can stay."

Steve didn't like that, and he argued with Brandie about it. But she didn't want a fight all over her parent's multi-million dollar living room, so she figured it was better to have the uninvited guests. Steve said something really nasty to Brandie and stalked off into another room.

Things just went downhill from there. The dirtbags kind of drifted into the kitchen where they started passing around the bottle of Jack Daniels. Bill and Cindy stood by the front door getting louder and angrier. Meanwhile, boys and girls began to pair off and head for the bedrooms.

That's when it got worse. Cars started to pull up outside, and kids started coming in. Obviously, the word was out that Brandie was having an open house. It always happens. You can't have a closed party if your parents aren't home.

So within ten minutes you had Bill and Cindy screaming at each other, and the dirtbags cursing and drinking (one of them threw an empty vodka bottle against the refrigerator), and about forty or fifty new kids all over the place.

I sat there for a long time, and wondered how I'd ever get

home. Mom and Dad were in the city and wouldn't be back until about three in the morning. I considered calling up Kimber or somebody and asking them to pick me up, except it was now after midnight, and I'd get *them* in trouble.

When Bill smacked Cindy, it got me up in a hurry. The sound was like a gunshot. You'd think everybody would stop what they were doing and turn around, but this bunch was so out of hand that only a few people bothered to look. Cindy was holding her mouth and there was blood between her fingers. She was staring at Bill with this insane look. Bill was saying "I'm sorry, I'm sorry. . . ."

Then one of the jocks came *hurtling* across the room—I swear to God—and he bodyslammed Bill. The two of them went to the floor, pushing a chair over. They started to whale on each other. All I could see was blood where Bill's face was.

I heard somebody say, "Call the police!" and someone else said, "No way!" but all I wanted to do was get out of there. I didn't care how I got home. My head was pounding from the two stupid wine coolers I had, and my stomach churned. The trouble was that Bill and the jock were fighting in the front hallway, blocking the door. I stepped over bodies and headed for the family room, which had sliding doors.

The family room was dark, except for the glowing lights from the stereo unit. You could also see the outlines of bodies on the floor and you could hear them moaning and breathing. It was bizarre.

Fortunately, the sliding doors were open because people were out on the patio screaming their heads off and throwing beer bottles all over the grass. Lights were going on in other houses and I thought I heard someone scream, "You damn kids! I'm calling the cops!"

I was suffocating by that time. I groped my way to the fence gate, and across the front lawn. Behind me, Brandie's house was all lit up, and I could hear glass breaking and screams and loud music. I ran, but Brandie's lawn is a sloping hill and I tripped and nearly did a somersault. Pain shot through my lower leg and I grabbed it and rolled back and forth, crying.

And then I threw up on the grass.

So I was now an absolute mess, with my leg sprained and grass stains all over me, and blood on my clothes, not to mention puke. And I hadn't *done* anything. Meanwhile, they kept trashing the house.

And that's when I saw the headlights. At first, I thought it was the police. I held up my hand to cover my eyes and I started to *whimper.* You have to really know what kind of shape I was in, so you can understand what happened. Not that *anything* happened, because it *didn't,* and that's one reason I'm agreeing to tell all this, so it's clear that nothing happened. But you can understand why people *thought* something happened . . .

You're babbling, Deena.

Yes. I am. I'm so defensive and I don't know why.

The car had stopped right by the edge of the lawn. I heard the car door open and then footsteps and male voices. I thought, oh God, more of them. And then I wondered if they were going to come after me. I'd read stories about girls being thrown into cars and raped.

So I tried to get up, but the second I put pressure on my leg, the pain flamed up. I screamed and dropped down again. I tried to crawl, dragging my bad leg behind me. The grass was soaking wet, and my hands came down on slithery things.

Then the guys from the car were all around me. I curled up into a ball and said, "Please don't hurt me, please don't hurt me . . ." over and over again.

And then this voice said, *"Deena!"*

I kept sniveling because it didn't register for a minute that he'd called me by name. Then it penetrated. I looked up and there was Lou standing over me. At that moment, he was God. He was Rambo. He was the Lone Ranger. How would *you* react?

He was wearing this neat shirt with a hundred zippers on it, and Bugle Boy jeans, and his hair blew softly in the breeze. He was the most beautiful man in the world at that moment. But you can understand why, can't you?

So I croaked, "Lou . . ." and then I threw up again.

I heard a siren in the distance and then I heard Lou saying, "Come on, Deena. Get up."

"I can't move," I said. "I broke my leg or something."

Lou cursed, but then he and his friend Doug picked me up and supported me between them while I hobbled on one foot down the lawn. One of the windows in Brandie's house shattered, and there was a shriek. Lou glanced over his shoulder and said, "Let's move."

I think I half blacked out, but I remember being loaded into the car and Doug sliding in next to me. Lou got behind the wheel and the car doors slammed shut. I heard the motor rev, and the tires squeal, and I was thrown back as Lou booked out of there. I looked out the window and saw people on Brandie's front lawn. I caught a glimpse of red lights as Lou made a left turn, and then we were on a quiet, dark street.

I could feel every part of my body shaking uncontrollably. Doug said, "You stink," and Lou's other friend, Neil, said, "Open the windows! I'm going to barf!"

Windows hummed open and damp spring air blew hard into my face. I shut my eyes and felt the rocking motion of the car. Lou said, "Deena, what the hell were you doing there?"

"Nothing," I mumbled. "I swear. I was trying to get away."

"Unreal," Lou said. He and Doug and Neil discussed what a mess that was going to be tomorrow, and how Brandie would be punished for the rest of her life.

I said, "What made you show up there?"

They all laughed. Lou said, "We were bored, and we knew Brandie was having a party, so we figured we'd cruise by. Not a swift idea."

"Thank God," I said. "You saved my life."

"Yeah, well, no sweat. What are you going to do about your clothes and your leg? Are your folks home?"

I shook my head. "Not yet. I don't think so, anyway. I'll throw the clothes in the wash."

"And your leg?"

I couldn't really think straight at that point. I said, "My mom and dad will know I was at Brandie's house. I'll tell them the truth, that I hurt myself trying to get out."

"Sounds good," Doug said. They all laughed again.

I said, "Can I tell my parents that you picked me up? I mean, you're not supposed to be somewhere else or anything?"

"Nope."

"Thanks." I sank back against the seat, disgusted with my own smell. I was shuddering but my heart was slowing down. I didn't feel much of anything then, just grateful that I was away from the house.

So whose idea was it for Lou to go back to your house with you?

It wasn't anyone's idea, Kimber. It just made sense. Lou drove me back home, and my leg was throbbing like crazy, so he helped me inside. That's not exactly sinister.

How come he dropped off Doug and Neil first?

Oh, come *on*! Boy, I'll bet you didn't subject Martha to this, and she deserves it a lot more than I do.

Don't avoid the question.

I'm *not* avoiding the question. The reason he dropped off Doug and Neil first is that they were all tired from riding around and they'd been drinking and they wanted to get to bed. Lou said he could get me into my house without help. And then *he* intended to go home also.

We got to my house and it was about one in the morning. Lou pulled onto the driveway while I fumbled my keys out of my pocket. Lou took the keys from me and opened up the door and helped me inside. Now is any of this really arousing? I mean, does it sound *fiendish* enough?

Keep going.

He helped me turn on some lights, and he helped me upstairs to my bedroom. Yes, that's right. He actually saw my frilly curtains and my stuffed animals and the poster of George Michael on my closet door. Then he stood *outside* the door while I undressed. I opened the door a *crack* and handed out all the dirty clothes to him and he went downstairs and threw them into the washing machine.

Then he sat in my family room and watched TV while I limped into the bathroom and took a shower. Except for my leg, I felt human! Then I brushed my teeth and limped *back* into my room and put on a nightdress *and* a robe and then I kind of swung myself downstairs a step at a time.

And Lou waited for me because he wanted to make sure I didn't hurt myself. Boy, this must be boring for all you scandal fans.

Finish up, Deena.

I went into the family room and he kind of jumped up and said, "Why don't you let me help you?" and I said, "You've done enough for me, Lou."

He grabbed me to make sure I didn't fall, and I held onto him. And for that second, it felt glorious to hold him. I was so incredibly grateful and relieved that I would have felt glorious if Freddy Kruger had saved my life. All the strength drained out of me and I looked into his eyes, and then I kissed him.

Yes, this is the big revelation Kimber is so hot to unleash on the world. We kissed. And I thanked him and he said it was okay, and then he sat me down and helped me get some ice in a towel and he propped me up on the couch so I could hold the ice pack on my leg.

And then he bent down and kissed me again, very tenderly, and he said, "Sure you'll be okay?"

"Yes," I said. "Thanks again, Lou. I really owe you."

He said no I didn't, and he left. I sat watching videos for half an hour, holding the ice pack on my leg. Then I got hungry so I limped into the kitchen and took some Oreo cookies and some milk, and then I shut the light and hauled myself upstairs and into my room and into my bed. And I shut my little bed lamp and put my head back and in about four seconds I was asleep.

And that's the whole story. Another moment of infamy in the life of Deena Russo, *femme fatale*. Gee, Kimber, do you hear everyone laughing at you?

No, Deena. But of course, that *isn't* the whole story, just an episode. So you can relax now while we go on. And don't *you* interrupt *us*.

Chapter Ten

Now, if you can't see what was happening here, let me fill you in: Lou was entering the separation stage of our relationship. That's when the guy is really ready to end it, but won't. So he starts to cheat. Not blatantly, but like rescuing Martha and kissing Deena.

Well, cross out rescuing Martha. He rescued Martha for a whole other reason. But *after* rescuing Martha is what's important. Notice the way he and his friends were cruising around looking for parties? He was sending me a message: I want to be with my friends. I want to be free.

So I'd have to be pretty stupid not to read the signs, but remember where *I* was coming from. It was now May, and I was scared to death about facing college. My brother was a mess, and my dad had told me that he never loved my mom. I was not feeling self-sufficient. Lou was the only thing in my life that made me feel important and worthwhile.

Which is why I pretended that nothing was wrong. The Prom was coming up, the trees were green, and I had Lou. Of course, *everything* was wrong, and it all started to come down on my head.

Let's fade in on Monday morning. I'm by my locker, staring at it, my hands sweating. Why? Because in the locker are three bags of candy. It's been a week and I haven't had the guts to sell any of it. But the weather is getting warm and this stuff is going to melt, and chocolate sauce is going to ooze out of my locker.

So there I stand, but not alone. The hallway in the morning is like Christmas at Macy's. Busses pull in, one after the other, and kids come pouring into the building. There are hundreds of bodies now in the hallway. Girls are kneeling by their lockers, pawing through notebooks. Guys are talking about cars or girls. Lovers are kissing.

So there's this whole scene of screaming and clanging, and I was this island of repose. My stomach was flip-flopping. I'd been avoiding Jason, and getting obsessed with the whole thing. Finally, I blew out a breath, opened my locker, and grabbed a bag of candy. It rustled and it sounded to me like a bomb exploding. I shut my locker, hefted my books against my chest, shrugged to make the shoulder strap of my bag stay on, and started off to my first period class, which is Creative Writing.

This class is in the Business wing because it's in a room with computers. The teacher is Mr. Alterson, but he wasn't there yet. So I dropped my books and my handbag on the floor and stood by the door with the bag of candy in my hand. Naturally, kids started asking me what I was selling. I opened the bag, and they started pawing through and took stuff out. I took the money and for a second, it was exciting. This was working! I was selling candy! I had this greedy vision of making hundreds of dollars just standing by classroom doors.

Then Lou came by. Usually, I didn't see Lou until third period Physics, which we take together. But of course, since I was illegally selling this candy, that's when he decided to pay me a surprise visit. I didn't notice him at first because I was busy grabbing money and holding out the bag. Then I looked up and there he was.

"What are you doing?" he said.

"Selling candy."

"For who?"

"*Expressions.*" My face began to burn and I got infuriated. I couldn't believe he was going to get righteous at this moment.

"Since when are they having a candy sale?"

"Since I said so. Would you shut up?"

I wished I could put the stupid bag away but it was like I had drugs. Suddenly everybody was starving for Snickers. The warning bell rang, and I knew Mr. Alterson would be coming by, but this whole ring of kids was around me, looking through the candy while I held out the bag. Lou watched with a little smirk.

"Making a little money on the side, huh?"

"Will you shut *up*?"

Everyone started moving to the classrooms and this business teacher, Miss Forte, yelled at stragglers. I felt like everyone was watching me. Then Mr. Alterson strolled in, with his black tote bag. I almost choked. "I have to stop selling now," I mumbled, but nobody listened.

Lou said, "See you third," and chuckled as he walked away. I wanted to stab him. Mr. Alterson wedged himself in between the kids and glanced at me. "Hi," he smiled.

"Hi."

He turned the key and opened the door. I let this nerdy little kid throw his fifty cents into the bag and then I crushed it closed and hurled myself into the room. Mr. Alterson was at the teacher's desk, taking folders out of his tote bag. I went to the disk file on the desk and pawed through, looking for my disk, and *not* looking up.

"You have peanut butter cups?" he asked.

I nodded.

I heard him wriggling his hand around in his pocket. Change jingled. "Nope," he said. "A few cents short."

I looked up like I'd been shot. His face was apologetic, not angry. "That's okay," I said. "I trust you."

"Oh, God, *thank you*," he said. "At two o'clock, I'm going to need my fix."

I smiled weakly and dredged a package of peanut butter cups out of the bag. I handed him the candy and he dropped thirty five cents into my cupped palm. I clutched the money and grabbed my disks and scurried over to my terminal. I couldn't believe I'd just sold illegal candy to a teacher. Not just a teacher but *my* teacher, and my club advisor. I felt so sleazy.

I felt sleazy all day. I felt double sleazy in Physics because Lou kept looking at me and smirking and chuckling. At the end of Physics, we were at the doorway together. "Sold it all?" he asked.

"Drop dread."

"I won't turn you in."

"Thanks."

He saw I was pissed off, so he put his hand on the wall to lean over me and he said, "Are we hanging out later?"

I shrugged. "If you want."

"Maybe we can watch a tape or something at my house."

"Sure. Call me."

He kissed me, one of those quick kisses that get you half on the mouth and half on the chin. I was not as cool as I sounded. I was pretty shaky, in fact, because Lou and I hadn't gotten together for a while, and I was hysterical with worrying. I was now ecstatic and grateful. With two words, Lou had folded me back into his heart. That's how insecure I was.

You have to know all of this because of the way things went. That night was pretty terrific, too. I did the dinner dishes and skipped homework, which is pretty easy for a senior to do when May rolls around. Then I drove over to Lou's house. It was a warm, damp night, and I rolled the window down and played loud music. I felt good. I'd actually sold the candy.

And Lou had asked me over. Maybe I was being stupid about Lou and Martha (I didn't know what had gone on with Deena yet, only that there had been a wild party at Brandie's house). It's pretty simple to lie to yourself when you need to.

Lou's house is a ranch on a kind of sloping hill in a magnificent development. You drive down a curvy road with incredible trees all around. There aren't a million cars parked along the curb—in fact, there isn't a curb. And there aren't hundreds of little kids roaming the street. With Lou's house, you have to park on the driveway, and then walk up about forty steps. Inside, there's a flagstone foyer, and a living room that's all peach and off-white, with original paintings and no dust on anything.

His folks were out and we sat in the den and watched MTV for a while. He kept the sound low so we could talk. We drank Cokes and grabbed chips from a bowl on a coffee table. He had his arm around me and his feet up on the table, with his sweat socks on.

"How come you're selling candy?" he asked.

"Boy," I said. "You don't let it alone."

"It isn't like you."

"I needed some money," I said, stuffing chips into my mouth. I looked at the TV screen.

"I could lend you money."

"Not a loan," I said. "My own money."

"You work at the mall."

"Not enough. Come *on*! Lay off."

He was quiet for a minute and we watched. He kind of scrunched down a little more. So did I. He said, "So where are we going from the Prom?"

I shrugged again. "I don't know. Where did we decide?"

"We didn't decide yet." He took some more chips.

You know, there's a kind of *pattern* to these meaningless conversations you have when you're not really in love anymore, and you don't have much to say. Like, Lou and I were really bored at that moment, but if you just sit there and watch TV and breathe, it's embarrassing. So we talk about stuff, and we do things to fill in the spaces between the words. The conversation goes something like this:

PERSON	WORDS	ACTION
KIMBER	I thought we were going to the city?	crunch crunch
LOU	That's okay with me.	reaches for can of Coke
KIMBER	Do you *want* to go to the city?	takes more chips
LOU	Makes no difference to me.	drinks from can
KIMBER	Well, do you want to go out to Montauk?	crunch crunch
LOU	I told you, it makes no difference.	puts down can
KIMBER	Have you talked to Rob and Phil?	reaches for can of Coke
LOU	I don't even *see* them.	takes more chips
KIMBER	Well, we have to get together on this at some point.	drinks from can
LOU	So figure it out with the girls.	crunch crunch
KIMBER	I don't get to see *them*.	puts down can

We kept it up for a while, going back and forth about plans for Prom weekend. The thing is nobody wants to make the decision in case it falls apart. So you keep passing it around like in a game of hot potato, and finally you have a big argument and half the people in your group are pissed off.

Then we went from boring conversation into the next phase, which is making out. Making out is pretty easy when you're infatuated and you can't wait to get your lips and bodies together. But when it's the twilight of romance, usually you start making out because you're bored or you think you have to. There are specific actions that lead you right in:

PERSON	WORDS	ACTION
LOU	So how come you were selling candy?	arm on back of sofa
KIMBER	You're really asking for it.	lick chip salt off fingers
LOU	You *never* do anything illegal.	fingers rub nape of my neck
KIMBER	I was desperate.	run tongue over teeth
LOU	Who put you up to it?	fingers move to shoulder blades and under shirt collar
KIMBER	You think I can't have my own ideas?	slither closer to him and lean head against his neck
LOU	Not criminal ideas.	arm around my shoulder and lips at my ear
KIMBER	I can't reveal my sources.	eyes shut, breathe faster
LOU	What *can* you reveal?	tongue in my ear, hot breath in my eye
KIMBER	Don't be crude.	turn face slightly to receive his kiss
LOU	Why not?	3-2-1 contact!

So we made out, and I was enthusiastic about it. Maybe it was the warm spring air, or the music thumping from the TV, but I remembered that I'd been in love with Lou for all these months, or most of these months, and that he made me feel excellent a lot of that time. I didn't know he was being a slime at that moment, seducing me again just to show himself he could get three girls interested in him at the same time.

But it's not *easy* to know when a guy's doing that. If you're a girl, you need to be loved, no matter how smart you are, and you'll go through life blindfolded if you can get that need taken care of.

This was an outstanding evening. When Lou's folks got home, his Mom got out ice cream and home-baked brownies and we sat around the kitchen table joking and eating and I felt so good I wanted to cry. I felt like I was *home*, like I was practically married, like my troubles were over.

Talk about being set up.

It was the next morning, and I was back in the cafeteria for my bagel and juice. Remember at the start of this saga how I told you about the cafeteria? Except now it was disgustingly warm in there, with a kind of liquid slime in the air. It was one of those pale sunny days where the sky and the trees and the buildings are all the same shade of dirty yellow.

Martha was not there because she wasn't getting up early anymore. She wasn't even coming to school that much. But I'll get back to her later. Deena was there, huffing and sighing over her social history homework. Cindy was also there, from Brandie's party, remember? She was giving me looks, the kind of looks that mean only one thing: "Girl, you are a victim."

I drank my orange juice and pushed back my hair and tried to keep my eyes open. I'd gotten into bed at one-thirty in the morning. Deena said, "You look awful, Kimber."

"Thank you."

"Well, you do. What were you up to last night?"

"My old tricks," I said.

Deena looked puzzled. Cindy said, "Ha ha."

I shook my head and stared at the filthy windows and the teachers walking into the building. It occurred to me in a blinding revelation that they probably have problems getting through the day, too. Except they get paid for it.

"Were you with Lou?" Deena asked.

I gave her an inquiring glance. She was nonchalantly shuffling papers around in her Strawberry Shortcake folder (yes, she has a Strawberry Shortcake folder), but she was doing it nervously, like she didn't want me to wonder why she was so interested in Lou's whereabouts. See how subtle this all is? Also notice how Deena was lying about that kiss meaning nothing.

Anyway, I didn't hear any warning bells yet, probably because no nerves in my brain were functioning. I said, "Yes, I was with Lou. Do you want a review?"

"Never mind," she said.

"At least I wasn't at an orgy."

Her head *shot* up. "Not funny," she said.

"Oh, wow," I said. "I see we're all pretty touchy today. Cindy, was that not an orgy?"

Cindy chuckled. "I passed out before the real good stuff."

"That's the talk of the town," I said. "I'm sorry I missed it."

"I'm sorry I *didn't* miss it," Cindy said. She was drinking chocolate milk and a soggy donut sat on a plate in front of her. "I'm grounded for a month, and if I didn't have my dress, I wouldn't be going to the Prom, either."

"I think there were mass groundings," I said. "What's your version, Deena?"

Deena was nearly quivering. I couldn't figure it. Everyone knew Deena was at the party, and that she hurt her leg and got a ride home. So what was the big deal?

"I don't have a version," she said.

"Deena left early," Cindy offered.

Deena now gave *Cindy* the evil eye. I said, "Good thinking. But you'd messed up your leg by then, huh?"

She began to put together her stuff. "I tripped on the lawn."

"I know," I said, staring at her. "I wasn't doubting you."

Deena sighed and tried to compose herself. Cindy was leaning way back in her chair, kind of shaking her head. I caught the action and now little fuzzy things began to crawl up and down in my stomach. "What's going on?" I said. "Is there something I don't know?"

Deena pierced Cindy with a furious glance. Cindy slurped the last of her chocolate milk and shrugged. I looked back and forth at both of them. Then Deena exhaled and said, "Okay. Here we go. This is going to be another major fiasco. Lou took me home, okay? That's the whole secret."

I wasn't sure what to feel. Inside my chest, it was like I'd dropped a dozen eggs. "Lou was at the party?"

Cindy said, "No. He just showed up. Someone saw him and Doug and Neil put Deena in the car."

"*Put* Deena in the car?"

"I was *hurt*," Deena said in her best whine. "Lou and his friends were driving by, and I was out on the front lawn . . ."

Well, not to cut Deena off, but you've already heard the whole story, which Deena now told in an extremely condensed version. By the time she finished, it was twenty-five after seven and the warning bell rang for first period. Since the cafeteria was about twelve miles away from my Creative Writing room, I was going to be late.

And I didn't really care. Deena gathered her stuff together and flounced out. I sat there feeling used. Cindy said, "It's no big deal. From what I hear, she really *was* hurt and the guys were helping her out."

"Swell guys," I said.

Cindy laughed. "Don't sweat it. Deena's catching hell for escaping before the cops came. Brandie still wants her to help pay the damages, but her folks are saying no because she didn't do any of it. So she's probably going to get her ass kicked."

"Can I help?"

That made Cindy laugh again. I felt the rage come up in my throat but there was nothing to slam. The creep. Who cared if he'd driven Deena home? It was that he didn't *tell* me. And if he didn't tell me, that meant he felt guilty about it. And if he felt guilty about it, there had to be a reason.

So the slow, terrible progression of doubt and suspicion began. I thought about Lou being so loving last night. Sure. He was softening me up, figuring I'd hear about him and Deena. And *Deena.* Forget *that.* Of course, it's always one of your friends who eventually goes after your boyfriend because you're always around each other, but Deena was just—well, you didn't want your boyfriend stolen by Deena. It made you look like more of a jerk than you were. And the way Deena threw her body at guys, you had to figure that he'd cheated within *seconds*.

So there I sat, cutting class, three weeks from the Senior Prom, selling illegal candy, with my life in pieces. Cheated on. Lied to. And was it the first time? Oh yeah, that's the next step, you see. You go back through every month of your relationship and examine every word, every gesture. How long have you been a dimwit? How long has everyone been laughing at you?

Yup, there I was. And little did I know that Lou hadn't even warmed *up* yet! Because, on that sludgy May morning, Martha Sullivan was being called into Mr. Sachs's office, and that was the beginning of the betrayal of the century.

Martha? Over to you, kid.

Chapter Eleven

Well, I *was* the one in the principal's office, so I might as well tell it. Come to think of it, I was the one with Henning on the Senior Weekend. I was also the one who *really* betrayed Kimber, unlike Deena who's just a confused mass of hormones.

I wasn't confused, I was just self-destructive. I knew I'd catch trouble by hanging out with those Swedish guys, and I *wanted* to catch trouble. I guess I was suicidal. Who knows?

By the time I found myself in a chair in the Main Office, I'd bounced off rock bottom. I hated Rob for blowing me off in the hallway. I know why he did it. And, yeah, I'd cheated on him with Henning, though not the way everyone thought. But I still hated him. That was the worst moment of my life, standing there at the mercy of those jocks, *stared* at like a freak. At that instant, I truly wanted love and affection.

I know what you're thinking. Lou came along and gave me what I wanted. You're right. He timed it perfectly. But Lou does that a lot. It's how he got to be a lacrosse star and a prize student and a hunk. Why do you think guys like that have ego problems?

So there I was. It was a windy, rainy spring day, the kind where you think about different ways to die. I looked like the wreck of the Hesperus: raggy denim jacket, wrinkled concert T-shirt, old jeans, wild hair, red eyes. Total scrub.

I watched people come in and out for a while, and chewed at my fingernails. I had to go to the bathroom but I was too shot to bother. Then Mr. Sachs came out of his office and beckoned to me. I got up with a lot of insolence, to show I wasn't afraid. He wasn't afraid either. Sachs is a killer. He's short and stocky, with cropped hair and a potbelly. He always wears a white shirt and tie, and reading glasses halfway down his nose.

So I followed the hanging judge into his chambers. He shut the door behind us and said, "Sit down, Martha."

I sat down in this big leather chair by a conference table that butted up against his desk. Ever sit in a principal's office? The whole school is like cinder block and linoleum and acoustic tiles, but the principal's office is panelled, with thick carpeting and heavy drapes and soft lighting and hanging plants. How much can you care about kids in that kind of womb?

Well, Sachs eased into his chair, which was a massive executive jobbie, and he peered at me through those half-glasses. He had a file folder open, with all the reports that were written up on me after the weekend. My intestines were rolling over. Martha the Brave was losing it.

"I'm not going to rehash this situation," he said. "You know what you did. You know it embarrassed the school, and your family, and you."

I kept my eyes down and played little finger games. I could hear the rain blowing against the window beyond the drapes. "Yeah," I said.

"You may have endangered the future of the Senior Weekend."

I shrugged.

"Does that bother you?"

I looked up. "I don't think I endangered the Senior Weekend."

"You don't, huh?" He slid the file away from him with a brusque gesture. "Martha, I have had at least ten phone calls from parents who want to know why we need to take our kids down to Washington to sleep in hotels."

I made an incredulous noise. He plowed right on.

"Don't look shocked. This is a blue-collar district. They're conservative. We have to sell our activities, and sell them hard. These people think kids should be doing reading, writing, and arithmetic all day, every day. For the most part, I agree with that. But I also believe in our co-curricular program. One thoughtless, selfish act like yours jeopardizes that program. That's why people are mad at you. Can you understand that?"

He was punching me out. I had no reserves left at this point. Remember, I had no real home, with my dad an alcoholic and my mom finding herself. Not that Mom was that supportive of me even before she lost herself. But I was drugged out and depressed. It's my insanity defense.

"No, I don't understand it," I said. "I know I wasn't supposed to hang out with those guys after curfew. I know I wasn't supposed to sneak into the bar and have drinks with them. I know I wasn't supposed to walk Henning back to his room. But I don't see where that kills Westfield's image."

"That wasn't all that happened, Martha."

"Yes it was, damn it."

"Watch your temper."

I slammed myself back in the chair. I was suffocating in this office. It reminded me of my shrink's office. "This is so stupid. Some kids lie about me because I'm radical and I don't mousse my hair. And you guys swallow it."

Sachs looked at me with his little drill-bit eyes. "You were seen walking the young man to his room, and going in. You weren't seen coming out. And the hallway duty teacher reported that you never returned to your own room."

"I know." My fists were both clenched. "Man, I've said this a million times. I stayed in Henning's room with Henning and another guy, and we kept drinking. I finally left the room, but I couldn't find my way down the hall. I made it to the ice machine and passed out. I woke up the next morning and by the time I got back to my room, everyone was down having breakfast."

Sachs tightened his lips, which were pretty tight to begin with. "But nobody *saw* you by the ice machine. Not the whole night. That's pretty unlikely, isn't it?"

"I don't know. Maybe nobody needed ice. But it stinks that you believe the sluts who turned me in."

"Watch your mouth."

"They were sore at me because *they* were hot for Henning. And they didn't like me because I wasn't a cute little Westfield coed and I wouldn't wear the Senior Weekend T-shirt. Man, you're an adult. Can't you see *through* people like that?"

Wrong approach. You don't cast aspersions on the principal's psychological expertise. "I can see what I have to," he said coldly. "The problem is, Martha, that you're not just an innocent victim. You've compiled a record of disruption, truancy, and insubordination that stretches back to seventh grade. You've been suspended eight times in the last two years. I have to consider patterns, Martha."

"Yeah? What about my pattern of being ranked fifth in the class? What about my pattern of winning the science fair? What about my pattern of raising money for that kid's heart surgery, or running the Christmas party in the nursing home? How come *those* patterns don't mean anything?"

"They mean a lot," he said. "They tell me what you *could* be. The other things tell me what you've *decided* to be. But none of that really matters, Martha. You compromised yourself and the school. That's what I have to deal with."

So now I was out of the game, with no cards to play. Except one. But forget it. I'd have to tell Sachs that Lou Ross had seen me by the ice machine, at about two o'clock in the morning. And I couldn't. Because Lou had asked me not to, and I couldn't turn him in. First of all, it would be the most cowardly stinking thing I could do; and second, Sachs would peg it as a desperate attempt to get out of being punished.

Actually, I took comfort in my loyalty. I was going to die, taking Lou's secret to my grave. I'd be noble while he remained a snake.

Sachs leaned forward and said, "At Senior Orientation in September, you were told that misbehavior on the Senior Weekend would result in loss of other privileges. So, as of Monday, you will have to surrender your parking permit . . ."

For a second, my heart jumped up. That was *it*? Loss of my almighty senior parking spot?

But he kept going. ". . . and you will not be permitted to attend the Senior Prom. I'm genuinely sorry about this, and none of it is done vengefully. But honors students are expected to follow the same rules as other students, and your behavior was not acceptable. Now, is there anything you want to add, or question?"

I hadn't heard him after the word "Prom." It rammed me in my belly. It paralyzed my limbs. Which was ridiculous. Like, *what* prom? Rob had walked away from me. I had no date. This was the *least* damaging thing they could do to me.

But it was everything. I don't know why. Maybe because the Prom was my one lifeline to being sober and straight and pretty and in love and happy. I remembered how phenomenal I felt at the Banquet, discovering Rob, loving my bare shoulders. Yeah, it was inside me, that dream. It's inside every girl. And I'd blown it.

So I stared at his paper clip holder and it glistened because I was crying. I felt myself shudder all over as I clasped my hands together. Finally, they'd gotten to me. Tough little Martha had stood toe to toe with the Big Guys all her life, spitting and snarling and punching. Little Orphan Annie, they used to call me. Now I was just a dirtbag in the principal's office.

I hated Sachs. *Sleazy old man,* I thought. *I bet you're getting a charge out of imagining me with Henning. I bet you wish there were videotapes.*

It didn't help. Sachs said, "I know you're upset, Martha. You want to sit in here for a while?"

I shook my head savagely. "Can I go back to class?"

"Sure. But you should pull yourself together."

I looked at him, snuffling and tearing. Pompous ass. If you wanted me together, why did you pull me apart? But I didn't say anything. I was still pretty respectful. I got up and opened the door. The fluorescent lights of the office hurt my eyes. All of a sudden there was a clatter of phones and typewriters and voices. And I could *see* the rain dribbling down the windows and the wind tossing the trees.

I bulled my way out of the office and into the corridor. I realized I hadn't even gotten a pass back to class. Good. I *wanted* to be challenged. I stopped in the hallway, turned toward the windows and sobbed like a jerk. But I kept it quiet so nobody would come over and comfort me. A few kids passed by and stared, but they didn't say anything.

So I'd been barbecued. I'd been denied the Senior Prom. It was official recognition of my failure. My body gaped like a screaming wound, and I hurt in every nerve and muscle. I knew if I got into my car I'd drive off a bridge.

See it? Hopeless. Desperate. Empty. Crawling in the pits. I was now going to go to Lou, to tell him this, to try to prevail on his decency, on his sense of fair play, on his code of honor.

But Lou *has* no decency or sense of fair play or code of honor. So he wouldn't reassure me and do the right thing. What Lou *did* have at this point was a powerful need for another girl. And what I had at this point was a severe need for love.

So if I went to Lou, there was every probability that he and I would do the *wrong* thing.

So I went. And we did.

It was even romantic. We met by this lake that is one of Westfield's great attractions. Back in prehistoric times, it was a summer resort for Italian people from Brooklyn. Now there's developments all around it and it's polluted. But it's a great hangout for kids.

So we met at the lake at about four in the afternoon, which is too early for most of the crowd to be there. We chose a little beach, mostly pebbles and dead grass. I skimmed rocks across the gray water of the lake. Nasty clouds slid across the sky, and a cold wind slammed my back.

Lou stood next to me, his hands jammed in his jacket pockets. His face looked blue-white. He has a beautiful profile. Like a fashion ad. I'd always put him down as a typical prep, and I'd always thought Kimber was a fool for going out with him. I knew he was brilliant and he was easy on the eyes, but mostly I dismissed him as an establishment stooge.

But now I was vulnerable. I told him what went on in Sach's office. He listened. We didn't look at each other. He just stared out over the water.

"So what do you want me to do?" he asked.

"I don't know. You saw me by the ice machine."

He sighed, real tense. "You want me to tell Sachs I saw you?"

I shrugged. "I know you can't do it, Lou."

Lou kind of picked up his chin and breathed in. His jaw pulsated. We could hear cars humming by on Market Road. My heart was fluttering, and I didn't really know what I wanted to happen.

Lou turned to face me. "If you really want me to tell Sachs, I'll tell him. I don't want you to hang."

You students of how to make it in a wicked world, take note. See what he did? He didn't get huffy and say, "Look, Martha, I can't get myself into trouble." He didn't get virtuous and say, "But Andrea's reputation is at stake." An amateur would have said those things.

Not Lou. He turned the screws on *me*. Now, was I going to let him destroy himself? No way. Lou understood the teenage code better than anybody. I said, "I'm not asking for that, Lou. I'm really not. I just don't know what to do."

His eyes got soft and caring and he put his hands on my shoulders. I was wearing my stiff denim jacket, so he couldn't transmit a lot of tenderness, but his touch went through me like high voltage anyway. "I'll do what you want me to do, Martha."

I nodded and sniffled away tears. "It doesn't matter. It wouldn't do any good."

He gave a rueful laugh. "Yeah, you're right about that. Sachs would say that *my* sins don't excuse yours."

"Probably."

"What a pisser. Half a million bucks in drug deals going down every day and Sachs goes after *you* for giving Westfield a bad image!"

"I got the publicity," I said. "The dealers don't."

"And that's what matters, man. The dealers might come after Sachs and shoot his kneecaps."

That made me laugh through my tears, and that gave Lou an excuse to gather me in for a hug. And oh, man did I need a hug. They've done research on hugs, you know. They do things to your body, release some kind of chemical or something that makes you feel better. Well, Lou released my chemicals. I hugged him back and I buried my face in his neck. The wind pounded us and rain spattered down.

"I'm sorry," I blubbered. "I don't usually fall apart."

"Bull," he said. "Everyone falls apart."

He kissed my hair and rubbed my back. He'd snowed me. He'd let me know that I was going to twist in the wind while he kept his reputation unstained, and the way he'd done it, I was falling in love with him. What a flimflam man. Most likely to run the world.

It was all over by then. I looked up and he looked down. His eyes went soft like cheese melting. That's the kiss signal. I was sucked up like Dorothy into the cyclone, and I shut my eyes and opened my mouth and threw my arms around his neck and kissed him with Mach 5 passion.

And that's where I'll fade out. Want to know how I felt that night? Forget it. Guilt about Kimber, overlaid with love for Lou, overlaid with guilt about Rob, overlaid with hatred of Sachs. I'm shocked I didn't fragment into six personalities.

But I didn't have much time to get introspective. Because, like I said, the lake is a big hangout. And Lou and I were observed. And it all hit the fan.

Chapter Twelve

"Kimber, when did you find out that Lou had made a play for Martha?"

Not for a while. Later I found out it was Joanna Reilly who saw them. Joanna knew me from Gym, but she didn't have any reason to tell me. Of course, she told *her* friends, and it slowly got around.

"What would be a reason for telling you?"

To destroy us as a couple. From the time you start going out with a guy, somebody's trying to break you up. Usually it's some other girl who wants that guy, but sometimes it's a friend who's jealous because you're spending time with the guy and not with her, or maybe it's someone who just doesn't like you.

"So you have these huns and vandals lurking at the borders, waiting for an opportunity to strike?"

That's pretty good. Huns and vandals.

"Yeah. I should be a writer."

Ha ha.

"But getting back to this betrayal business. I'm fascinated that a friend could also be a spider woman, patiently waiting for your boyfriend to cheat on you."

Oh, they're not always so patient. If another girl wants to break you up, she'll just start a rumor.

"You mean lie?"

Through her teeth. Sometimes she'll lie right to *you*, and tell you she knows your boyfriend has been fooling around. Of course, you don't want to believe her, but you have all these doubts about yourself, so you think *maybe* it's true. You can't enjoy yourself anymore until you talk to the guy. Naturally, he gets pissed off that you believed the rumors and sometimes that's enough to end it.

"Logical. Once the seed is planted, you're never sure."

Of course, it goes the other way. If your friend is interested in your guy, she'll go to *him* and say that *you're* cheating, and the same scene happens in reverse. Guys get really incensed over it because they see you as property. Girls mostly get depressed.

"And all this begins when the romance begins?"

Not so much at the start. You're still infatuated then. But once you're in love, and you're unloading four hundred bucks at the jewelry counter at A&S, that's just about when you start to get bored with each other, and your ears perk up at gossip.

"It all sounds so sad."

Tell me about it.

"Well, you're doing a better job telling *me*."

You sound just like Jason sometimes.

"Don't forget, I created him. Every character I create is part of me."

Oh, God. Including Lou?

"Well, he's a *small* part."

And I bet Jason's a big part. Even though you weren't going to give him a lead.

"I didn't want to admit that. But he's an important part of your story, so I have to let him loose."

Well, he's a more important part than I like to admit. He was there when I found out about Lou.

"I know. Want to talk about it?"

I guess I should, but . . .

BULLETIN! BULLETIN! WE INTERRUPT OUR REGU-LARLY SCHEDULED NARRATIVE TO BRING YOU THIS IMPORTANT NEWS! KIMBER DELANEY HAS DISAP-PEARED! SHE MAY HAVE GONE TO BRAZIL!

Uh oh, Jason.

Yes, Kimber. It's Uh-Oh Jason, with his newest hit, "I've Got Tears In My Ears From Lying On My Back In My Bed As I Cry Over You!" Solid Gold from 1963!

Let me guess. *You* want to tell this part.

No, I *have* to tell this part. It's my humiliation and I'll cry if I want to.

But you'll make *me* look like some kind of shrew.

Nonsense! Come on and Kiss Me, Kimber!

Be serious!

Okay, I'll be serious. I'll be grim and morbid and lugubri-ous. Then you can go back and talk about cheating and gos-siping and other teenage stuff.

You see, I don't get to partake in that game. I've been in love a few times—every other Thursday, in fact—but I never got far enough to be the victim of rumors. Remember, I'm not mint or hot or cute or built. I look like the stunt double for *Revenge of the Nerds*. And let no dimpled coed feed you a line about looking for intelligence and humor in a man. They look for bulging biceps, blue eyes, and tight buns. End of shopping list.

Hey, you want to know how many times I've sat with a sobbing damsel while she sang a sad song of abuse? And each time, my beady little eyes gleamed with hope. Ah yes, this one will fall into my spindly arms, and her flesh will meld with mine.

We're sorry. You didn't Win the Wench this time, but you get these wonderful consolation prizes: (A) a grateful kiss on the cheek; (B) a big sisterly hug; (C) a glowing thank you! We know they're not as much fun as sex and worship, but your little love object has returned to her grunting ape for more beatings.

Because they always *will* go back. As long as his lips pout, he can tie her up with Band-Aids and play badminton with her head. Oh, guys like me *do* get married, catching some maiden in the midst of Higher Aspirations. Yes, dear Bernard is so sensitive and steady. And dear Bernard hires a private eye a year later because wifey is dating a stevedore. The girls can't help it. It's genetic. I'm an evolutionary error, meant to die out, but protected by laws against stomping schlemiels.

I know that all sounded bitter, but it felt good to get it off my chest. Not that I have much of a chest, but it felt good, anyway.

As the mother said to the child who just puked on the rug, what brought all *that* up? Well, it's what happened when Kimber learned about Lou's treachery and came to me.

Let me set the scene:

Kimber had just learned that Lou had driven Deena home

from the wild party at Brandie's house. She knew in her heart of hearts that Lou was no longer interested in her, but she kept fooling herself. She had to. The Prom was fast approaching. Half of the swaying couples at any given Prom are pretending. There's the girl with her cousin from Seattle, or the couple that broke up last Tuesday, or the friend acting as a mercy date. Tradition says you're supposed to step into adulthood that night, with stars in your eyes.

Bah. Humbug. And Kimber was humbugging along with the best of them. I knew it because Kimber was the most important thing in my life. I studied her. I could tell by the angle of her chin or the flick of her eyebrow what she was thinking and feeling.

Why did I love her so much? Let me count the ways:

1. She was small and pretty.
2. She could write terrific stories and essays.
3. She could draw.
4. She understood puns.
5. You could talk to her seriously about subjects other than MTV, makeup, and parties.
6. She'd actually cry over news stories about crack or racial violence.
7. She sang off-key in a whispery little voice.
8. When she wore big sweaters and pulled the sleeves over her hands she looked so cute I went into cardiac arrest.
9. Her eyes got wide when she was excited.

I could list about a hundred more reasons, but none of it matters. I loved her. Hopelessly. Month after month, I watched her traipse around with Lou and be ignored, belittled, mocked, and dominated. I'd watch her take it, sometimes with her eyes cast down, sometimes with a brave little smile. And I'd punch the wall in my room. I wrote sonnets and songs for her and kept her picture in my notebook. I kept hoping that she'd wake up and see who was the right guy.

I thought I had a pretty good shot when I found her in the Music Suite and came up with the candy deal. I knew Kimber needed something outrageous to get her engine started again. I always know what Kimber needs.

The hour we spent going to Cheap John's and driving back to the school was like a movie montage. We laughed. We talked. I made believe she was my girlfriend. Then I said good night and she wasn't. But I'm used to that.

Still, I kept up my fruitless vigil. And let me tell you, a vigil without fruit is pretty dry. But I knew she and Lou were on the edge, so I clung to a little sliver of hope. Two months left to the senior year, two months before I went away to Cornell and she went to Geneseo. Two months to capture her heart. Hey, I work well under pressure.

So there we were, with Kimber suffering doubts, and me just suffering. And then she finds out that Lou took Deena home. She is raging inside. She feels ugly and dirty and stupid. She thinks everyone's laughing at her. She's disillusioned, she's frightened, and she's hurt.

H-E-L-L-L-O-O-O-O-O-O, KIMBER!!!!

Sure she came to me. The broken blossoms always come to us nerds. *That's* when they need sensitivity and intelligence. We're like the clubhouse on the golf course. Great for unwinding, but come morning, it's out on the fairway again. So we supply back rubs and wisdom and send them back for more bruises.

I was in Room 60, debugging a program for Advanced Computer Science, which wasn't easy because it was my program and I'd bugged it in the first place. It was about two-thirty. The halls were silent. The sun heated up the room. Suddenly, I sensed a presence. And it wasn't even my birthday!

(Okay, I'll go quietly.)

Anyway, I knew someone was there. I kept hacking because I was deeply involved with this problem. I hack at home until two in the morning sometimes because I have to have an answer. This is considered good in some quarters of the commercial world. But for the social life of a high school boy, it's the pits.

Kimber stood there for a long time, watching me. Then she said, "Jason?"

My heart perked up at the sound of her voice. I stopped clicking. My head was still filled with assembly code, but I didn't want Kimber to go, so I turned around. "Hi."

She was trembling. It scares me a little. When a girl is emotional, she's like a mainframe with a glitch; one wrong keystroke can crash the whole system. And Kimber was emotional. She had all the symptoms: glistening eyes, arms hugging books to her chest, blotchy skin.

"What's wrong?" I asked.

She tightened her lips and shook her head. I got up and went over to her. I could smell the last wisps of her perfume.

I never know what to do with touching. Sometimes I'll rub a girl's neck and she'll throw her head back and say, "Oh, that's perfect." But sometimes she'll twitch and say, "Don't, I'm too tense."

I tried locking eyes with her and sending her deeply moving messages of my love: *I love you, Kimber. Release your tears. Share your pain. Take off your clothes.* She returned my gaze, but she was still looking inward.

"I'm going nuts," she said, still clutching her books. "I have had the worst day of my life."

I gestured toward one of the desks. "So sit down. Talk a while."

She gave a faint smile and shook her head again. I began to get ticked. Had she just stopped in to let me know she was unhappy, without any intention of letting me help? How dare the woman! I *needed* to help. It was the basis of my existence.

"Is it a teacher problem?" I coaxed.

She shook her head, and pushed back her hair.

"Home?"

Head shake.

"Friends?"

Head shake.

"Romance?"

She gave a knowing smile and lowered her eyes. My heart began to pound fiercely in my little techie chest. *Ohboyohboyohboyohboyohboyohboy! She had a fight!*

"Did you have a fight?"

She gave a little laugh.

"Does that mean yes or no?"

"It means not yet."

"Uh oh. What happened?"

She looked up toward the ceiling, sighed, and kind of sucked at her teeth. *At least put down the books so I can hug you! I'm going bananas here.*

"Can I help? Carry your books? Shave your legs?"

She laughed, and hefted the books in her arms. "Jason, you're my savior."

"Bless you, child. But what am I savioring?"

She thought about it for a minute, "He took Deena home from a party." *The brute! The demon! The fiend! The rogue! He took Deena home from a party! HALLELUJAH!*

"When?"

"On the weekend. He just *happened* to be driving by . . ."

At this point, Kimber told me what she'd found out that morning in the cafeteria, and you already know the story. I listened with mounting anticipation (always mount anticipation from the left side). I admit it. I didn't care about Kimber's pain at that moment. I cared about my own. For the first time, opportunity knocked.

"Wow," I said solemnly. "That stinks."

"Yeah," she agreed. Tears streaked her face. But she still

held her books. That was a signal. She wasn't here for a hug. She was struggling with her feelings, and her self-esteem. She needed my company, my words (maybe), but not my touch.

I missed the signal. At that point, I would have missed it if she waved semaphore flags. I saw the girl I loved vulnerable and in tears. Lou had cheated on her. All bets were off. Open Season had arrived.

I stepped to her and put my hands on her books. "Want to go somewhere?" I suggested.

She shook her head and she *didn't let go of the books.*

"Sit down. You look beat."

She shook her head again. Now I was in trouble. I was standing right in front of her, with my hands on her books. But she didn't want to let go of the books. I tugged slightly. She held on. Now what? Did I lift my hands from the books and step back? Did I wrench the books from her hands and order her to sit? Did we *both* continue to hold her books, in a kind of literary communion?

"Kimber, I feel so bad for you," I lied.

"I can't believe this is happening."

That made two of us. "You need to rest," I said.

"Rest won't help."

"Standing here in pain won't help either," I said.

She looked tenderly at me. "Tell me a good joke, Jason. That's what I need from you."

Watch out! We're going D
$$O$$
$$W$$
$$N$$
$$!$$

Remember, I was tired. I had let myself rise to the heights of fantasy fulfillment. And now I stood, with my hands on her books, and she asked for a joke! Not a hug, not a rubdown, but a joke!!

I panicked. Blood rampaged in my undeveloped little

arteries. My paralyzed hands moved up from her books to her arms. I looked savagely into her confused face. I lost control.

"No jokes," I said in a voice that was meant to be Clint Eastwood but came out Kermit the Frog.

"Jason, what should I do?" she asked.

"Stop letting him destroy you."

"I know."

"Then do it."

"How?"

"Just say no."

See? I made a joke. Right at that moment when maybe I *could* have succeeded, I made a joke. It's fear of success. I read about it in *Psychology Today*. It's a built-in destruct mechanism that resides in my brain like a killer cell.

But when I said the words, they didn't sound funny to me. I followed immediately with a kiss attempt. I moved into her, but of course she was still holding her books, which rammed into my stomach. I tilted my face so I could find with her mouth.

Except that *she* had heard my words as funny, and she laughed. The little explosion of merriment coincided precisely with the landing of my lips on hers so that she actually laughed right into my open mouth. This was so startling that she jerked her head back and stared at me. Then she laughed harder.

I let go of Kimber, and my hands stayed in the air, as if I were surrendering to the cops.

"Jason? . . ." she said.

"I'm sorry," I murmured.

Then she laughed again. Totally mortified, I tried to back up and turn around at the same time. My foot came under the wire that led to the terminal plug. I lifted my foot, yanked the wire, and the plug sprang from its socket. With a little gurgle of horror, I looked at the screen. It was black.

I'd wiped out an hour of work.

I gaped at the screen. Kimber said, "Oh, no! Did you unplug it?"

I said, "Abba abba abba abba abba," and laid my hands on the monitor, as if to resurrect the program by healing.

"Oooh," Kimber said. "I'm sorry."

I turned and looked at her with such anguish that she blanched. I couldn't function. In front of me was the girl I just tried to assault and behind me the computer I'd tried to outwit. Both had rejected me. I wanted to run from the room and scuttle down the hall like a mad dwarf. But I just stood there, incoherent.

Kimber shifted the books again and said, "Jason, I'm really sorry. I think I'll leave you to deal with this mess. Thanks for cheering me up."

The heartless wanton gave me a sunny little smile, as if nothing had ever troubled her heart, and bounced blithely out of the room. I didn't even go to the door to watch her. Even when Lou had cheated on her, even when she was pulverized, even *then* she wouldn't accept me. Better the pain than the nerd.

Every hope had been dashed. Every fantasy devalued. Every dream demolished. Loving Kimber was now a sick joke. I turned back to the blank screen and proceeded to throw a tantrum, whaling on the monitor, kicking the wall, and flinging disks like boomerangs.

And a few hours later, I was dreaming of her again. But that moment had set up the next crisis, because Jason Goldman had been trifled with, and that turned out to be a more dangerous problem than anybody expected.

So, Kimber. Didn't I tell it stunningly? . . . Kimber? . . . Are you there?

Yes, Jason. I'm here.

No response?

You asshole.

Ah. You liked it.

Damn you, Jason. Damn you to hell.

Chapter Thirteen

You know, Jason, maybe this isn't the time to say anything, but if you wouldn't keep putting yourself down and calling yourself a nerd, you might get the love you want.

Another lecture. Thank you.

See what you're doing? Everything's a flip answer. A lot of people like you, Jason. But you make it impossible for a girl to get close to you.

Why? I use deodorant. I brush and floss. I squeeze my zits.

Forget it. I'm not going to be made a fool of. And I really resent being characterized as a heartless wench. I came into that room looking for some friendship. I wasn't expecting to be attacked. And you looked so pathetic and ridiculous that I couldn't help laughing. You know, if you wanted to make a play for me, Jason, there are traditional ways to do it.

Right. Which friend of a friend should I ask if you're interested? How far would I get?

(Sigh) All right, let's drop it. You're determined to be offended. But I don't have to feel guilty. I love you very much, Jason. I'm sorry it's not romantic or lustful, but like we're all trying to prove here, life isn't a fairy tale. The fact is . . .

Well, I'm getting ahead of myself. Let me jump from Room 60 to about a week later. This was a week of sleepwalking through life. Remember I'd just been hit with Deena's ride home in Lou's car. I managed to avoid seeing Lou all week, and he didn't exactly come after me.

Now I know why, of course. He was whooping it up with Martha. I was unaware of this. I was also unaware that news of their rendezvous by the lake was flashing around the school. It wasn't just that Lou was cheating on me, he was cheating with *Martha*, and Martha was the hottest item in Westfield. Sure it's hypocritical. You know and I know that half the kids in the school are messing around and doing drugs, but that's how people are. Societies need scapegoats. I learned about that in Sociology.

So how did *I* find out? No, not from Joanna Reilly. No, it wasn't any of her friends who told me, either. Come on, three guesses.

Well, let me lead up to it. I knew that Lou had taken Deena home. I didn't know that he'd kissed her goodnight, but it didn't matter. I was burning with jealousy. This whole year of my life had been a downhill run. I couldn't make my father happy, I couldn't control my brother, I couldn't afford to go to the college I wanted. So Lou was my only success. *I had Lou.* See? That made me okay.

But now I couldn't pretend anymore. Bye, bye Lou. Bye, bye happiness. Jason had tried. When he got me to buy that candy and sell it, he was sending me a big message, which I ignored. Oh, I sold most of the candy (unfortunately, I ate a lot of it, too), and I put the change into coin rolls and bundled up the dollar bills and put them in my bank account. It felt good. But I *still* didn't get the message. I mean, how could Jason's good sense ever compete with my irrationality? So by the time I spoke to Martha, I was blind, deaf, and dumb. (Nope, it wasn't Martha who told me about Martha. Good guess, though.)

But just before that happened, things came to a head at home. It was bound to happen, anyway, but the timing was perfect.

It was the day I went into Room 60 to get some humor from Jason. I left Room 60 more confused than when I went in. I got home and there was nobody in the house. Sometimes I like that.

I wanted it when I came home on this particular afternoon. It had gotten real warm, the sun spread over the neighborhood like syrup, and the sky was soft blue. A wet wind made the new leaves shiver on the trees. Kids rode their bikes and screamed. Actually, it made me pretty sad because of the way I was feeling.

So when I came in and yelled "Hello!" and nobody answered I figured I'd zonk out for a while. I dropped my books on the kitchen counter and opened the refrigerator. I could hear the battery clock ticking and muffled kids' noises outside. I was getting sleepier by the minute. I grabbed an orange, shut the fridge door, peeled the orange, got a napkin, and started eating.

While I lunged and slurped at the orange, I wandered into the foyer and glanced upstairs. Corey's door was closed. My heart sank a little. If Corey was home, I couldn't really enjoy my leisure. He'd blast his stereo and come downstairs to get snacks.

So before I got comfy on the couch, I trudged upstairs to see if he *was* home. I knocked on his door. "Corey?"

No answer. Which didn't mean he wasn't there, since Corey goes into trances and wouldn't hear a bulldozer knocking down the walls. But then again, I didn't hear his heavy metal tapes blasting. I knocked again. *"Corey?"*

Still no answer. I held the orange and napkin in my left hand and turned the doorknob. The door was locked. Now, this isn't unusual. Daddy installed a key lock for Corey about two years ago when the prince wanted his privacy. Mainly he didn't want his big sister barging in when he was naked (like I'd really go out of my way to see him parading around admiring himself). So he got the lock. The key hangs on a hook by the side of the door, so that Dad can get in if there's a fire.

Or I can get in if I'm suspicious.

I don't know why I was suspicious. There were no fumes coming from the room. But remember, Corey had been getting more and more rebellious. That night at the Sumpfest, I got scared. Then when I found Dad drinking and had that talk with him, I realized that Corey was really on his own.

And I just *felt* suspicious. Woman's intuition, right? Only with Corey it didn't take a lot of intuition.

So I lifted the key from its hook and opened his door. My heart started fluttering because I'm not a great criminal. I scanned the room. Corey isn't gross, but he isn't exactly neat. There were unwashed sweats on the bed, and the bedspread was bunched up. He had his old soccer trophies in a hutch, along with some car models and his deodorant stick. His fish tank gurgled, and his one gray fish swam around morosely. Corey's had about a hundred fish in the last five years, but he kills them. Sometimes he cuts them in half, and sometimes he starves them to death and sometimes he takes them out and flushes them down the toilet.

I was about to walk out of the room, when I saw his sock drawer slightly open. You know how it is; you probably wouldn't go around *opening* drawers, unless you're a burglar, but you can't resist a drawer that's slightly open. *Why* is it slightly open? What's in there? So I went over and pulled the drawer all the way open, which isn't easy because it was off its track.

There were lots of sweat socks in there, some of them clean and some of them not. Right away, I saw the edge of the plastic baggie. It was sticking up from between the socks. My throat clutched because I knew right away what it was. I grabbed the edge of the baggie (I was still holding my half-eaten orange in my left hand) and pulled it out. There was still enough grass in there for a couple of joints.

The sun pressed hard on the closed windows, making them into smears. I looked over at the television set, which was covered with thick dust. I looked at Corey's VCR, on a shelf underneath the set. He'd bought that set, and the VCR, by mowing lawns. I took him to Crazy Eddie's for the VCR. He was so proud of himself. He carried the box to the car and kept looking at it on his lap all the way home.

I started to cry. I slammed the remains of the orange into his New York Mets garbage pail and sat down on his bed with the baggie clenched in my hand. He was a *kid*. He was an obnoxious, bony, zit-faced little boy. It tore me up. I mean, there are about a million kids smoking pot, and half my friends do it, and I know it's no big deal, but Corey was only fourteen. And this wasn't a joint, it was a dime bag. Like, was he *dealing* it?

My face was on fire, and my head throbbed. That's when the front door opened, and I got up like I'd been shot (actually, you would *fall down* if you were shot, but you get the idea). I had no time to think, because you can see Corey's door from the foyer, and Corey yelled up, "Who's in my ROOM?"

Usually, I would be so scared at being caught that I'd get inarticulate and come running out with some excuse like, "I thought I smelled smoke." But I was in a crisis.

"*I'm* in your room," I yelled back.

He slammed his book bag down on the floor with a thump. "WHY?"

"Come up and I'll show you why."

My adrenalin kicked in and I got pumped. Corey hammered up the steps and loomed over me. And I mean *over* me. This kid is over six feet tall, and he looked enormous now, with his arms dangling and his face contorted and his hair in his eyes. In his gray sweats, he looked like a flapping stork.

He saw what I was holding right away, and whatever he was going to say got caught in his throat. I looked right into his eyes and said, "What the hell goes on, Corey?"

"Where'd you get that?"

"Give it a rest. Are you totally brain dead or what?"

He made a swipe for the bag but I yanked it out of his reach. I could see the rage that shook his whole body. "You went through my DRAWER?"

"It was open."

"What'd you do, open my DOOR?"

"Yeah, I opened your door. I thought you were dead."

"Who the hell said you could open it?"

"I *told* you why I opened it. You're a total waste, you know that?"

"I'll kick your ASS!"

He lunged at me, and I pushed him away. I don't know what was giving me the courage, because Corey's pretty strong and I didn't have any reason to think he wouldn't beat me insensible. But I was rolling now. I just placed my hand in the middle of his bony chest and shoved. He shuffled backwards and stared at me.

"You won't kick anything, creep," I said. "You're over the line. You're going to straighten up or I'll put your butt in jail."

He must have figured I was serious, at least for the moment, because he changed his strategy. He kind of shook himself out and put on a little smirk. "Jeez, what's the big deal? Everybody does that stuff."

"Who's everybody? Greg and Scott?"

"*Everybody.*"

"Are you dealing?"

The smirk got bigger. "Yeah, I'm dealing, all right? I'm a freakin' drug lord."

That's when I broke. My face was burning from the crying I'd done. This was not a great moment to give me snotty comebacks. So I stepped up to Corey and I slapped his face. Now I'd *never* slapped anyone's face in my life. I'd only seen it in movies and on TV. I found out that it hurts like crazy. My fingers started throbbing and swelling up.

Corey's cheek showed a perfect red imprint of my hand and he stared at me, bug-eyed. Then he said, "What the hell is the matter with you?"

"You're the matter," I said. "This whole damn house is the matter. Daddy won't see what you are, but I'm not going to look away. Maybe your father's afraid of you, but I'm not. I'm going to be on your rear end from now on. I'll trash your room every day, and I mean *trash* it. I'm going to watch you in the house, on the street, in school, everywhere. You want to go down the tubes, you'll have to work at it."

My stomach was flip-flopping and I tasted rancid orange in my mouth. Corey blinked faster and faster, which he always did when he was cornered. "Are you going to tell Dad?"

"Yeah, I'm going to tell him."

Incredibly, he started to cry! Not real sobbing, but his eyes got wet and he swiped at them. "Don't tell him, okay? Just don't tell him."

"Why not? You don't deserve any chances."

"JUST DON'T TELL HIM, OKAY?"

He turned away, softly banging his fist on the dresser. "Look, just don't tell Dad. I'll stay clean. I'll do my damn work. You can hire a private detective. Okay?"

I was confused. I never would have believed that Corey was afraid of his father. Then again, the few times Daddy got angry enough, he got pretty violent. Or maybe Corey was still the screwed-up kid he was when Mom walked out.

Anyway, I believed Corey was really upset, at least for the minute. Maybe he was acting, but it was good acting. And to tell the truth, I felt pretty decent about confronting him. I'd *made* him upset. I'd stood up to him. I'd *done* something about the problem. In a way, I was finding out exactly what Jason tried to show me with the candy, but I didn't put anything together yet.

So I said, "All right, I won't tell Daddy for a while. As long as you know that I'm on your case."

"Thanks," he said, and he sounded really grateful. He gestured aimlessly toward the baggie. "I'm sorry about that."

"Get off it," I said. "You're not sorry about anything. But it's too bad, because you're on enforced good behavior. And I mean B's and A's, kid, or I lower the boom."

I was drained. I mean, this was not exactly cookies and a nap on the couch. I went out of Corey's room and into the bathroom, where I flushed all the pot down the toilet. Corey stayed in his room, but I could hear him cursing. Trashing the marijuana probably hurt him worse than anything I said because he must have saved up for a few weeks to buy it. I took the baggie downstairs and threw it away in a garbage pail outside. Then I came in and washed my hands with soap and water and flopped into one of the big chairs in the family room—the same one Daddy always used. I thought about how *I* needed a drink, but I didn't take anything.

I felt my heart banging away, and my legs shaking. This was all going to hit me now. I saw that my right hand was purplish and I could hardly move my fingers without pain. So I went back into the kitchen and wrapped ice cubes in a paper towel and held them against my fingers. I also cried again.

But I felt pretty good. I was determined, angry, and making plans. That was the way I used to be. I *almost* called up Lou and told him to suck ice. But I wasn't *that* transformed yet.

Now, *that* was the mood I was in when I saw Martha. Why did I see Martha? Well, little known to Kimber, Martha had not *stopped* with the tête-à-tête down by the lake. That could have been written off as a mad moment. Martha and Lou had *continued*. They'd seen each other a couple of times, and they were starting to get serious. Obviously, this was not good. As I explained, there are only two ways to fall in love if you're a teenager: the "legal" route, with all its procedures, or the "illegal" route, by cheating with someone else's partner.

So Martha was going illegal. It was preying on her mind and she needed to talk to me. She called me a few days after the blowout I had with Corey. I found out later she was *supposed* to go to Lou's house, except his folks were home. But at the moment, I was ignorant.

Chapter Fourteen

Martha grabbed me in the hall during passing, with eight thousand bodies crushed together, and said, "I have to talk to you."

"Sure," I said. I knew she wasn't kidding. Usually, she holds everything inside and suffers, so when she tells you she wants to talk, you *know* she's hanging by a thread.

"I'll pick you up at seven," she said.

"Okay." I watched her get sucked into the mob going upstairs and continued on, very unhappy. I should *not* have said okay to Martha driving. I knew that she'd been drinking pretty heavily, and was probably suicidal. I wasn't enchanted with life at the moment, but I didn't want to die in a ball of flame.

But I couldn't figure out a way to get out of it, or to tell her I'd drive. That would be letting her know I didn't trust her. I *didn't*, but I couldn't let her know. You understand.

So I went home and did my homework, sort of. Then I changed into sweatshirt, old jeans, and a denim jacket, brushed out my hair, and fixed my makeup as Martha pulled up on the driveway.

Outside, it was dark, but right at the tree line was a band of blue. It made the black part of the sky look like an Astrodome sliding back to reveal the rest of the universe. I felt dizzy and excited all at once. The air smelled grassy and all the front door lights on the block glowed like fireflies. Martha's headlights burned my eyes.

I slid into her '82 Mustang, and shut the door. Which isn't easy because you have to pull real hard and do it about three times. And the window rattles because it won't close all the way. "Hi," I said.

"Howdy."

Martha looked the way she usually looked, which was kind of a relief. I'd half expected her to be in all black with whiteface makeup and green hair. She jammed the automatic into reverse and left rubber on my dad's driveway. She got about three feet into the road and stomped the brake. I lurched forward and heard the other car pass by.

"Glad to see you're calm," I said.

She smiled and backed into the street, then bolted forward. Martha's actually a good driver, but she gets impatient.

A few blocks later, she pulled into the 7-Eleven parking lot, and said, "I'm buying Hostess cupcakes."

I looked at her because she's hardly ever sentimental. "Good thinking."

I stayed in the car and watched her go inside. The usual army of jacked-up trucks idled in the parking lot, and the usual group of dirtbags hung out just behind the store. I caught myself scanning for Corey, and turned away.

Through the store window, I saw Martha on line behind a big muscular dude with a pony tail and tattoos all over his arms. He was buying beer.

Martha came out with a paper sack and jumped in. She tossed me the sack and I dug out the cupcakes. I peeled off the plastic while she drove down Center Avenue. She actually *inched* down Center Avenue, because it was wall to wall cars. I tossed a cupcake to Martha and we both stuffed our faces happily.

Maybe not so happily. The cupcakes reminded me of times gone by, and of the obvious fact that Martha wasn't a pudgy little troublemaker any more and I wasn't a hyper elf. Daddy once said that when he passed forty he began to feel the weight of his life. Well, at seventeen I wasn't feeling *tons*, but there *was* a difference.

"So what's doin'?" I asked.

"No prom," she said.

"Sachs really said no?"

"Sure did."

She told me what went on in his office, which you've already heard from Martha. I said, "It's so stupid. All those jocks who got wasted and trashed the hotel just got reprimanded. Man, if you're a football player at Westfield, you've got it made."

She gave a rueful laugh. "I wonder if John Brody and Greg Fratelli got barred from the prom."

"I doubt they were even suspended for assaulting you."

"No way," Martha said. "They had a lacrosse match that Saturday."

"*Forgive* me."

Martha threw the blinker on and edged into the right turn lane. She actually snuck onto the shoulder fifty yards *before* the right turn lane, which is a Long Island tradition.

"Where are we going?" I asked.

"Ocean Point Harbor."

She made the turn when the light went green. I saw a silver oil truck careening down the curve and for a second I didn't think it was going to stop for the light, but it did. My whole body shivered. Martha's lead foot took over now that we were on County Road 93, which is two lanes each way, curvy, and *fast*.

The wind whipped past the broken window and I huddled in my jacket. "What are you going to do?" I asked.

"Stay home."

"But that *stinks*. We have the limo and everything."

"*You* have the limo and everything."

"There's got to be some way. Maybe Sachs is just giving you a hard time, and he'll relent at the last minute."

She gave a little laugh. "I don't think so."

I leaned back, feeling angry. "It won't be fun without you."

"Sure it will."

"No it won't."

She leaned forward to wipe her lips on her sleeve without taking her hand off the wheel. I glanced at her profile, edged in passing headlights. The inside of her car smelled like mildew, and a little like rum.

"Nobody's indispensable," she said. "I won't leave a hole in the evening."

"Hey!" I gave her a sharp glance. Naturally, I was attuned to suicidal references.

She laughed openly and shook her head. "Take it easy."

"Sorry. My life has been crumbling, and I've been watching *your* life crumble."

"Well, I'm crumbling faster than you are."

Her face tensed, and she accelerated with maniacal determination. The light at Midland Avenue was turning amber and Martha was not going to get caught.

Martha ran the light just as it turned red, which is another Long Island tradition. I got a rush of adrenalin. Anyway, three cars behind us also ran the light.

Martha had that look like she wanted to say something. She thought it over for a while, then said, "You remember all those times we drove this baby into the city?"

"Uh huh."

"Like the Def Leppard concert. Remember the Def Leppard concert?"

"I could never forget."

With a slightly hysterical laugh, Martha said, "Man, that was wild. First Gina comes out in that half top and those tight spandex pants, remember? And we all discussed whether we were going to get raped or killed or raped *and* killed? And then we parked fifty miles away at the Meadowlands and got on the bus but it was a *training* bus and it wasn't going anywhere?"

Yeah, I remembered. I hated Def Leppard (forgive me, fans!), but going to a concert with Martha was the real show anyway. "And Gina," I added. "Remember how obsessed she was? How she stood up with her mouth open and grabbed the mike stand when it came sailing into the audience?"

Martha nodded and laughed merrily. She was not merry, of course. I could tell because she was driving faster and faster, which wasn't intelligent on this part of 93. It was dark as the inside of a sock, and the road whipped back and forth. We rocketed past the college and under the Long Island Railroad trestle and then Martha hooked a thrilling left turn onto Arcadia Road, about three inches ahead of an oncoming line of cars.

With infuriated horns at our asses, we kept going. "I wish I could have that back again," Martha said. "It was so great. Just cruising, and drinking, and joking, and going nowhere. *Man.*"

I felt frustrated because I knew I couldn't make her feel better. And she was getting *me* troubled. "You're not exactly a hundred and three," I reminded her. "There's a lot of good times ahead."

"Not the same. Now it'll be, 'What time do we have to be back because we have to get up for work?' and 'I don't want to drive into the city because the car'll get scratched.' It'll never be *free* again."

I lifted my eyebrows. "Since when are you planning a responsible life? You'll *always* be free."

"No I won't."

She got silent and grim. I slumped back and watched bars of light slide across the roof. *That* brought back memories, of being a little kid and riding with Mommy and Daddy. I used to curl up in the back seat and feel the rhythmic bumping of the car and watch the lights pass across the roof. I used to guess if we were turning left or right. It was so soothing and safe. You really trust your folks at that age. Daddy could have been driving off a cliff and I wouldn't have known.

I started to talk about this to Martha. "Once we were riding home in a hurricane," I told her. "I remember we were on some kind of bridge and Daddy had to stop and look under the hood. I remember waves crashing up over the side of the bridge."

"I love old memories," Martha said. "You can see them again and again, the same colors, the same sequence."

"And you're never sure if they were dreams, right?"

"What about old *dreams*?" she said. "From when you were two or three years old?"

"Yeah!" I said. "I still remember one where I was trying to find this comic book I wanted—it was an Archie comic book. In the dream, I went into this drug store by a bus terminal and the comic book was on the shelf, but I never bought it."

Martha was silent, which deflated me, because a conversation like this needs a lot of talk, or else you feel silly. Martha had turned right onto Harbor Road and now we drove past baronial homes, set way back on sloping lawns, with willow trees and brick entrance gates. The road was narrow and rough. Through the trees on our left, we could glimpse the harbor, and all the boats tied up.

When Martha spoke, it startled me, because I thought she'd forgotten about the conversation. "I had a recurring dream," she said. "I was on a green bridge, except it was flat, like Colorforms. Remember Colorforms?"

"Sure," I said.

"It was a green Colorforms bridge against black night, but the night was flat, too. And I always fell off the bridge. Over and over again."

"That's supposed to mean something, falling."

"It's supposed to mean death."

I *knew* it was supposed to mean death, but I didn't want to say it. "They also say that dreams don't really mean *anything.*"

Martha's profile was so dark it was unreadable. "I don't know if it meant anything, but it scared me. I know I'm going to see that bridge again, and I'm scared."

We'd gotten to the harbor. The road ended in a gravel parking lot. Martha pulled in and stopped the car, which relieved me a little. We got out and stood in very chilly air. The wind slapped the flags by the yacht club, and made the boats creek. I could hear the *slosh slosh* of water by the pilings.

I buttoned up my jacket and shoved my hands in the pockets. We walked on the gravel and then on the narrow boardwalk. My teeth chattered. Some boats had lights on. Martha said, "Making nookie on deck."

I laughed. "It's so *cramped* on one of these things."

"How far do you have to move?"

That made us both laugh. I was nervous walking between the boat slips. I always have this fear that I'm going to fall. We reached the end and looked out at dark oily water, rippled with cold moonlight. There were heavy clouds on the horizon. This had to be the loneliest place in the world.

I sensed that Martha was crying and I rubbed her back. She was shaking and she felt hot, even through the layers of clothes. "Can't your mom talk to Sachs?"

Martha shook her head.

"What about Rob? Have you talked to him at all?"

She chewed on her lip. Remember, I didn't know what was *really* tearing her apart. Not that the prom thing *wasn't*, but that's all I knew about. So I moved closer to her and said, "Maybe we'll all boycott the prom."

Laughter puffed from her lips. "That's unbelievably stupid."

"Well, I feel bad going. And I feel bad that you're not."

She didn't say anything for a minute. Then her words gushed. "I never expected to care this much, Kimber. I mean, big freaking deal. The *prom*. Why do I *care* so much?"

"It's still a big thing," I said. In a crisis like this, I didn't fool around; I went right for the cliché.

Martha spun around with tremendous force. "It's *not* a big thing," she said. "It's a game. *Sachs* is playing a game. *You're* playing games. I'm so sick of it."

I clawed for something to say. She'd come out of nowhere and

I wasn't even sure what she was talking about. Her eyes were on fire.

She grabbed my arm and turned me back toward the parking lot. "Come on," she said.

"Where are we going now?"

"Nowhere."

Oh boy. I followed her, half running because she was taking long strides, and I'm not tall enough to take long strides. She swept through the parking lot and flung open the passenger door of the Mustang. "Get in," she said.

"Martha, chill out."

"Get in or walk home. It makes no difference to me."

Don't you love these decisions? She was obviously disturbed. But if I let her drive alone, she might kill herself *plus* I had no way of getting home from here and I'm not brave enough to go knocking on the doors of extremely rich people who probably had killer dogs.

So I took a deep breath and got in, slamming the door three times with mounting anger. Martha nearly stripped the gears as she started the engine, and she tore ass out of that parking lot, spewing gravel halfway to Connecticut.

I grabbed the hand grip and leaned back, feeling a little like an astronaut on lift-off. "Cut the crap, Martha," I said. "This doesn't impress me."

"I couldn't care less about impressing you."

Terrific. She was totally irrational. Well, so much for sharing childhood memories and forging a closer bond. I didn't know why in the blazes she'd suddenly turned into Mr. Hyde, but I was terrified. Martha took the narrow curves practically on two wheels. Her tires squealed like mad and I heard the *pht-pht-pht* of trees flashing past. My blood drummed in my ears.

She cut off oncoming traffic again, making the right onto 93, and now she *really* got in gear. She began to weave around other cars, clipping across lanes, deliberately cutting people off. She reached into her jacket (while I had a heart attack because she was now speeding recklessly with only one hand on the wheel) and drew out a flask!

"MARTHA!"

"Say good-bye, Kimber."

She began to swill at the flask while spinning the wheel back and forth with her free hand. This was a big show. Even when she drank and drove, she didn't do it like this. But at that particular moment, I wasn't into analyzing her sincerity. The Mustang was skidding into eternity.

"YOU ASSHOLE!" I screamed.

I lunged to my left and wrenched the steering wheel back the other way. Martha fought me for it. I heard her grunting. I bit down so hard on my lip that I bled. I could not believe that I was fighting for my life like some stunt scene in a movie! I'm even more amazed that I *did* it, instead of just shutting my eyes. But like I said, there are moments of crisis, and catalysts.

Also, not to make myself sound like Wonder Woman, Martha didn't *really* want to kill us; she was just being obnoxious. The thing is, being obnoxious at seventy miles an hour can kill you pretty dead. So I fought and as we fought I knocked the flask out of her hand (that was accidental). Then I punched her in the face (that was deliberate). And I started to scream. Nothing intelligent or meaningful, just animal noises.

Whatever I did, it worked. She suddenly stopped tussling and grabbed the wheel. More importantly, her foot eased up on the gas and the car slowed down. She was crying hysterically, and then she yanked the wheel to the left and the car slammed off the road and *thumped-thumped* onto the median, which was a wide grassy ditch. Martha stopped the car at a lunatic angle and I could hear steam rushing out.

For a few seconds, I was still speeding. Then, slowly, my body accepted the fact that it was sitting still. My heart pushed my chest out each time it beat, which was about a hundred and twenty times a minute. Martha's sobs sounded loud against the abrupt silence. The Mustang shuddered each time a car on the road went past.

Martha looked at me, her cheeks crisscrossed with wet tracks. "Kimber . . ." she burbled. Then she pitched toward me and I hugged her while I cursed. We rocked back and forth like that with Martha saying she was sorry and me saying she was crazy. I loved her more than anyone at that moment.

And the very next morning, I understood everything that had gone on, and a lot more. But you know, even though I hated her guts when I found out, I think I'll always treasure that deranged car ride and the way we both said good-bye to our girlhoods in ways we didn't even comprehend.

Forget the prom, man. *That* was our graduation party.

Chapter Fifteen

So there I was, shaken to my roots by Martha. But I'd stopped her from killing us. I'd *done* something. Right after I'd done something about Corey. The comeback started when Jason got me to sell the candy. That was the first thing I *did* all year, on my own. So keep all this in mind because it was priming me for the Biggie.

It happened in the parking lot of the McDonald's on Market Road. Everyone in McDonald's got a show, let me tell you. And if you haven't already guessed, the person who let me know about Lou and Martha was . . .

Don't even bother. It was me. Deena. And this time I'm not going to just sit here while you peel off my skin. *I'll* tell the story about the fight, so we don't see it from *your* distorted point of view.

Cool off, Deena. First of all, it wasn't a *fight*, and second of all I'm not going to *peel* your skin, so don't get hyper.

I'm not hyper. I'm just tired of being painted as a fool. Yes, I ratted on Lou because I was tired of seeing you hurt. We were all supposed to be going to the prom together as friends and meanwhile we were falling apart.

Deena, we were falling apart because you and Martha were cheating with *my* boy friend! I mean, come *on*! If we're telling the truth, we might as well do it.

Your version of the truth is not always mine, Kimber. And let's not call what I did cheating, okay? *Lou* did the kissing, and one kiss out of sympathy isn't exactly an affair. If you were so insecure about his love, that's not my problem.

That's a laugh! *You're* the insecure party, Deena. I mean, it's so obvious. You hate your parents for just having *you* and then running all over the place, and you hate *yourself* . . .

Oh, come *on*!

You do! You're always on another crash diet, you fix your stupid makeup every five minutes, you buy clothes three times a day, and you carry on about true love until everybody throws up. Meanwhile you're throwing yourself at one guy after another! That's *classic* insecurity, Deena, and you know it!

It's nice to know what you've been saying about me.

Don't get self-pitying, Deena . . .

Shut up, okay? It's really terrific to know that you've been *pretending* to be my friend while you were laughing at me. What did you guys do, analyze me when I wasn't there? I guess I provided many moments of fun. Well, maybe you ought to think about *why* Lou got bored with you. Before you criticize someone else, you should fix your own problems.

Don't worry, Deena, I know what my problems are. I don't draw little roses as the answer to everything. But this whole thing is ridiculous. I wasn't bringing up *your* problems, I was getting to *my* problem, when I found out about Lou and— *Martha*! What are *you* doing here?

Well, *I'm* the one who should tell it.

You weren't in the car when I found out.

But I *caused* the blowup, so I should tell the story.

Thanks, but I'd really rather do it myself.

Man, you've changed. Back at the beginning of this, you didn't want to be bothered.

So I want to be bothered now, okay? I don't believe how I'm getting hassled. You know, if you really want to get down to it, girls, you were *both* rags, so I think I should at least get first shot at rehashing it.

And let you paint us as *rags*? Yeah, you'd love that.

Deena, for God's sake, stop being paranoid!

I'm paranoid? Give me a break! You spent the whole . . .

"OKAY, BLUE PENCIL TIME":

~~And let you paint us as *rags*? Yeah, you'd love that.~~

~~Deena, for God's sake, stop being paranoid!~~

~~*I'm* paranoid? Give me a break! You spent the whole . . .~~

Huh? What's going on? Why is everything we say being crossed out?

"Because I'm stopping all three of you before this becomes a fist fight."

You're the author, right?

"Well, I *used* to be, Kimber. I'm enjoying the way you're revealing yourselves, and I like your different viewpoints, but this little donnybrook isn't helpful. First of all, it's impossible to know who's talking, and second of all, you're being hurtful without being informative."

You're right. We're not supposed to act this way.

"Well, you can act that way in rough draft, but we're trying to get this in final shape. *Anyway*, I think I . . ."

Ooh, *that's* where I get it from!

"Get *what* from?"

My habit of saying "anyway" all the time. *You* do it.

"Yes, Kimber, of course. You *all* get your habits from me. Now, I think I ought to take over the scene, like I did with the fight in the hallway. Since you're all involved, we need *all* points of view, *and* objectivity."

I'm willing to let you do it.

"At this point, none of you has any choice. Just sit quietly, and don't interrupt."

Now . . .

What happened was that Martha and Lou discovered love— new, burning love. Martha, who had been lower than a groundhog's navel, suddenly felt girlish and hopeful (when she wasn't tormented by guilt). Lou, who had gotten nastier and nastier, suddenly exuded tenderness and warmth.

So Lou and Martha made out down by the lake, with the kind of fury that characterizes an illicit fling. Of course they *had* to see each other again. Now Lou wasn't about to ask her to the movies, where everybody would see them.

So they watched and waited for parents to be gone, and they made whispered phone calls, and they drove to each other's homes. Lou had the advantage of a double garage, so Martha could stash her Mustang. Lou's TransAm had to stay unhidden when he went to Martha's house, so he parked a block away and walked through backyards.

And what did they do together? A lot of frantic clutching and kissing, a lot of TV watching, a lot of conversation about college plans, and a lot of time planning the *next* meeting. There was nowhere for the romance to go as long as they were keeping it a secret. They couldn't date openly and get to know each other because Lou was *taken*. He'd have to break up with Kimber so that they wouldn't be going together any-more. Or at least he'd have to tell Kimber that he wanted to *see* other people. Then he could at least *see* Martha, even if he couldn't go *out* with her.

Am I getting this right, Kimber?

Yeah, that's pretty good.

Thanks. Anyway, Lou was not ready to make any drastic moves. First of all, he still liked owning Kimber, because Lou was pretty insecure himself. Second, Martha was hardly a prize girlfriend. Her reputation was stained, she'd been barred from the prom, she dressed like a scrub, and she was probably deeper than Lou.

So he was willing to sneak around and enjoy the rush of *amour* with none of the responsibility. Martha was not stupid. She knew what he was doing, and she knew what *she* was doing. She was cheating on Kimber.

Now . . .

Cindy had let on that Deena was driven home from Bran-die's party by Lou. Kimber was seething about it because your boyfriend was not supposed to drive other girls home at one in the morning and *take them into their houses.*

Kimber was jealous, and filled with self-hatred. But she's told you all about that. Deena, meanwhile, was smarting from this new slap at her reputation. She hadn't *meant* to entice Lou. She hadn't *meant* to kiss him. She hadn't even meant for him to come along and drive her home. (Deena never ever thought along the lines of maybe not allowing Lou to come in, or refusing the kiss.)

And don't forget Phil. He was plugging away at Stony Brook, and desperately trying to book a motel room for Prom Night. Was Deena still in love with Phil? Well, feelings of love bubbled up inside her when she thought about him.

When she thought about *Lou*, feelings of love bubbled up for *him*. But unlike Martha, Deena couldn't make house calls.

So Deena found herself *hating* Martha because Martha was cheating with Lou. Deena thought about how morally wrong this was and how it was going to hurt Kimber.

So when she began to realize that she was going to *tell* Kimber about Martha and Lou, she didn't think of it as revenge. She thought of it as a public service.

The time was ripe. The details about Lou and Martha had been circulating feverishly in school. The crowd was delirious to have a *new* Martha Sullivan scandal on top of the *old* Martha Sullivan scandal.

Nobody had told Kimber yet. Letting the victim know is an important job. It can't be done casually, or you risk losing the full effect. First of all, you want to suck the juices dry from the victim's ignorance. Once you're ready for the spectacle of the victim breaking down, you need to tell her when the most vivid fireworks can occur.

In this situation, the locale was the McDonald's on Market Road. Kimber, Deena, and Martha had each agreed that final preparations for the prom had to be made. The limo route from house to house, destinations after the prom, costs, and so on, had to be hammered out. This was before Martha got nailed. Now the powwow would include strategies to get Martha into the prom—even though Rob had abandoned her.

Deena knew that there would be no better moment, not only because Kimber and Martha and Deena would be together (so Deena could watch the results) but because Lou had said he would stop by during his free period. That meant that Deena could break the news, let Kimber and Martha go at it, and then watch Lou arrive at the perfect instant. None of this was plotted maliciously, of course.

The day arrived. It was a loathsome Wednesday. The sky glowered, filled with tumorous clouds. The air smelled of rotting things.

Deena asked if she could ride with Kimber, and Kimber said sure. When the bell rang ending fourth period, Kimber waited for Deena at the entrance to the school. Deena came huffing along a few minutes later, pushing back her hair, and they both walked to the student parking lot. Deena waited until Kimber had started the car and pulled to the entrance gate.

"Kimber," Deena whispered.

Kimber looked sharply at Deena, while she tried to check the traffic left and right. The way Deena had said her name made every organ in Kimber's body shrivel.

"What?"

Deena sighed and looked straight ahead. She wore a cute tangerine dress with puff sleeves and looked very spring-like. "Make the turn first."

Kimber went ashen and said, "What's wrong?"

"Make the turn first."

With an exasperated breath, Kimber swung left onto Post Road. "What's with you?"

Deena moistened her lips. "Give me a minute."

"Deena!"

I realize that you might be a little puzzled by this. Why is Kimber reacting so violently when Deena hasn't said anything yet? Actually, she's saying a great deal. Here's the same exchange with translations in parentheses:

"Kimber," Deena whispered. (*I'm about to tell you that your boyfriend is a cheat and shatter your whole world.*)

Kimber looked sharply at Deena, while she tried to check the traffic left and right. The way Deena said her name made every organ in Kimber's body shrivel.

"What?" (*I've been suspecting this.*)

Deena sighed and looked straight ahead. She wore a cute tangerine dress with puff sleeves and looked very spring-like. "Make the turn first." (*It's even worse than you thought!*)

Kimber went ashen and said, "What's wrong?" (*Oh God, not with Martha!*)

"Make the turn first." (*You got it.*)

With an exasperated breath, Kimber swung left onto Post Road. "What's with you?" (*Let's have the gory details.*)

Deena moistened her lips. "Give me a minute." (*I want you to suffer first.*)

"*Deena!*" (*Tell me or I'll pull your hair out by the roots!*)

So by the time Kimber crossed into the left turn lane to travel down Adler Avenue to Market Road, she already knew. Bad news like that can't be in the air all week and not go unnoticed by the victim. She'd pushed it out of her mind, but now it was confirmed. Still, Deena couldn't tell her flat out. It was bad form.

"I'm sorry, Kimber," she said. "I really am so sorry."

"Sorry about *what*?"

"I wanted to talk to you all week, but I never got the chance in school. I started to dial your number about eighty times, but I couldn't do it. I'm such a coward when it comes to that."

Kimber kept her hands steady on the wheel. "Deena, I'm not in the mood for your bizarre monologues. If something's wrong, tell me."

Deena tipped her head back and sighed again. "I'm so impressed with the way you're handling it. I mean, the way you kind of freaked when you found out that Lou drove me home from Brandie's party, which was totally innocent and meaningless, I figured for sure you'd be in a straitjacket by now. But you are so cool."

If you watched Kimber's hands, you'd see them tighten, perceptibly, which made the car swerve. "Deena, if you want to live past the next block, spit out what you want to say."

Deena turned slowly to stare at Kimber. She did this part elegantly, with widening eyes. The turquoise color of those eyes made the effect stunning. "Kimber, you *know* what I'm talking about. You found out from Joanna Reilly."

Remember Joanna Reilly? Joanna first saw Lou and Martha by the lake. Joanna told her friends, and the story spread. Deena got it from Michelle Epstein, who was on the third level of the gossip pyramid.

"Found out *what* from Joanna Reilly?" Kimber demanded.

Deena's jaw dropped, and simultaneously her hand went to Kimber's shoulder. "Oh my *God*," she breathed. "Oh my God. Oh . . . Kimber . . ."

Kimber jerked the car to a stop at the intersection of Adler Road and Market Road. This portion of Market Road was in the heart of Marion, a town south of Westfield.

Kimber was trembling visibly. "Deena, Joanna Reilly didn't tell me anything. I don't even *know* Joanna Reilly. Could you make sense?"

Deena was wet-eyed. "Oh God, I'm so sorry. I thought you knew. I could have *sworn* you knew."

"Knew WHAT, damn it!"

I always liked those movie scenes where a character is told something astonishing but you don't hear the words. You see the two characters and the sound track has traffic noises or helicopters or whatever, and you just see mouths moving and the character's reaction.

So let's do that here. Let's turn up the traffic sounds at this intersection, especially as the light turns green and the cars behind Kimber start honking wildly. Let's watch Deena tighten her grip on Kimber's shoulder and quickly, awkwardly, speak to her. Let's watch Kimber slump back in the seat, her eyes filling, her hands dropping from the steering wheel.

But no time for emotion. Because the car begins to roll. Deena screams, and points. Kimber alertly jams the brake, and grabs the wheel. The car lurches and cars behind Kimber also lurch. Drivers are cursing and getting out of their cars. Kimber stamps on the gas pedal and roars into her left turn, with McDonald's a block away. And Martha is in the third car behind Kimber.

Chapter Sixteen

By the time Kimber made a right turn into the McDonald's parking lot, blood had flamed her face. Deena winced as the front end scraped the curb. Kimber nearly sliced the rear fender off a Mitsubishi as she parked.

Kimber sat back, shaking her head. "Turn off the car," Deena suggested.

With a vicious twist of the key, Kimber shut down the engine. The car shuddered and hissed. Scattered rain drops bubbled on the windshield. "This is so stupid," she said. "I can't believe she did this. I can't believe she didn't *tell* me."

"I feel terrible," Deena said. She touched Kimber's shoulder. "I really thought you knew."

"Don't con me," Kimber snapped.

"Okay, okay."

Deena was scared, but awed by the response she produced. Now she noticed Martha's Mustang clattering into the parking lot. Kimber's head popped up. "Slut."

"Don't say anything here," Deena told her. "It's not worth it."

"Don't tell me what's not worth it."

"Fine. Be a jerk."

Kimber wasted no time listening to Deena. She pushed open the car door and slammed it behind her so hard that the Nova rocked. Martha had just glided into a parking space vacated by a van. Kimber watched through the fine, warm rain as the Mustang's parking lights flashed off.

Martha ducked out of the Mustang and started to run for the restaurant. She drew up short when she saw Kimber. "Why aren't you inside? What's wrong?"

Kimber was tongue-tied. She'd never had this kind of fight before. But emotion pushed her, like a reluctant gladiator, toward the confrontation.

"Is it true?" Kimber blurted.

"Is *what* true?" Martha knew exactly what Kimber was talking about.

"You know exactly what I'm talking about."

"I do?"

"Come on, Martha. Just spit it out. Or are we going on another car ride?"

"Cool down, babe."

"Don't tell me to cool down. Was that why you almost killed me? Were you trying to get up the guts to confess? This is your chance. I'm all ears."

The rain darkened Kimber's hair. Martha's mane frizzed. "Kimber, I drove here to meet with you and Deena about the Prom. Is that what's happening? Because if not, I have things to do."

"SHUT UP!" Kimber screamed. "How could you make me look like such a fool? How could you *do* it?"

"Screw off," Martha said, and tried to edge past Kimber. Kimber grabbed Martha's arm and threw her back against her car. The impact made a low thud that caused Deena to yelp. Deena had decided to hide in the Nova.

Martha gaped at Kimber. Then she came raging off the side of the car and pushed Kimber with both hands. Kimber's heel caught in a pothole and she twisted her foot. "You're crazy," Martha said.

Kimber was crying hysterically. "Yeah, I'm crazy. You're not crazy, though, huh? You're fine. Everything you do is fine. You have such a lousy life, you can do whatever you want, and everybody's got to feel sorry for you."

Martha wiped rain from her lips. "You want to rant and rave, go ahead. But I'm getting soaked. I want to have lunch and get back to school."

Kimber looked brokenly at Martha. She seemed a bedraggled elf with her hair in wet strings over her eyes and her nylon jacket clinging to her body. Her immediate fury had passed and she felt a thick, heavy sadness.

"What's the purpose?" she said. "It's just us out here. You know what I'm talking about. You got caught. Admit it, for Pete's sake."

Martha blinked away rain and looked defeated. To confess now, without forcing Kimber to make the accusation, was bad form. But Martha was suicidal with guilt. "Are you talking about me and Lou?"

"*Why*? That's all I want to know."

"I don't know why," Martha said. "Can't we talk about it inside?"

"I want to talk about it here."

Martha's eyes flickered. "Who told you, anyway?"

"It doesn't matter."

"I'm just interested."

"It doesn't matter who told me."

Martha had remembered, right in the middle of fighting, that Kimber had driven here with Deena. Martha further remembered that as of third period this morning, when she'd said hello to Kimber in the hallway, Kimber didn't know the truth.

"Where's Deena?" Martha demanded. "Didn't she come with you?"

"Never mind Deena," Kimber said. "We're talking about *you*."

Martha looked hard at the Nova. "What is she doing in there? *Watching*?"

Furiously, Martha swept Kimber aside and splashed over to the Nova. "She's *watching*! I don't believe this!" Martha rapped on the window. Then she grabbed the door handle and rattled it. "She locked herself in! I'LL WAIT, DEENA! AS LONG AS IT TAKES!"

Kimber felt the moment slipping away. "Forget about Deena. I don't want to deal with her. I want to deal with what you did to me."

Martha spun. "What do you mean what I did to you? I didn't do *anything* to you! Lou was the one who hit on *me*!"

"He just kidnapped you, huh?"

"LISTEN to me! I had to talk to him. There are things you don't know."

"Like what?"

"Man, if *he* didn't tell you, *I* can't tell you!"

"Bull."

Martha whirled again, and slammed both palms against the glass. "Get out!"

"What things didn't I know?" Kimber insisted.

Martha kept glaring at the Nova's door, as if she'd melt it open. "Things about the Senior Weekend."

"What about it?"

"Private things."

"Between you and Lou?"

"No!" Martha turned to Kimber again. On Market Road, cars drove with headlights bright and wipers clacking. Kimber's face reflected the glow of the McDonald's sign.

"Then what?"

Martha pushed a hand through her frazzled hair. "This is crazy. I didn't want you to find out about me and Lou from someone else, especially not"—she punched the door—"*that* thing. I *wanted* to tell you about it."

"Well, you're telling me now."

Kimber was surprised at her own tenacity and strength. Martha was cowed by it. Seeing no escape (especially since Kimber was planted flat in front of the Mustang), she continued to turn her frustration on the locked Nova. "I'm not saying anything until she comes out."

"Deena didn't tell me, if you really want to know. She thought I knew already."

"I want her out here."

"Oh, cut it out, Martha!" Kimber fished in her jacket pockets and came out with a bunch of keys. "Here! Unlock the damn door if you want it open so badly. What's the difference? You're still avoiding it."

Martha sniffled, looking back and forth between the Nova and Kimber. The rain had let up momentarily. "You want to know why I saw Lou? You *really really* want to know? I was going nuts about the Prom. Sachs destroyed me. I couldn't hack it."

"And you went to *Lou?*"

"I went to Lou because he's the only one who can prove I didn't spend the night with Henning."

Kimber wrestled with that bombshell for a long moment. The implications were so awful that she felt her stomach heave. "What are you saying?"

"What does it *sound* like I'm saying? I spent the night passed out by the ice machine. Lou saw me there. He's the only one who saw me there. He knows I wasn't with Henning."

A thump from the Nova made Martha cry out and lift her hands in alarm. She saw the door tremble.

"It sticks," Kimber said. "Rattle it a few times."

"No!" Martha leaned against the door.

"You were just going hairy to get her out of the car!"

"She can't hear this!"

Kimber dropped her keys back into her drenched pocket. "Well, she can't get out if the door's stuck."

"Good." Martha wiped her lips. They both had to dance out of the way of cars coming and going. "I woke up by the ice machine. I was looking up at Lou. He was wearing sweat pants and no top. Extremely hot, I might add."

"I don't *believe* this!"

"Sorry. He was getting ice. And he was polluted. He was laughing at me and asking me what I was doing there. He'd dropped a couple of ice cubes on me, which is what woke me up. I told him I'd passed out. He said he hoped to do that pretty soon. I asked him what was going on. He said there was a mint party in his room. A few babes had come in by the little balcony outside the room, and they were partying."

"A few babes, huh?" Kimber felt her emotions flat-line. "Is that thrown in for my benefit?"

Martha shrugged. The Nova door thumped as Deena pounded on it from inside. "You don't want to believe me, don't. I'm telling you what he said. And one of the babes was like the valedictorian, you know?"

"Stacey *Coleman*?"

"Yeah, Stacey Coleman."

"She is a total geek! She wears Peter Pan collars!"

"Well, I don't know what she was wearing, but she was in Lou's room at two in the morning—he told me what time it was—and if anyone found out, she wouldn't be valedictorian anymore, and Lou would be barred from the Prom and his father and mother wouldn't like that. So the next day, Lou pushed me into a dinosaur exhibit at the Smithsonian and asked me what I remembered. I told him. He asked me not to tell anyone. I said sure. I didn't know I'd be bagged later on."

The rain started again, pattering gently on car roofs. Kimber chewed over this second revelation about Lou, which didn't seem so surprising at this point. Lou and Stacey. Lou and Deena. Lou and Martha. Lou and the guys. Lou and anyone but Kimber. She was just his girlfriend, available when nobody else was around.

Self-pity welled up, sweet and terrible. "So you still didn't tell me why you went to Lou."

Vaguely, Kimber could hear Deena's muffled voice. Martha

said, "I was going to ask him to go to Sachs and own up. I wanted my Prom ticket back. And he said he'd do it. But somehow he got me to tell him not to. I don't remember exactly why. But that's when we . . . got interested in each other."

It was no use. Kimber kept imagining Lou and Martha together, and the vision twisted her throat. But even more ferocious than her fury at Martha was her hatred of Lou, which was growing now like a virus.

"You suck," she said to Martha.

"I didn't want it to happen, and I didn't want to tell you about it in a parking lot."

"You *never* would have told me."

"Yes. I would have."

"Bull."

"Believe whatever you want."

"What am I *supposed* to believe? I asked you straight . . ."

Kimber had looked at the window of her car and saw three wet finger marks suddenly streak the haze. "She's going to die!" Kimber yelled. "Let her out!"

Martha looked around. "Oh, damn." She yanked on the door handle, uselessly. "Give me the keys."

Kimber dredged the keys out again and tossed them to Martha, who pawed through them, cursing, and then jammed the right one into the lock.

"It won't open!" she said.

"It *has* to open!"

"I'm telling you it won't open!"

Kimber strode over. "Let me do it." She braced one hand against the water-beaded door and twisted the key. The lock remained locked. Annoyed, Kimber twisted harder. "This is ridiculous."

"What about the other side? Can't she get out the other side?"

Kimber shook her head. "Not if she locked it. There's something wrong with both locks."

"How can you drive around that way?"

Kimber bit her tongue as she concentrated. "Usually I can open one of the two doors."

"What a jerk."

"Listen, I'm not even talking to you."

"Don't threaten me. I'm not going to be punished for this the rest of my life."

"Which means you don't think it was wrong."

"I didn't *say* it wasn't wrong."

Kimber straightened up and blew out a vexed breath. "*Damn it!*"

"Let me try again."

"You can't do it."

"Well, you're not doing any better."

"Get out of my face, Martha."

"I'll get out of your face, Kimber. I'll get out of your face for good."

"Great. I'd appreciate it."

"You got it."

Martha really didn't want to leave. She procrastinated just long enough to allow Lou to arrive. Martha's chest pulled taut when she saw the black Trans Am, gleaming with rain, stabbing the gray morning with blazing halogen lights.

"It's Lou," she said.

Kimber was so engrossed in opening the lock that she didn't appreciate the emotional impact of the words. "Maybe he can do something with this."

Lou smoothly sailed into a parking space and gave Martha a secret look when he got out of the car. The flirtatiousness dropped away when he saw how water-logged Martha was, and when he saw Kimber bending over the door to her car.

"What's going on?" he asked. He looked so jaunty and together, in his *dry* jacket, sweater, and slacks, that Martha felt murderous.

"Deena's stuck in the car."

"What?" Lou chuckled. "How'd she do that?"

"It's a long story," Martha said.

"Let's see."

Lou sauntered over, pausing alongside Martha to graze her hand. Martha shuddered. Lou stood behind Kimber and said, "Need a man's touch?"

"I can't get the key to turn," Kimber said.

Lou flexed his fingers dramatically. "I can open many doors." He placed his hands on Kimber's small waist and nuzzled the back of her neck. "C'mon, babe. You're drowned rat. Let me do it."

Kimber stood up and Lou smiled at her as he bent over to work the key. She watched him with seething intensity. She felt drawn to him like a spectator to an accident.

"Aha!" he cried. Kimber could hear the click of the lock opening. Lou straightened and tugged open the door. Deena sprawled in the passenger seat, staring insanely. "Hi," Lou said, as he tossed the keys to Kimber.

Deena looked maniacally at him for a long moment. "I could have *died* in there," she said hoarsely. "Why didn't you let me out?"

"We were trying," Kimber said.

Deena gingerly got out of the Nova, slumping as she tried to stand. Lou braced her. She never stopped staring at him. He became uncomfortable and glanced quizzically at Kimber and Martha. He couldn't know that Deena was boggled beyond speech, that he was calmly standing between the girl he betrayed and the girl he'd betrayed her with.

"So," Lou said. "Are we going inside, or what? Like there's only twenty minutes left to the period and we're all going to be late."

Kimber looked from Lou to Martha and from Martha to Lou. She envisioned them kissing. It gave her excruciating pains in her chest. She began to tremble, and realized that she'd lose it within seconds.

Lou gave her an odd look. "What's with all of you? Is there something I'm supposed to know?"

Kimber said, "I know about you and Martha. Okay?"

If he was scared, he didn't announce it. But he was quiet. He looked quickly at Martha, who looked away. He looked at Deena, who looked down at the puddles. Lou toyed with loose change in his jacket pocket, and exhaled. "Who told you?"

"Man, you're a piece of work," Kimber said. "That's the most important thing? Who *told* me? God told me! He appeared in a burning bush and gave me the whole story."

"*O*-kay," Lou said. "I think we'd better reschedule this."

"Unbelievable," Kimber said. "Totally unbelievable. I'm getting the hell out of here."

Deena's eyes widened. "I almost *died* in your car!"

"Almost doesn't count," Kimber lashed back. "Get a ride back with Lou. You're used to *his* car."

She stalked around the Nova, stepping into a huge puddle and spattering herself with muddy water. Cursing, she pulled the door handle, which, of course, did not open. With Lou, Martha, and Deena watching, Kimber jammed the key in the lock and twisted it back and forth. She began to perspire and it began to rain harder.

Martha said, "Go in on the other side; it's open."

Kimber stopped, one hand on the window frame. "I *know* the other side is open," she growled murderously. "I want to open *this* side!"

At which point Kimber stepped back and began to kick the Nova. Each time she kicked, she cried out. McDonald's patrons sitting by the windows watched with rapt attention. Lou nervously backed up and eyed his own car. Deena gawked. Kimber went on kicking and screaming until finally she stood panting with her eyes shut. Then she came around the car, not looking at anyone, and slid in on the passenger side. She slammed the door and the car rocked as she scrunched over. Kimber backed up in a series of lurches, straightened, and accelerated out of the parking lot. She had to brake to a skidding stop, though, because cars were passing on

Market Road. Her dramatic exit ruined, she eased into traffic and was gone.

Deena blinked rapidly and Martha uttered an obscenity two or three times. Lou caught Martha's eye. He shook his head and as he shook his head he insinuated his fingers between Martha's fingers. He closed his hand over hers. He locked onto her eyes. He stepped close to her and pulled her gently toward him. He wrapped his arms around her in a commiserating hug. She hugged him back. Then he kissed her, passionately. She kissed him back. You see, Martha needed to win a battle. Any battle.

Deena watched the two of them (as did the McDonald's patrons). Jealousy bubbled. But this time, she couldn't tell anybody. She needed Phil very much at this moment.

Or somebody.

Jason—are you there?

Chapter Seventeen

Of course I'm here. Where else would I be? I don't exactly have a lot of hot dates (I *do* like warm raisins, though).

Now, all of your readers are wondering: What does Jason have to do with *Deena*? Once again, it was timing. Or in this case, two-timing.

I was depressed. Kimber had rejected me. My fantasies didn't work any more. After that infamous day in Room 60, when she *knew* my feelings and jumped up and down on them with hob-nailed boots, it was no good lying on my bed, looking up at the stars, and imagining her cool lips on mine. I kept hearing her laugh.

What stars? Oh, when I was about nine, I cut out little pieces of glow-in-the-dark material and made constellations on my ceiling. I was into astronomy. I remember quivering with excitement when I could see Jupiter out my window. Every night for a week, I'd kneel by my window and look out at Jupiter. I'd call in my parents, who were *not* interested. I had a red telescope I got for Hanukkah one year. You couldn't see *anything* through it. But I pressed my little throbbing eyeball to that lens night after night and looked at blackness, hoping to see Jupiter up close. I never did.

See, I always believed in miracles. Like the telescope would work. Or Kimber would love me.

But she didn't. And as I digested that, I got a pristine white envelope from RPI telling me I was rejected. That was my number-one college choice, but my math wasn't strong enough. I was crushed. I sat in my room, looking at my glow-in-the-dark constellations and crying. I refused to eat more than four meals a day. I became heavily involved with peanut butter Twix bars.

Not that I showed my pain. I bounced cheerily through the day (until Cheerily got dizzy from being bounced), I joined in the spring madness by wearing the most garish Jams and tropical shirts I could buy, along with sunglasses on a rope. But I was hurting. Meanwhile, Deena had witnessed the fracas with Kimber, Martha, and Lou (heck, she'd *caused* the fracas!), and was steaming with jealousy. Deena expected Lou to be made a soprano by Kimber. She *didn't* expect him to wind up playing tonsil-hockey with Martha.

So she came into school depressed. Now when *Deena* gets depressed, she draws elaborate foliage and her eyes are misty. All day she walks around with misty eyes. And her head down. When you ask her, "Deena, what's wrong?" she gives a bitter little smile and says "Nothing." And she keeps her head down and draws more flowers.

Okay, so here we were in English. This was Alterson's class, and Alterson was by his desk, sliding out folders from his tote bag and freaking because he couldn't find anything. Also, twelve kids in the class were waving overdue papers at him and he was saying "Don't give me papers until I call for them!"

I strolled in and saw Deena sitting in her seat, which is against the blackboard, first row. Her head was down. She was drawing a huge forest in her sketch pad. I saw the way the fluorescent light gleamed from her hair. I saw the way her narrow shoulders hunched in her peach-colored top. She was upset! Hey, who you gonna call, when you don't feel good? MOROSE BUSTERS!

I stopped at her desk and said, "Hi? What's wrong?"

She gave a bitter little smile and said, "Nothing." And she kept her head down and drew more flowers.

I swung gracefully into the seat next to her (good thing Gracefully doesn't weigh much) and rubbed her neck. I waited through that heartstopping minute to see if she told me to stop. She didn't.

"Love troubles?" I asked. She gave a bitter little smile and said, "No." And she kept her head down and drew more flowers.

I expanded my rubbing territory, in widening ovals across her back. Her top was scooped out so once during every oval my hand touched her skin. For a man doomed to celibacy, this is a major event. "Did Phil break up with you?"

She gave a bitter little smile and said, "Nothing." And she kept her head down and drew more flowers.

This was getting critical. I'd have to stop rubbing pretty soon, and either go into a two-handed massage or just leave. The bell rang, so a full massage was out. I went to a joke. "Okay, Deena," I said. "This is shock treatment. A bunch of ants are in a bakery. They're eating bread. Suddenly, the head ant yells, 'Let's get outta here! The baker's coming!' And one little ant says, 'Don't stop me now—I'm on a roll!' "

Deena stopped drawing. The corners of her mouth tugged upward. She said, "Jason, go away."

I rested my rubbing hand on her right shoulder and drew closer (while Closer drew somebody else). "Meet me later by the school store," I whispered. "I'll buy you a brownie. You deserve to forget."

Her eyes were misted. She looked incredibly beautiful. "Thanks, Jason," she said.

"No problem." I smiled.

Alterson was addressing the class. I squeezed Deena's hand and scurried to my seat. I sat gripping the edges of my desk, feeling the sudden May warmth across my back, smelling cut grass and soft, wet sky. It was springtime! The sap runneth!

I *know* I'd bought Kimber a brownie. But Kimber had kissed me off, so why not buy a brownie for Deena? I *know* Deena was going with Phil. But Phil was at Stony Brook, and Deena was here. I didn't think about Phil.

Yes, I *did* think about Phil. I thought about acing him out. I thought about seducing Deena and taking her from him. I thought all of those evil thoughts.

The longer I sat in that seat with little cirrus clouds wisping through the sky, the more excited I became. I wanted a conquest. I wanted to go where every man had boldly gone before. I wanted to win one for the Gipper. I wanted to know who the heck the Gipper was, and who he Gipped. I'd given my brains and heart and soul to others. I wanted something for myself myself myself (sorry, I'm repeating myself).

So I spent that period fantasizing rich, sweet fantasies with Deena in the starring role. Alterson must have wondered about the sick smile on my face. I didn't care. I just knew that I wanted Deena . . . I wanted Deember . . . I wanted Dimber . . .

Well, you get the idea.

And so did Deena, for a moment. But it was the moment that set the stage for the Prom.

The Art Wing is opposite the Music Suite, down by the Gym lobby. There is something about that whole area that inspires romance. You have the lighting booth above the auditorium, the loft above the stage, and the practice rooms in the Music Suite. After hours, these become dark, empty places, littered with old Burger King wrappers and stained with spilled soda.

In other words—Make Out City.

The Art rooms aren't usually part of the sin strip because they're tightly locked. Wayward students can't be allowed near X-acto knives. But sometimes, if a student is working on a project, an art room *can* be open late.

So it was that afternoon. I playfully prevented Deena from leaving Alterson's room, and I said, "Are we on for the brownie later?"

This was another critical moment. If she gave me a "Be real" look and rolled her eyes, the illusion was over. But I was driven by forces beyond my control (usually, my mother drove me, but she was busy). I waited for her response.

She looked directly at me, and said, "Sure. I'd like that."

I smiled gently. And I thought:

SHE SAID SURE SHE'D LIKE THAT!!

I said, "Seventh period? School store?"

She chewed the corner of her lip (O beauteous corner! O ravishing lip!) and said, "I've got Economics seventh. How about after school? I'm finishing my portfolio project in Room 102."

I nodded amiably. And I thought:

SHE'S GOING TO BE ALONE IN ROOM 102 AND SHE WANTS YOU TO BRING THE BROWNIE!

I said, "Great. See you then."

She smiled brightly and shifted her sketch pad against her chest (O beauteous sketch pad! O . . . never mind) and skipped out. I won't bother describing my state of mind for the rest of the day. I was obsessed with images of Deena, lying nude on a drawing table while I painted her in acrylics.

I purchased the brownie during seventh period and kept it in my folder through eighth. I had to periodically cool down my fevered body by thinking of Calculus quizzes.

At last the piercing electronic whine signaled the end of the academic day. In 3.6 seconds, the classrooms emptied and the hallways filled. Like buffalo herds, they stampeded past the door to my Social History classroom. This was in the hallway where Lou rescued Martha. In fact, this was the very room where John Brody was made to cool his heels!

I adjusted my tropical shirt, popping an extra button to show more skin. I brushed back my wedge of dark hair. My tongue probed my teeth for traces of lunch. Then I tucked my folder under my arm and walked through the Gym lobby. I entered the Art Wing. I saw the light from Room 102.

Slowly, I slid the wrapped brownie from my folder. I clutched it in one sweating hand. My heart slammed against my ribs. I hadn't been this nervous with Kimber. But that's because I really hadn't expected Kimber to succumb.

I entered Room 102. The strong smell of fixative filled my nostrils. I stood in the entryway, between the paper cutter and the metal supply cabinet. Wooden easels loomed over my head.

I went all the way into the room. There she sat, coloring a huge flower bed with pastels. Rose-colored dust stained her fingertips. She looked up and smiled.

"Hi, Jason. Got my brownie?"

Disappointment. I'd hoped she would bypass the brownie and declare her passion right away. I'd envisioned her eyes smouldering, her lips parted, her chest heaving. She was too cheery.

"As promised," I said. "Sweets to the sweet."

"Thanks," she said. "I'm starving."

Worse and worse. I kept my step jaunty as I walked to the table and set the brownie before her. "Nuts to you," I quipped.

She flashed a quick smile, and unwrapped the confection. She shut her eyes as she bit off a piece, and chewed soulfully. "Mmmmm," she murmured. "I needed that."

I came around the table, and glanced at the pastel. She was really very good. I pride myself on feeling genuine appreciation for her talent while at the nadir of my hopes.

But my nadir was postponed. Deena looked over at me, daintily holding the half-eaten brownie. She glanced down at the pastel. "It stinks," she said. "I'm just trying to get it done."

"I think it's amazing," I said honestly.

She gave a self-deprecating little laugh. "Yeah, amazing."

"Come on, no false modesty. You know you're good."

She shrugged. "I guess I am. Well, yeah, I *am*."

"That's a good little egomaniac."

"Stop!" She laughed self-consciously and finished the brownie. She brushed her hands together to get rid of the crumbs. A tiny shred of nut clung to the corner of her mouth.

"Are you going to art school?" I asked.

To my surprise, her eyes filled and she kind of twittered her hands and looked down. "I don't know."

"Don't you want to?"

"Yes."

"Is it money?"

Now her lip trembled and she started to cry.

"Deena?" I moved to her, really concerned. I put my hands on her shoulders. "What'd I say?"

She shook her head, and her hand came up to cover mine. She took a deep breath. Her whole body was hot. She turned to face me; my hands stayed on her shoulders. "It's stupid."

"So am I."

She laughed. "Jason, you're the only person I can trust."

"So trust me."

She sighed. "My folks won't pay for art school. They want me to go to Suffolk Community."

"*What?*"

She nodded. "They don't want to shell out all that money when I might not be a professional artist."

"How would you know unless you went there?"

"Don't ask me."

I pushed stray hair back from her forehead. I do gentle things like that. "Why don't they apply for financial aid?"

Her eyes suddenly flared. "They *have* the money! They're using it to buy land upstate."

"Huh?"

"They're buying all this land upstate because it's all going to be developed. It's a big investment. First it was the stock market, and then it was some real estate group, and now it's land upstate. Oh, and of course there's the Lincoln Town Car which they must have and the vacations in South America. They have to unwind a lot. I don't know from what."

All of this came gushing out in a few breaths. She was shaking when she finished. Finally, I said, "You really hate their guts, huh?"

She shook her head violently. "No, I don't hate them. I just *resent* them. It's like they had me and they're pissed off because I didn't die young or something. They have this incredible romantic marriage, always together, always holding hands, and I'm nowhere. Except when they're laying down all these stupid rules and telling me I'm not that good at art. I idolize their marriage. I want my marriage to be just like theirs. But I want my children to be *part* of my happiness."

When she stopped, I hugged her, which seemed like the thing to do. She hugged me back and rested her cheek against my jaw. I could smell her perfume.

"What a duo," I said. I rubbed her back with one hand. "What you need is for them to have a nice, juicy divorce, and fight over you."

"No," she murmured into my neck. "I don't want them to get divorced. I just want to be *there*. I'm not making any sense."

"You're making sense," I assured her. "You're making dollars, in fact. And if you don't try for an art scholarship, you're an idiot, because you're good."

She hugged me tighter.

"Yeah," I said angrily. "And when you become a hot artist, wipe all your childhood drawings off the walls! Take back your mother's day cards! They can't do this to you!"

She laughed. Then she looked me square in the face. That is powerful wampum for me, boy. I don't usually get those full-face looks from girls. But she kept gazing, her eyes full and damp. I watched her nostrils flare. She tilted her face, shut her eyes, and opened her mouth.

Wait a minute . . . tilted face, eyes shut, open mouth . . .

Oh my God, that means something! What does it mean? Spock, search the computer banks, quickly! Tilted face, eyes shut, open mouth . . . I know it means something, Spock! *What does it mean?*

Captain, it is part of an illogical human response to physical attraction. It is a form of labial oscillation . . .

In English, Spock!

Your race quaintly refers to the process as a "kiss" . . .

Kiss! That's it, Spock! She wants to be kissed! Battle stations! Lock phasers! We're going in!

And so our lips met. I felt like a star ship hitting warp speed. My thigh pressed hard against the drawing table, and my hands clutched at her back. I tasted chocolate brownie and I heard her breathing. All the time I was consciously aware that I was kissing Deena. I was *passionately* kissing Deena.

We went on for some time, and I'll leave out the more spine-tingling details. But at last, we broke apart and held hands and I grinned dumbly as she swallowed me with her sea-foam eyes.

And then she said, "Oh, Jason. I miss Phil so much!"

Now you have to know, so you won't feel too sorry for me, that only Deena could say that, at this precise moment, with total innocence. She meant no harm. Her dizzy, romantic little heart tumbled in those few seconds and Phil was there when it stopped spinning.

I said, "What?"

She realized her gaffe and wrung my hands. "Oh, God! I'm sorry, Jason. I didn't mean it that way."

"How many ways could you mean it?"

She let go of my hands and clenched her fists. Turning away, she sighed deeply. Then she turned back. "Jason, this was . . ." She swept her hand to indicate the brownie wrapper and me. ". . . all of this . . . it meant so much to me." She looked tenderly at me. "I've never told anybody how I feel, ever. Not even Phil. You helped me so much, Jason. You've given me the motivation to go on. I love you, Jason. I wish everyone knew how incredible you are."

"We could print leaflets."

She laughed, and said, "Stop. You're always putting yourself down. Be proud of what you are. I am."

"I'd rather have physical affection than pride."

That brought a sweet smile. "Jason, I'd love to be your girlfriend, I really would. But . . ." And here her voice took on a tone of wonderment. ". . . I'm really in love with Phil. I want to see him *right now*."

"Well, just click your heels three times and say 'I want to have my Phil . . . ' "

"Nut!" She laughed again and hugged me with that ecstatic fervor the girls always display when I've convinced them to return to their boy friends. She kissed me hard. "I'm so happy right now. I feel content and fulfilled and *right* for the first time. Thank you, Jason. I owe you my life."

"How about your body as down payment?" I joked. Of course, she laughed.

And soon after, I left the art room, rejected again. But this was different. Even though it was the same dreary scenario, with me bringing joy and revelation to a girl, but not *getting* the girl, I wasn't despondent or frustrated (well, maybe a *teensy bit* frustrated). First of all, my heart wasn't totally into seducing Deena because she *was* attached, and I still loved Kimber. Second, I felt kind of good about finding out that Deena hated her parents and was truly human. She'd released her demons and I *had* changed her life.

That's kind of worthwhile, you know? If my role in life is to be fairy godmother, I might as well be a good one. If the wand fits, wave it!

And it may have *been* magic because Deena's epiphany started the trend of reconciliation that led to the night of the Senior Prom.

When all hell broke loose.

And that's your cue, Kimber.

Chapter Eighteen

So, Jason, *you* had a little fling with Deena! Not that the idea is
so incredible, since *everybody* has had a little fling with Deena.
But it's nice to see that you have some wickedness in your heart.
And you're right. Your May madness knocked us back into our
slots.

Also, we had to be practical. The Prom was in three weeks.
We'd reserved a limo. The girls had bought dresses. Hundreds of
dollars had been sunk into this ball. So we gritted our teeth and
crawled back to our slimes!

Actually, Phil is *not* a slime. He's a genuinely nice guy. In fact,
Rob is a nice guy, too. You remember Rob, Martha's boyfriend
until the hallway fight. Yep, she went back to *him*.

Lou, of course, *is* a slime.

I'll get to my reconciliation with Lou in a minute. First, let's
set the scene for Prom Night. Deena, tell how you got back with
Phil

You forget, Kimber, I never *broke up* with Phil.

True. You just cheated on him a little.

If two kisses are your definition of cheating, fine. I cheated. I was going through a lot. I didn't know Jason was going to repeat what I told him, but as long as he did, you can see that I wasn't the romantic little ditz everyone thought I was.

And Jason *is* a fairy godmother. When we were together in Room 102, I realized how much I loved Phil. Actually, I realized it the night Lou took me home, but I didn't realize it *consciously*.

So when I went home after seeing Jason, I toasted an English muffin and made chocolate milk and took it upstairs to my room. I turned on my TV and watched soap operas, but I kept looking at Phil's picture on my dresser. I remembered the day I met him and the candlelight dinners we'd had and the long talks.

And I knew right then that I wanted to marry him.

It just kind of spread over me, like a warm blanket. I wanted to have his children. I wanted to show them the love I never got. I imagined us sitting in our family room, with a crackling fire going, and the kids playing Nintendo. It felt so *good* to imagine that.

I was totally calm about all of this. It felt so right, so perfect. It was like walking into a warm house after driving through a storm. I opened up my English notebook and wrote "Deena Pizer" over and over again, and I drew wedding bells:

And pretty soon, I started to cry. It was dark out, and cold, and I heard clocks ticking and water dripping and the refrigerator motor humming. I was used to these sounds because I was alone in the house most of the time. But this time they frightened me.

I was enough of a basket case to call Phil. I'd vowed not to. Phil hadn't called me for *weeks* and I told myself if he was tired of me, or angry with me, it was up to *him* to let me know. My vow worked for a while, but not on this night, not after Jason made me realize how much I loved the guy.

It was just time to break the rules, you know? To stop playing the game. Anyway, why am I making excuses? I'm *always* making excuses.

I sat on my bed and held my hand over my phone for about a half hour. The soap operas were still going on but I didn't even hear them. I pushed around the black muffin crumbs on my plate and looked at the little globs of chocolate syrup at the bottom of my glass. My hand hovered and my stomach tightened up. I tried to plan out what I was going to say.

I remember suddenly hearing loud music on the TV and realizing that the six o'clock news was coming on. I yanked up the receiver and punched out Phil's dorm number. I pushed the receiver hard against my ear and held my breath. This whole thing could have been a waste because you never know if anyone's going to pick up in the dorm or if the person you're calling is there.

But it was time for magic. A guy's voice said, "Miller Hall," and I said, "Hi! Is Phil Pizer around?" and he said, "Hold on, I'll check."

So I had to wait again while my chest tied up in knots. I yanked my gold chain back and forth, practically sawing through my neck. I looked at the chips in my nails.

Then he got on. "Hello?"

My mouth dried up and I choked. He must have thought it was a prank call. He kept saying "Hello? Hello?" getting more and more annoyed.

I got some of my voice back and I said, "Hi."

"Who is this?"

"Deena."

There was a *long* silence and I nearly died! Then he said, *"Deena?* Hi! How are you?"

"Pretty good. Yourself?"

"Numb. I've been putting in all-nighters. We've got finals."

"Right! I forgot."

"I wish *I* could forget. Listen, I'm sorry I haven't called for a while, but I have no concept of time any more."

"Well, I kind of missed hearing from you."

"So you should have called *me.*"

I could feel a fight coming on and I didn't want to fight. Actually, part of me *did* want to fight and part of me didn't.

So I said, "I guess I was waiting for you to make the first move."

"That's a pretty dangerous game, Deena. I just assumed you'd lost interest."

"That's what I assumed about *you.*"

I felt like laughing and I imagined Phil smiling. "Well, we'd better start being more honest."

"Fine with me."

There was another long silence. We both wanted to scream out "I LOVE YOU! I LOVE YOU!" but we didn't want to risk it. My skin got hotter and hotter and my emotions got lower and lower. I was about to say "Are we going to the Prom?" when suddenly his voice said, "Deen, there's not one room available for that night, unless you want one at the Hilton for $220, and I don't have that kind of money."

He was still talking about going to the Prom! "That's okay," I said. "We'll find a place to be alone."

"We might be able to come back here."

"Anywhere is okay, Phil. I just want to be with you."

I couldn't believe I'd said that! It came out so naturally. He said, "I want to be with you, too, babe. I've really missed you."

"I've missed you too. I've missed you so much."

"I want to see you before the Prom, Deena! I'm going crazy without you."

"Not as crazy as I've been. I need . . ."

Uh . . . come to think of it, I don't really want to go through the whole conversation we had. Even though it was a beautiful conversation, it's really private. It was everything I wanted to say and everything I wanted to hear. By the end of that phone call, Phil and I were stronger than ever. We both knew we were in love and that the Prom would be the most magical night of our lives.

Which it didn't exactly turn out to be.

I know that, Kimber. But it doesn't change what I felt and what he felt. It doesn't change the fact that I stopped needing to be kissed and hugged by somebody once a day. I was finally secure about myself and about loving one guy. That was pretty terrific, and Jason made it happen.

Well, I won't argue with that. And the magic continued. Because the next day, Deena was so radiant with love that she waltzed over to Martha in the cafeteria and told her about it! And that continued the chain reaction. Martha?

I don't want to make Deena sound magical because I still think she's a platinum airhead. But I will admit that I was in a state of flux that morning. I was in the whole *country* of flux. I was in the cafeteria that early because I couldn't sleep anymore, so it was easier to get up and go to school than to be hassled at home.

And I was ready for reform. I mean that word exactly as it sounds: *re*-form. Form again. Into what I was. I wasn't always a druggie and a derelict. I once had a sense of humor. I had moral integrity. I ate Hostess cupcakes and ogled hot guys. I really wanted to be normal more than anything else in the world.

It just didn't work out. First I got into the Gifted and Talented Program, and got labelled as one of the Geek Squad. My red hair didn't help me keep a low profile, and neither did my big mouth. As I got older, I saw the corruption and hypocrisy around me, kind of like Hamlet. So half of me was running bake sales to raise money for the Seeing Eye Foundation and half of me was cutting class. I was schizoid. And I hated myself for it. (That was a feeble attempt at humor, but I don't have Jason's wit.)

I truly wanted to join the teen world when I went out with Rob. I *tried*. I just couldn't. It was my karma that got me talking to Henning and his friends. I wasn't hot for the guy (he was fantastic-looking, though). I was just *interested*. Rob was not exactly scintillating to talk to. Okay, I could have said no to the drinks at the bar, but that's where Henning and his friends *were*. Could you see me yelling in, "Hey, guys, I'm jailbait, so come on out and let's talk by the pinball machine!"

So I had my four glasses of Absolut (well, *they* were hoisting straight vodka!), and I had a great time getting to know them. And when Henning was too wasted to walk straight, I helped him back to his room. Sure it was stupid. But it wasn't *evil*.

And the rest just kind of happened. Well, okay, I helped it happen. I didn't have to make out with Lou by the lake, or all the other times, including in the McDonald's parking lot. But in a way, I *did* have to. I think with my heart, not my brain.

So that morning, I was a mess. I brooded over a container of orange juice, looking like hell, with a cracked, froggy voice from a cold, and Hefty bags under my eyes. I was praying I didn't see Lou because he was all over me, trying to make *me* make *him* forget about losing Kimber. I felt totally disgusted about my inability to resist him.

All this on a buttery May morning with stupid birds twittering and leaves bursting out and blue skies above. And speaking of buttery May mornings, there was Deena, in a springy little white dress with orange polka dots, and her eyes like two swimming pools.

I clenched my jaw and mentally told Deena not to come near me because we'd have a knockdown fight and get suspended. But I heard her little clickety footsteps. I couldn't believe she was really doing this.

She pulled out a chair and sat down next to me. I could smell her perfume. My organs churned like they were in a washing machine. Then she folded her hand over my wrist and began this little speech, which went something like this:

"(Deep breath) Martha, don't hit me until I say what I want to say. (Deep breath) I am so incredibly sorry about everything. I acted like a total asshole at McDonald's and I know it. (Slower breath) I *did* tell Kimber about you and Lou, but I really thought she knew already and I did it because I couldn't stand that she didn't know. (Quick breath) I wasn't trying to get you in trouble, I was just trying to save Kimber from being really hurt. If I messed up your friendship with Kimber, I'm really truly sorry and I'll do anything to help you make it up with her."

At this point she ran out of air and I looked up at her. "How about if you lay down and I run you over?"

She blushed and tightened her lips into a thin line. She blinked a million times and her eyes sparkled. I hated those eyes. I hated her smashing little body which looked sexy no matter what she wore. I felt like the swamp beast when I was next to her.

Deena didn't flinch. She said, "I know you're really really angry, Martha. I know what you've been going through. But I've been doing a lot of thinking and last night Phil and I reminded each other of how in love we are, and I just wanted to be friends again before the Prom and the end of our senior year. I don't want to end with bad blood."

I gave a little rueful laugh. "Too late."

"Don't say that, Martha!"

"Come on," I said. "I appreciate your attitude, Deena, and I'm not going to spend the rest of my life actively hating you, but telling me how you and Phil are in love and reminding me about the Prom is not going to make my day."

Deena got this really earnest expression. "I wasn't trying to rub anything in. I want you to be happy again, too. That's my whole point."

"Want to bribe Sachs?"

She half smiled, but nothing was going to derail her crusade. "Martha, why don't you try to get back with Rob? Even just until graduation? No, listen to me. I'm not being crazy. This is what came to me after I talked to Phil. It's so silly to be stubborn. In a few weeks, we'll scatter all over the country and never see each other again."

I suffered acid rebound from the orange juice and gave Deena my one-eyebrow-raised glare. "Deena, you're being obnoxious."

She blushed again. "I don't care if you insult me. I came to apologize and to try to get you to go back to Rob. I think it would work out."

Understand: she meant this. In Deena's mind, my going back to Rob would get me away from Lou so Deena could get Lou and Kimber back together. That would tie up everything in a pretty bow, and Deena liked to think of life that way.

Sure it was dumb and childish. But it lit a spark in my burnt-out husk. Not a totally honorable spark, either. Rob, my thinking went, was a jock. Sachs, like most of the administrators in Westfield, drools over the jocks. *S-o-o-o-o*, if Rob wanted to take me to the Prom, maybe Sachs would relent.

I know it was low-down and dirty. I can't pretend that I felt a resurgence of love for Rob (or that I'd ever felt a surgence in the first place). But it was May, I was at rock bottom, and I was trapped in the world of high school romance.

So I said, "Deena, I don't think Rob is exactly panting to come back to me."

"You might be surprised."

"Why?"

She gave a cute shrug. "I heard that Rob still likes you and wants to get back together."

"You're lying."

"I am not lying." Her face pouted. "I heard it around."

"A guy who likes you does not walk away from a fight and leave you to be abused by two football players."

"He feels lousy about that," Deena insisted. "Why don't you just talk to him?"

Already, I was rehearsing opening lines. It had to be the sweet spring air washing in from the open windows. It was madness. Rob had dropped me because of pressure from his friends. Now I was barred from the Prom and even *more* of an outcast. If he saw me coming, he'd run screaming down the hall.

But, like the eternal fourteen-year-old I am, I asked Deena, "You think he'd talk to me?"

"I *know* he would." She was absolutely luminous now. She clamped *both* hands on my wrist and pushed her face into mine. "He and his friends hang out by the Deli at two o'clock, because he goes to practice right after. Why don't we kind of show up there and you can feel him out?"

Yes, I was excited! "I can't show up looking like this," I said. "I'm a total scrub."

"So go home and change during your free period."

My mind raced. "My only free period is fourth, and that isn't enough time. But I have Concert Band fifth, and LaFleur will never miss me." I stopped myself, feeling moronic. "Deena, this is stupid. I'm screwed up enough without getting harassed by my ex-boyfriend and his Neanderthal friends."

"If they start anything, we'll just get back in the car," Deena said. "And you don't have to pay any attention to them."

I looked at her. She was eager and credulous. It's what I'd liked about her from the beginning. Deena and I were opposites, and Kimber kind of combined qualities of both of us. It made us a tight little trio. I wanted to be a tight little trio again. No less than Deena, I wanted things back the way they were. I believed at that moment, as if fairy dust had been sprinkled on me, that I was going to go to the Senior Prom, and Kimber, Deena, and I would hug each other and laugh and cry and have a Happy Ending.

So I planned to cut my fifth period class, go home, change into something cute and spring-like, and hit on Rob after school. To spare you the suspense, I did, and it worked. The scene with Rob isn't even worth telling. Here's a sample:

Rob is on the side of the Deli, eating sour cream and onion potato chips. His friends are there too, with sodas and junk. Rob's in his cut-off jersey and shorts, his muscles bulging in the sun. It's eighty degrees and the air is heavy. Deena and I have gotten out of the car. I'm wearing a green sleeveless blouse and black shorts (they have a slimming effect, which my thunder thighs badly need). I've put on makeup and brushed my hair. I have shades on. I'm sweating like an entire pigpen. My heart is banging against my chest.

Deena and I walk slowly past Rob and his friends. Our shoes crunch on the gravel. I look obliquely at Rob. He looks at me. His friends look at me. It is extremely tense. I search his face for signs of hatred. I see only curiosity. Not that Rob's eyes were ever that expressive.

And here's the exciting, romantic, thrilling reconciliation:

I say, "Hi."

He says, "Hi."

I say, "How's it going?"

He says, "Good."

I say, "Practice today?"

He says, "Yeah."

I say, "Maybe I'll watch."

He says, "Why?"

I say, "I have a dentist appointment and I have to hang out until four."

He says, "Oh."

I say, "So, maybe I'll watch."

He says, "Okay."

I say, "See you."

He says, "Okay."

I say, "Bye."

He says, "Bye."

Are you palpitating? I was. Man, I read the code. He said okay.

It was okay for me to watch his practice. It was okay for me to be visible in the stands while he bared his awesome torso. I looked wildly at Deena who grinned like an idiot and we both went into the Deli and burst into idiotic giggles. I bought Hostess cupcakes and we stayed in there until we heard Rob and his friends drive off.

So I'd found Rob again. Nothing too magical about it. Rob felt putrid about ducking the fight, and the scandal with me and Henning had died down. Everyone knew that Prom time was truce time. You had to have a date and if the date was somebody you didn't want to be seen with in March, well, your friends kind of looked the other way in May. Rob, as I learned later, had asked two other girls who were already taken. My timing was right.

Which, maybe, *was* magic, considering that my timing has never been right.

Not that the magic lasted very long, as Kimber will tell you now.

Chapter Nineteen

All right, everyone. Now you've seen the reconciliation between Deena and Phil, and the reconciliation between Martha and Rob. Here's the Main Event: the reconciliation between me and Lou. Now sit back with a box of tissues because this will wrench your hearts. Okay? Are you ready? The Reconciliation Between Kimber and Lou! Here it is:

Well? Are you limp with emotion?

What do you mean, "Where was it?" Didn't you see it go by?

You didn't? Don't be surprised. Because there *was* no reconciliation!

That's right. There was no heart-to-heart talk, no long walk on the beach, no wine in a restaurant. And it makes sense. Lou had cheated on me. Any trust between us was shattered. To rebuild that trust would take months, and we didn't *have* months. If we tried to talk things out, we'd have a rip-roaring fight, and there'd be no chance of us going to the Prom together.

But if we just let it alone, and stayed away from each other, we could be civil, dance, eat, and go out with our friends. Then we could break up formally. So the entire script between me and Lou was played out in front of my classroom door and it went like this:

KIMBER: What time are you coming for me?

LOU: Limo's due at six, so I'll be around at about six-fifteen.

KIMBER: Okay. Then we'll pick up Deena because she's closer, and then Martha.

LOU: All right.

KIMBER: Did we decide on going into the city after?

LOU: Fine with me.

KIMBER: Uh oh. That's the bell. Talk to you later.

LOU: Right.

We said other things to each other before the Prom, but nothing important. And we didn't go out with each other. Why should we?

Okay. All together now:

HOW COULD YOU GO TO THE SENIOR PROM TOGETHER IF YOU DON'T LOVE EACH OTHER?

What? Nobody's astonished? Come *on*! Aren't your illusions shattered? What about our beloved author? You were going to make this a fairy tale of true love. Aren't you disenchanted?

"Well, I'm too old to be disenchanted. But I think *you're* disenchanted."

Nah. I'd seen this kind of junk go on every year. I'd seen my friends betray each other, abuse each other, hurt each other, and get trapped in lousy relationships.

I guess I *was* a little surprised that it was happening to me. Or maybe I was embarrassed that I hadn't seen it coming. But I was realizing a lot of stuff. I hurt like crazy, but I wasn't *numb* the way I'd been. I was on Corey's butt every day, making him do his homework and grilling him about where he'd been. He hated my guts, but he was humbler, man.

I felt a forward motion I hadn't felt all year. I still wasn't talking to Martha, but I was weakening. I couldn't forget all the years we'd shared, or that car ride when she'd begged me to save her life. Maybe *that's* why she cheated with Lou. Martha was always good at getting attention.

No, I wasn't disenchanted. Half the kids at the Prom weren't in love. But the Prom was THERE. You were supposed to go. You were supposed to spend a thousand bucks. You were supposed to turn into a princess for one night. And if you had to go with your cousin, or a mercy date, or a guy you hated, you went. Hey, it's a fitting finale to all the years of idiotic romance.

"Kimber, I really feel sad for you. I'm sorry that there were no happy endings."

Whoa! I never said there were no happy endings!

"But you told me . . ."

We told you that there was no fairy tale romance! But we *can* learn. I was learning like mad. So was Martha. And Deena. And Jason. And the Prom was our final exam.

"All right, Kimber. Let's go to the Prom."

You got it.

Now the Westfield tradition was heavy rain on Prom night. For the last three years, there were major T-storms. For us, the forecast was just as gloomy: a typical Long Island weather system of overcast and afternoon rain. It rained on Tuesday afternoon, it rained on Wednesday afternoon, it rained on Thursday afternoon, and it rained on Friday morning.

On the Friday of the Prom, there is another tradition: the Exodus. School policy says seniors have to be in school on that day or they can't go to the Prom. So all the seniors show up in the morning and report to homeroom, and then they get sick. Boy, do they get sick. There's a line of seniors out the door of the Attendance office, and a line of cars in the parking lot. That's all the parents picking up their sick seniors.

By fifth period, the senior girls are at the hair salons. I don't know what the guys do. I hit the salon at about twelve-thirty. Back at the beginning of this epic, you said I had cascades of glossy hair, which is a romantic way of saying my hair hangs all over the place. It's not naturally curly either, so I had to sit for two hours while they made me look like a model.

I got home at about three, and the house was empty. The rain had slacked off and the streets smelled good. I thought I saw cracks in the clouds. I started to feel butterflies, in spite of everything. I watched some soaps and made some phone calls. And I cried. I wanted Mom to be home, to be excited, to reminisce about *her* Prom. It wasn't fun spending this afternoon by myself.

Corey blew in from school and gave me a "Yo! Got your hair done?"

"Yes," I said.

"Looks good."

He pounded up the stairs and slammed his door. I looked up after him and almost wanted to hug him. I was getting dangerously sentimental. I made a tuna fish sandwich and coffee but I only ate half the sandwich. My stomach was churning and I felt light-headed. I got out my photo albums and my class books from seventh grade on, and I cried my eyes out. I looked out at the backyard where the old swing set still stood, rusted and bent. I saw the sun slowly spread over the grass and the chain-link fence.

If ever I needed Jason to snap me out of it, this was the time. But Jason was getting ready in his own house. He'd asked Stacey

Coleman (remember the valedictorian who was at the wild party in Lou's room?) at the last minute and she'd said yes. Don't get too excited. Love wasn't blooming; it was just that they both wanted to go.

Anyway, I showered at five, and got dressed in my room. Again, I missed not having Mom to sit on the bed and make comments. I tried to make a production of it, putting on makeup, daubing on perfume, s-l-o-w-l-y putting on my pantyhose and my slip and my dress. I played my stereo while I did it, and outside the sky turned blue and sunshine poured through my window. Of course, I cried hysterically again and had to redo my makeup.

Finally, I looked at myself in the mirror on my closet door. The lemony color of the dress looked pretty decent next to my skin, which is naturally dark. The way the gown was cut in front even suggested cleavage, which was a bonus. I pretended that the love of my life was picking me up, that I'd dance in the arms of my prince charming.

But not even Jason could go "Bibbity-bobbity-boo" and make *that* happen.

Dad came home and I came downstairs to show him how I looked. *He* looked terrible. His face was bluish and he looked old. He sat down in the family room and said, "Okay, princess, model for me."

I smiled. I know Dad never liked these mushy moments. I stood in the middle of the faded blue carpet and twirled. Shafts of sun made spotlights through the window, and the dust that danced in those beams was kind of like fairy dust. He applauded and held out his arms to me.

I knelt at the side of the chair and he gathered me in for a hug. I hung onto him and cried again (a princess with inflamed tear ducts). We broke the hug and I looked at him with the most love I'd ever felt. He wiped at my cheeks with his fingertip and his own eyes were moist, which is the same as wild hysteria in someone else.

"You're beautiful," he said.

"Thanks."

He held both of my hands. "Have a great time, Kimber. I know this is not the best possible Prom night, but make it terrific."

"Dad, you know I'll be out all night, okay?"

He smiled. "When you were a kid, I'd talk to your Mom about how strict we'd be when you were a teenager. But things change. I have to trust you. Whatever you are, you've done for yourself."

I rubbed his wrist. "You helped a little."

"I helped by staying out of your way."

"More than that." I felt so bad for him. I wished he knew about Corey or that he had a steady girlfriend or a little shred of luck in his work. But I knew he'd always be poor and alone. So did Mom, which was why she cheated on him and left him. She wasn't being cruel, just desperate.

I ruffled his hair—what was left of it. "I have to get ready," I said. "Lou's going to be here any minute."

He nodded, his eyes filled with the pain that all Daddies feel when their daughters go to the Prom. I was happy to see it.

Dad didn't know about Lou's escapades, so we could hold hands and keep up his illusions. Boy, if parents knew a fourth of what was going on with their kids, they'd all need intensive care.

The limo honked, and I took a deep breath and went out. Dad and Corey followed. Corey lounged on the portico, hands jammed in his dungaree pockets. He could not publicly show interest in his older sister's Prom. But the neighbors were all clustered at the curb. This was a BIG Prom tradition, everyone turning out to watch the couples and take pictures. Even Dad got out the camera and snapped a few. It's kind of like hope springing eternal. All these middle-aged people pretending that true love and happiness were possible.

The limo was gorgeous. It was black, Simonized like mad, with tinted windows. Lou looked gorgeous, too. He'd worn a yellow shirt and cummerbund to match my dress, and his tux was black. His hair glistened in the sunlight and his eyes gleamed. I almost fell in love with him again. It's a powerful potion, man. You can be rational and determined, but one laser beam from a guy's blue eyes, and you're a ninny again.

Lou said, "You look fantastic," and I said, "So do you." He pinned on my corsage. Dad posed us by the limo and took some snaps. I caught Corey's eye. He was looking hard at me, and his face was almost sad, almost caring. Then he looked away.

The limo driver was a mint-looking guy with a moustache. He obviously pumped iron. He held the door for me and I slid in. I giggled at the plushness of the seats. There was a little TV set and a CD player. No bar, though.

Lou shook hands with my Dad and got in. Dad bent down by the open door and said, "Have a great time, princess."

"I will, Daddy."

I touched my fingers to my lips and blew him a kiss and he caught it. Then the driver closed the door and I felt like I was in a space shuttle. Through the windows, everything looked purple and far away. The air conditioning blew cold against my face. I clutched my little beaded bag and leaned back as the limo backed off the driveway. Neighbors were waving. Dad was at the front door. Lou was next to me. None of it made sense.

"It got sunny," I said.

"Yep."

"Thank God. It's no fun running through the rain in these shoes."

"I'll bet."

"You smell good," I said.

"You, too."

He'd been drinking. I wished I had.

The Big Prom Production was in full swing in Deena's neighborhood. Deena's mom and dad were going bananas with pictures. Deena's mom looks like an older Deena, but her dad is bald. He was taking videos as we pulled up.

"Oh God," I said.

"Hurray for Hollywood," Lou added.

When we got out, we saw Deena and Phil standing by these tall shrubs in front of the living room window. Deena's mom took pictures of them, making them hold hands and turn sideways, and then stand with Phil behind Deena, and then kiss, and everything else she could think of. Deena kept saying *"Mom! That's enough!"* but Phil was being nice about it.

Once Deena was freed, she ran to me and we hugged and kissed. She looked phenomenal in her dress, which was peach, with as much gauze and flounce as you'd imagine Deena wearing. She honestly looked like a fairy princess. Her hair was piled up, adorned with baby's breath and combs. Phil wore a white tux with peach shirt and cummerbund, and it was like they were in some old Fred Astaire and Ginger Rogers movie.

Deena held my hands at arm's length and gushed. "Oh my *God!* Let me *see* you! Oh my *God!* You look so *fantastic!* Oh my *God!"* And on and on.

Finally, I said, "Shut up, Deena." But I was really glad she was being flowery, because I needed it.

We had to sit for about a roll of film in the limo. First we had to bend down by the open door and Deena's mother took us from the *opposite* open door. Then we had to sit *in* the limo. Then we had to stand *next* to the limo, and then in *front* of the limo. We were laughing hysterically by the thirteenth or fourteenth picture.

At last, Deena's mom and dad were done. We had to wait until they hugged Deena, separately and together. You'd never know from this emotional scene that Deena felt neglected.

We finally piled back into the limo, the four of us, and went to get Martha. She lived in an older neighborhood, which was a little run-down, with grass growing up in driveways and chunks of tar paper showing through where siding fell off houses. But Martha was out there on her driveway, and she looked *great*. She wore a mint green gown, strapless, with no flounces, so it made her look sophisticated. Her hair was beautifully done—I'd never seen it look that posh. Her mom was a worn out, old-looking lady, in a house dress. Rob was there, in a dove-gray tux with a top hat and white gloves.

"He looks like a waiter," I giggled.

"Shhh." Deena said.

Phil said, "She's taller than he is by a hairdo."

That broke us all up (except for Lou, who only smiled), and I gave Phil a surprised look.

This time *I* did the running when we got out of the limo. I grabbed Martha and bear-hugged her and she bear-hugged me back. I knew I was going to do it about a half mile before we got to Martha's house.

So did Martha. It felt excellent to hold her and start crying again. I could hear the guys making sarcastic remarks (except Lou, who only smiled), and Martha and I started laughing at each other's streaming mascara.

"We've destroyed ourselves," I said.

"Back to the bathroom!"

We went into Martha's house to freshen up. The guys didn't like that, and neither did Deena, but too bad. In the bathroom, we whispered and giggled some more.

"Did you catch Lou's expression?" I asked. "He looks like he's got constipation."

"He's *scared*," Martha intoned, as she bent over to re-apply her lip gloss. "If we're hugging each other, he's in big trouble."

I checked my eyes again and shut my bag. I turned to Martha and said, "No word from Sachs?"

She shrugged, and for the first time I can remember, she looked vulnerable and afraid. "Nobody stopped Rob from buying the tickets."

"Did he put down your name as his date?"

She hesitated.

"Martha!"

"Well," she said. "We didn't want to blow it right there at the sign-up table."

"But now you don't know!" I said. "What if they don't let you in?"

She kind of drew herself up and looked resolute. "They'll have to make a scene. Rob knows it's a risk. He's ready." She smiled. "He bought me a corsage and everything. He said yes right away when I asked if we could still go to the Prom."

"You asked *him*?"

"Time was running out. It just sort of came up naturally." She took a deep breath and let it out. Then she grabbed my wrist. "Kimber, I'm scared out of my wits. I don't even know why I'm doing this. I'm using Rob just to prove some point that makes no sense. What happens after tonight? What do I tell him?"

I seized both her hands, which were clammy. "Martha, nothing makes sense tonight. I thought I'd be miserable by now, but I'm actually excited. It's the Senior Prom! We waited for this for seven years."

Martha made a rueful noise and shook her head. "Yeah. What a turn-off."

"Come on," I urged. "Our chariot awaits."

"We who are about to die salute you," she said.

We went back outside and the sky had lit up in pink and gold. It was like one of those glowing Renaissance paintings. A fragrant wind riffled the trees. I looked around and saw the little kids. There are always little kids on Prom Night. They cluster by the driveways, and they stare. The skanky little brats are totally awed by their big brothers and sisters looking like fairy-tale royalty, getting into those big incredible cars and going off for adventure and romance.

I wanted to cry again, looking at those kids. They believed. I looked at Martha and squeezed her hand. She looked back at me. The looks said, "Remember?" We'd been there, anointed with jelly and mud, dreaming of the triumph of Prom Night. Now these imps were envying *us,* not knowing about the lies and the games and the broken dreams.

To hell with Lou Ross. I was going to my Prom for those kids, because they had to believe in us and in the magical beauty of this night. A lot of little girls were going to dream of limos and gowns because of me.

Martha kissed her mom goodnight and we got back into the limo. I paused, half in and half out, to take a last look at the fiery sunset. I wanted to remember it. Then I sat back and the door shut. The six of us scrunched together, perfumes and colognes mingling, dresses rustling, shoes blistering. The limo glided forward.

"We're on our way," I said.

We certainly were.

Chapter Twenty

Wait. How do we handle this? At the Prom, we split up for a while. Should the author take over again?

"Speaking as the author, I'd rather you guys do it. This was *your* Prom, and your moment of truth."

Okay. We're all here, right? Let's see—Martha, Deena, Jason, Lou, Phil, Rob—yeah, we're all here. Who starts?

"Let me set the scene for you, and then I'll just point."

All right. Boy, I can't believe we went through this whole story. It makes me shiver, bringing back those memories.

"It made *me* feel kind of strange, too. But let's not wander off the path. Let's go to the Woodside Manor on that beautiful Friday night in May:"

As Kimber said, Long Island is narrow, and local roads wind between strips of shopping centers. The Woodside Manor stood on one of those strips, off Central Avenue. It was a typical sub-urban catering hall: monolithic and tasteless. Its soaring windows and marble facade loomed over surrounding shops, and its trees glittered with thousands of tiny light bulbs. As your limo glided between the marble entrance gates (after waiting ten minutes to make the left turn), you saw monstrous chandeliers through the windows. The setting sun bathed the pink marble in golden splendor.

There was valet parking, which meant that some poor high school kid, gussied up in a comic opera uniform, waved your limo to the right. You got out . . .

Wait. As long as we have a dramatic sunset, let's make the limo the one our characters are in, and let's make this *their* grand entrance.

The limo driver tucked the car against an island ablaze with spring flowers and opened the doors. Everyone clambered out, the boys clumsily running around to offer their arms to the girls. Kimber smoothed her dress and her eyes darted, gulping in the beauty. Years later, she would recognize the decor as tacky, but tonight she was entranced.

As they stood for a moment, feeling the sweet evening breeze wash over them, other limos pulled in: white limos, black limos, blue limos, Rolls Royce limos. Swarming like army ants, they jockeyed for position as parking attendants cursed.

Phil said, "It looks like an OPEC convention."

Everyone laughed and Kimber gave Phil a second hard look. She'd never expected him to be amusing.

"Pictures!" Deena cried, as she held up her camera.

"Oh, no!" Martha moaned. But they all got into position on the island as Deena blocked traffic. They weren't alone. As each group of Prom-goers alit from a chariot, the cameras came out, flash-cubes sizzled, and hundreds of bejeweled teenagers grinned. At the entrance to the hall, a professional photographer posed quick group shots. Inside, three photographers had been hired by the school to take formal poses.

This was not a frill. Teenagers live for snapshots. They need the reassurance of glossies, to prove that they were *there*, that it *happened*, that it was *fun*. The formal poses would go into albums and one day would mock the balding, thickening adults who once owned the taut bodies and the faces that glowed with future.

After pictures, Kimber, Lou, Martha, Rob, Deena, and Phil clicked across the asphalt and under the canopied stairs to the hall. Behind them, traffic honked and snarled; ahead of them, glasses clinked and music thumped. They could smell body heat and canapés and feel the rush of excitement.

Kimber?

Okay. We were all pretty nervous about Martha. My stomach was jumping like a cricket. I held Lou's hand, more out of tension than affection. Lou and I were first on the stairs, then Deena and Phil, then Martha and Rob. And of course, there were about a million other people.

There was a line as we got to the entrance. Right inside the doors, there was a table. Behind the table sat Mr. Hanley and Mrs. Vecchio, the Senior Class advisors. They had database lists in front of them with everyone's name, and their dates, and whether they'd paid. Just behind the advisors, I could glimpse Mr. Sachs and Mr. Jaeger, one of the assistant principals. They were ready, boy.

I squeezed Lou's hand. "I'm scared for Martha."

Lou shrugged.

I hated his guts when he shrugged like that. Of course, he didn't know that *I* knew that *he* knew where Martha was that night.

Finally, we were inside. I looked around, and shivered at how luxurious it all looked. There was a huge lobby, and I mean *huge*, with this immense crystal chandelier hanging down. It was like a spaceship, all fire and glitter. There were two winding staircases, one on either side, leading up to a balcony. Kids were on the balcony, posing for pictures. The sun poured through the big windows. Waiters with yellow gloves walked around with trays of hors d'oeuvre. (Thanks, Author! You *knew* there was no way I could spell that!)

I gaped at how beautiful everyone looked. Kids hardly ever dress up, but on Prom night, it's like *Gone with the Wind*. Here are girls you see every day in class, with their sweats and torn jeans and dirty sneakers, and now they're in long gowns all spangled with sequins and trimmed with lace. Suddenly they're stunning, with smooth shoulders and proud chests and long legs. And all those ratty hairdos you get with a curling iron at 6:00 in the morning are ravishing upsweeps and cascading ringlets.

Even the guys look mint. Some of them were kind of funny in their top hats (with their long hair sticking out!!), but most of them looked dashing and distinguished. You could tell that everyone felt special—and uncomfortable. It was cute to watch these suave guys and girls mincing around holding little cheese balls.

You know, it's *worth* the money, even if you never wear the dress or the tux again. It feels different to dress up and dance in a big hall with chandeliers. Your body feels different. I know mine did. My heart was thudding and my face was on fire. And did it hurt that I wasn't in love.

But there wasn't time to brood. We were at the table and Mrs. Vecchio was smiling and saying, "Hi, Kimber. You look beautiful."

"Thanks," I said.

"Hi, Lou," she said to Lou. He smiled back. Lou thinks teachers are fools for being teachers because it doesn't pay enough, so he treats them like servants.

Mrs. Vecchio checked us off and we moved into the lobby. Mr. Sachs gave me a little smile, and I tightened up inside. He wore the same gray suit he always wears and he was drinking a glass of Coke. Of course, you can only get Coke or phony piña coladas at the Prom, but most of the kids were already pretty trashed by the time they got there.

I stopped Lou and we stood in the middle of all the kids and I watched as Deena and Phil signed in. I couldn't watch that closely because people we knew kept seeing us and we had to hug and kiss and squeal and say "Hi! You look *terrific!*"

Then Deena and Phil were inside and Rob and Martha were standing by the table. I couldn't hear anything because it was too noisy, but I saw Mrs. Vecchio look over at Mr. Sachs, who nodded and moved toward the table.

"*No,*" I said.

Lou didn't say anything, but his face got very pale. Mr. Sachs went over to Martha and said something to her. Martha's face got stormy. Rob said something to Mr. Sachs, and Mr. Sachs answered Rob. I could see the kids on line straining to see what was going on.

Mr. Sachs moved Martha and Rob away and the kids kept coming in. Martha joined in the conversation now, and it got kind of animated. Mr. Sachs didn't look mad, just determined. But I was watching Martha's face, not his. I could see her eyes fill up and I could see her bite hard on her lip to keep from crying. She touched Rob's arm and talked to him, and I knew she was telling him to go in alone. He shook his head. They both turned and went back out.

"He's not letting them in!" I yelled, a little louder than I wanted to.

Deena and Phil were with us by then and Phil said, "What's the story?"

I told him as quickly as I could. "This is so stupid," I added. "I *know* that Greg Fratelli and John Brody are here!"

Deena shook her head. "Why did she have to talk to those Swedes anyway?"

"Damn it," I exploded. "It's not her fault! She was stupid but not a criminal!"

Deena said, "Spending a night with a guy in his room is more than stupid."

I stared at her. I wanted to say, "You have the *nerve* to talk about spending the night with a guy!" but I wouldn't say it in front of Phil. *Especially* not in front of Phil.

The lobby was filling up and I could hear music from inside. Lou touched my elbow and said, "Come on, let's find our table."

Phil said, "Yeah, I want to get going on the fruit cup supreme."

Deena laughed and clung to Phil's arm. I felt myself go numb. I looked at the entrance, where kids were streaming in. I looked past them, at the glass doors, and outside, where it had gotten dark. Martha was out there. My best friend. And I knew that she *shouldn't* be out there.

I looked desperately at Lou. "It's not *fair*."

"I know it's not fair," he said. "What do you want me to do about it?"

I couldn't tell him. Not at that moment. I was too choked with fury. But this was Kimber in the spring, not Kimber in the winter. This was Kimber who had taken charge of her dirtbag brother and stopped Martha from killing herself and sold illegal candy in the school. This was Kimber who knew that she didn't need Lou Ross to make her life worth living.

"I'll be right back," I said.

"Don't be a jerk," Lou said.

"Go in without me. I'll find you."

I broke away and elbowed my way through the crowd (elbowing your way in a formal gown is not easy) until I got to the entrance. I saw Mr. Sachs standing with Mr. Jaeger by the window, looking out at the gridlock of limos.

I took a deep breath and went over to them. "Mr. Sachs?"

He turned around. His little hard eyes made me feel naked. "Yes, Kimber?"

I took another deep breath. I was close to fainting. "Listen, this thing with Martha. It's not fair."

He gave his little evil smile. "I can see why you think that, Kimber, but we're standing behind our rules."

"Fine, if she did what you say she did. But she didn't. I *know* she didn't."

"Really?"

I felt hot flashes all over my body, and I was sweating. Real elegant! "She *did* talk to those guys and she walked Henning back to his room, but she really *did* pass out by the ice machine. She never spent any time in his room. She's telling the truth, Mr. Sachs, and she should be allowed to be at her Prom."

Sachs looked at me, as if he were considering whether to have me torn apart by wild dogs. "Well, as I told Martha, I can't take her word for it, or yours. If you had evidence, I'd consider it."

My lips clamped shut. I turned, involuntarily, and looked at where Lou had been, but he was gone. I turned back. "I *have* evidence, Mr. Sachs, but it involves somebody else and I can't tell you who it is. Can't you believe me? Look at my record. I never cut a class. I never cheated on a test. I don't smoke or drink. And I wouldn't lie for Martha, not even for this."

Sachs glanced at Mr. Jaeger, who looked more sympathetic. He even smiled at me. Sachs said, " Kimber, I do trust you. But this is not a matter of trust. It's a matter of policy. If the person you're referring to comes forward with the evidence, I'll consider it. Otherwise, Martha can't come in."

My shoulders slumped. I looked outside, at the glittering trees and black sky. Martha was there, and I was here. And Lou could make it right.

I'd never felt so defeated in my life. And slowly, defeat turned to boiling anger. That creep! He'd used me for a year, he'd used Martha, he used everybody. And we all groveled for him, for *all* of these guys, because it was so awful to be alone. Well, I had nothing to lose at this point. I'd gotten to the Prom. I was here at Woodside Manor, and I'd had my picture taken. If I got thrown out, well, I'd had the experience. The rest of Prom weekend was no big deal: getting blitzed in Manhattan, sleeping at the beach, driving to Great Adventure with a hangover. I could skip it.

Yeah. It was a far, far better thing I was going to do now.

"I'll be back," I said to Sachs.

He nodded.

I spun and charged into the laughing, clinking, munching,

picture-snapping mob. I wanted Lou, and I was going to get him, even if it caused a riot.

Of course, I didn't know that a riot was already in the making. Because inside, Deena was running into a slight problem, Actually, *two* slight problems. Actually, three. But I'll let . . .

"Kimber, wait. Before you get inside, I think we're all interested in what Martha was doing *outside*. You left her hanging there."

Right. Martha, I'm sorry. Go ahead.

Oh, don't apologize. After I betrayed *you* and you risked everything to save *me*, I feel humble. Well, maybe not humble, but grateful.

I knew Sachs wouldn't let me in. Maybe I fooled myself for a while, but as Rob and I got to the door, I knew in my bones that I was doomed. I don't even remember the conversation with Sachs. I was heaving inside, and my head was filling up. I know that I kept telling myself I would not cry in front of this man, that I would not make a scene.

I also told myself that I was *not* going home. I'd stay out in the parking lot all night if necessary. And call the news media.

And then we were outside. We had to push against the incoming tide and of course I was recognized. Rob kept guiding me with a firm hand in the small of my back, until we were down the stairs and in the parking lot.

The sky overhead was brilliant yellow, sliding into a black horizon. The wind chilled my skin. I stood there stupidly, looking at the arriving throngs. Rob had taken off his ridiculous top hat and his hair blew. he seemed angry, but he didn't yell.

"I'm sorry," I said.

"It's okay. We took a chance."

"It isn't fair to you."

He shrugged.

I hugged myself because I was now getting goose bumps from

the evening chill. I looked out at the traffic and the lit-up store fronts. I didn't know what to do.

Rob said, "Let's sit in the limo."

Gratefully, I said, "Good thinking!" It took awhile to scan the sea of limos and find ours, but our driver had found a good spot at the front of the parking lot. He stood by the car, smoking a cigarette. We walked over and I felt even more feeble-minded.

"Leaving already?" the driver said.

Rob said, "She's not feelin' good. We just want to sit in the car."

The driver gave me a quick up-and-down look and nodded. I could see him smirk. He opened the door for us and said, "I'll warm it up for you."

I slid in, followed by Rob, and the driver shut the door. I slumped back in the seat, my head throbbing. I felt so incredibly *stupid* in this expensive gown, with my hair done, and my shoes dyed to match, and my corsage at my wrist. And here I was, sitting in the limo, not allowed in.

Rob switched on the stereo and the music washed over us. He leaned back. I could hear his tux rustle. I said, "Great night I gave you."

"It's not over yet."

I looked at him. "You have a secret plan in mind?"

He shook his head. "No. But it ain't over till the fat lady sings."

Whoops. I'd done it again. I'd forgotten that Rob was not a whip. Then again, if I was so smart, how come *I* couldn't think of a secret plan? Rob took something out of his tux and said, "Have a drink."

"Holy cow," I said. Actually it wasn't "Holy cow," but that's close enough. I took the flask from him and said, "What is it?"

"Vodka and Hawaiian Punch."

"What?"

"I had to disguise it, and there wasn't anything else in the house."

I laughed. "God. We used to drink vodka and Hawaiian Punch at sleep-over parties."

I uncapped the flask and took a long swig. It was Hawaiian Punch all right. But then I felt the vodka and it was warm and welcome. I do not recount this with any pride. Sitting in a limo and getting wasted was not my plan for the evening. But when you've been betrayed and you have no power to do anything about it, you go into denial, and vodka and Hawaiian Punch spelled denial right then.

Rob took the flask and drank, and then passed it back to me. I couldn't see anything out the windows because it had gotten dark out and the windows were tinted. The back of the limo became my whole world, with the rich stereo music and the sweet, potent drink, and my pulsating insides.

"Why did you say you'd go to the Prom with me?" I asked. This, of course, was a question that needed a lot of vodka and Hawaiian Punch to ask.

"I wanted to."

"Come on. You ran away from me. You thought I was a slut." (Yes, I said that. I was loose, man.)

Rob took another slug from the flask. I could hear it slosh. "I don't know, my friends were getting on me about it, and I didn't know what to do. You're not easy to know, Martha. Nobody likes you."

"Thanks," I said.

"You know what I mean. You're geeky."

"And you're jocky." I giggled. "Or Fruit of the Loom."

He giggled, too. He said, "I think you're pretty decent. If you wouldn't look so weird and use all those long words, you'd be more popular."

"With who? The cheerleaders? I've got friends, Bubba. Friends who appreciate me for what I am."

"Yeah. More geeks."

"The geeks will inherit the earth," I said.

"Huh?"

Whoops. His wit didn't improve with alcohol. "So once you ran out on me, how come you let me back in?"

"I told you. I like you."

"You also couldn't get a Prom date."

He shook the flask, which sounded just about empty. "Who told you *that*?"

"I heard it."

"It's not true."

"Yeah? So you chose me out of all the rest?"

"I said I'd go with you. Don't push it."

"I always push. I push until I screw up. That's how I do things, Bubba. You don't like it, lump it."

He laughed softly and put his arms back over his head, dropping the flask onto the thick carpet. "You're really weird, Martha."

I fished around for the flask, picked it up and drained it. Then *I* dropped it onto the thick carpet. "That's what they'll put on my grave," I mumbled. "Really Weird Martha."

He looked at me. "You're not into suicide, are you?"

"Well, only as a hobby, not a career."

"Come on!"

I put up my hands and made a face. "Okay, Bubba, shhhhh. Just kidding. I don't want to get you sore. You're a sweet guy. You're really brave to take me to the Prom and get kicked out with me. It's gonna mess up your whole social life."

He shrugged. "Nah. My friends are jerks anyway."

A warm, sticky flow of love buried me, like hot caramel. "I say you're brave, Bubba. And I appreciate it. No guy's been brave for me before."

"No sweat," he said.

Well, when a guy says "No sweat," my heart melts. So I lunged at him (actually, I half-lunged, half-fell) and started kissing his jaw and his cheek. Being no fool, he twisted around and gathered me up and we got our mouths more or less together. That first kiss in the steamed-up limo was about the most beautiful kiss of my life. I may have been blitzed, but I meant what I said. Rob was pretty damned courageous. It was his way of making up for not fighting. But it still took a lot of moxie because he had to face his buddies.

So for the next thirty minutes or so, I loved Rob. I loved him for making me feel like a woman, and like a human being. Lou had never done that, and never would, not for anyone. Jason did it, but he lacked sex appeal. Rob lacked Jason's intelligence and insight. Well, you can't have everything, right? Not all at once.

Tonight, in the limo, I took the sex appeal—and the crude gallantry that made Rob rise above himself. It wasn't a long romance, like I said. But it was real love.

And you can stand around here till the cows come home, but I am *not* describing any more!

Jason, help me out. Take us back to the Prom and Deena's Disaster. (No *way* are we letting *Deena* tell this one!)

Chapter Twenty-One

Okay, that was Martha Sullivan reporting live from the steamed-up limo. Back in Woodside Manor, we are about to introduce our Surprise Guest.

Kimber's shown you the lobby of Woodside Manor. Now step inside. Picture, if you will, a cavernous room decorated in putrid green wallpaper with silver foil accents. A titanic chandelier dominates the room, a megaton explosion of crystal that bounces each time the dance floor vibrates. Tables crowd the room, and to get from your table to the dance floor, you have to twist, squeeze, and climb.

At one end of the dance floor, towering speakers flank a rig that looks like the bridge of the Starship *Enterprise*. Bubbles flow, smoke billows, lights spin across the ceiling, and the deejay plays all the hits.

I was at Table 67, which was close enough to the dance floor to destroy my inner ear. Here's a diagram:

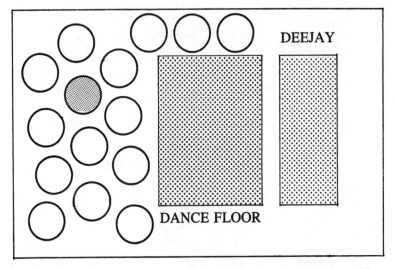

DEEJAY

DANCE FLOOR

My table was the shaded one. I won't list everyone at the table, but Stacey Coleman was there, and some of her friends and their dates. Stacey is a little taller than I am, with a pageboy haircut and a sweet face. Tonight, Stacey was wearing a light blue satin dress with spaghetti straps. So was I.

Just kidding. I was in your standard black tux with light blue shirt. I looked rather dapper. Of course, I was not the star of the evening or I'd be the Big Dapper.

Okay, okay! This is my last appearance, so I'm getting it all in!

It was a little later in the evening, and the Prom was merrily underway. Couples moved sensuously under the shifting lights, deep-kissing and whispering into each other's nostrils.

Most of the kids just wandered around, looking bored. They did this in great herds, moving from table to table, from room to room. Out in the lobby, the line for the photographer stretched back to the coat room. That's the goal of the evening: to get pictures taken and then get out. Within two hours, these debonair dandies and their dates would be trashing their livers and thrashing in the dunes.

But right now, it was the Ball. I wasn't having a bad time, considering that my heart ached for Kimber. Stacey Coleman just sat and gave me pale little smiles.

That's when Deena came over.

Actually, Deena *and* Phil came over. Actually, they were just en route to the dance floor. Deena looked so breathtaking that I stood up and ogled her. I remembered our few moments in Room 102. I was a frustrated man.

Deena and Phil were hand in hand, waving cheery hellos. Deena saw me, probably because I was waving frantically. At last, Deena was in front of me. I could breathe her perfume.

"God, you look radiant," I said.

"Thanks, Jason! You look handsome."

She smiled her alluring smile and tugged at Phil's hand. Phil gave me a condescending nod. They moved on. I couldn't stand it. I couldn't sit here and watch foxy women pass by all night and calmly munch prime rib. It was Prom Night.

"Come on," I told Stacey. "Let's dance."

She pushed back her chair and got up, sort of like a heron leaving the marsh. I grabbed her hand, which was clammy. I dragged her to the dance floor, searching for Deena. Kimber would be nice to find also, but Kimber was gunning for Lou.

I positioned myself as close to Deena as I could get, and started to gyrate. Stacey moved slightly, like she had mild convulsions. I was dynamite on legs, Mr. Movement, smart and sassy. I was trying to get Deena's attention.

She noticed me, and gave me a big smile and a wave. Phil glanced over with distaste. How jealous was Phil, I wondered? If I ran over and pinched Deena's butt would he rip off his jacket and fight? The thought was intoxicating.

Of course, nothing would have happened if it were just me out there. But it wasn't just me. As I worked up a sweat, I heard a male voice cry out, "Deena!"

I looked around, scanning the spiffy bodies. I saw Deena look around, too. And Phil.

"Deena!" the shout came again.

I zoomed in on a guy who looked almost familiar, the way people look who you haven't seen for awhile. He was tall and gawky, with Brillo hair and big hands. He wore a pale blue tux.

Deena stared at him the way a doe looks at a hunter who's taking aim. "Brett . . ." she said in a sick voice.

BRETT????

He swooped down on her like a condor on a rabbit. Deena kept dancing, but panic fluttered in her eyes. Phil had stopped dead, which was a dramatic sight on a dance floor filled with gyrating youth.

"How are you?" Deena said.

"Great! You look incredible!"

"Thanks."

I'm transcribing what I *think* they said, since the noise level made hearing impossible. Also, I was pretending to dance and not notice them.

Brett was not going to let Deena go without a *faux pas*. "Who are you here with?" he asked. I wondered who *he* was here with. None of us had ever considered the very real possibility that Brett would be at the Prom.

Deena looked with piteous eyes at Phil. "Brett, this is Phil Pizer. Phil, this is Brett Kamen."

Brett shook hands with Phil. Now, of course, he and Deena *and* Phil were standing still on the dance floor, getting jostled by revelers.

"How are you doing?" Brett asked Deena. "It's been a while."

"I'm fine, Brett," Deena whispered. (I'm taking poetic license; she could have screamed at the top of her lungs for all I know.)

"Great!" Brett kept staring at Deena with a goofy smile. "I'm here with Liz Battaglia." He jerked a thumb in the direction of the lobby. "She's in the girl's room."

At *that* line, I stopped dancing. Stacey stopped also. Deena looked ill, even in the colored lights. "That's nice," she said.

"Yeah, Liz and I are going out." He shrugged. "It's nothing serious. Not like us."

YIKES! CAPTAIN STUPID STRIKES AGAIN!

Phil said, "Look, I was dancing with Deena. You don't mind if we continue?"

Brett waved his hand. "No, no, no. I don't want to intrude. It's just that Liz is in the girl's room and I saw Deena and I wanted to say hello."

"Well, you said hello," Phil answered. "Now say good-bye."

Brett grabbed Deena's hand and said, "It's great seeing you again, Deen." He gazed raptly at the double strand of pearls around her throat. You *know* what Brett was looking for.

"Good to see you, too, Brett," Deena said.

Brett squeezed her hand and then his eyes traveled to her luscious little fingers. If there was no music, I would have heard her terrified gasp.

"Hey," Brett said. "You still have the ring!"

What is that man doing out there, Commander? He's running toward the detonator switch! If he throws that switch . . .

"*Brett!*" Deena warned.

Brett lifted her hand so it caught reflections from the chandelier. "Wow. I bought you that just when we started going out."

He's throwing the switch! It's too late!

Phil said, "What ring?"

Brett, in sublime idiocy, held Deena's hand under Phil's nose and said, "This opal ring. That was the first real gift I bought her. We used to go together."

At that moment, the music stopped!

It was like reverse thunder. Silence crashed over the room and the music lay in little glittering pieces all over the floor. There was a hubbub of talking and I heard silverware clink.

Phil said, "You're wearing his *ring*?"

"You asshole!" Deena told Brett.

"What?" Brett said. "What'd I do?"

Phil said, "Don't bother, Deena."

She spun to face him. "Phil, listen to me. It's just a ring. I have a lot of rings, and this one went with the dress."

"Well it doesn't go with me."

"Phil."

"Drop dead."

A crowd was gathering, thrilled to have a breakup happening right on the dance floor. I looked at Deena with aching compassion, and with hormonal envy.

Brett said, "I didn't mean to cause anything. I just noticed the ring, you know?"

"You've done enough," Deena sobbed. "Get *away.*"

"You might as well keep him," Phil said.

"Don't," she said, and grabbed his arm. He brushed her away, making her fall off-balance.

And yes, she fell toward me. I'd waited seventeen years for a beautiful girl to trip and fall into my arms, and tonight it happened, when I couldn't do anything about it. With irony like this, who needs O. Henry?

I grabbed her and pushed her upright. She looked at me with panic. I couldn't deal with that look. She was a ship going down in icy waters. "Jason," she said in a broken voice, "tell Phil!"

"Wh-wh-wh-wh-wh-wh-" I said.

"Listen to Jason," Deena begged Phil.

Phil's clobbered eyes turned on me. I cringed. No guy had ever given me that look. This was the look handsome guys got, guys who scored.

"Who the hell are you?" he said.

"Wh-wh-wh-wh-wh-wh-wh-" I repeated.

"Jason!" Brett said cheerily. "Jason Goldman! Hi!"

My eyes rolled over. Brett was waving!

Phil gave Deena a look of sublime disgust. "Is he another one of your johns?"

Brett said, "No, *Jason!*"

Oh my God, I thought.

Deena wrung my arm. "Jason, please tell him what I told you, please, please, please, don't let him walk away . . ."

I'd never seen Deena this way. An entire mob was around us now. Stacey Coleman had turned crimson and was backing off. Only Brett didn't notice.

I looked at Phil and said, "She's in love with you. Really."

Phil looked at me like I was a bloodworm. "How do *you* know?"

I felt Deena's hands cutting off my blood flow. "She told me. We were in Room 102 and she told me she was going to call you again because she was crazy about you."

You could see his eyes trying to comprehend. He looked at Deena, then at me. "Room 102?"

"It's an art room," Deena said. "He brought me a brownie."

Phil's lips slowly mouthed the word, "brownie," with no perception at all. And Brett sang out, "Room 102! Whoa! That's where we used to go after school!"

And

WHOOMPH!

—the deejay plugged in. The house lights went down, the colored gels spun, and all I could see was Phil twisting his neck to look at Brett, then twisting back to look at me. He yelled out something obscene. Then his hand whizzed through the air and smacked Deena's face. I heard the crack even over the music.

I lost all sanity as Deena's hand clenched over mine. I shook her off and threw myself at Phil. I think I would have beaten the crap out of him, except that he was already walking away and I missed him and went crashing into a dancing couple. I frantically shuffled to stay upright, and unseen arms helped me.

I looked around, straining to see in the spinning lights. A part of my ravaged brain envisioned Deena hugging me, kissing me, pressing herself against me. But she was gone.

She was chasing Phil!

The concept overloaded my circuits. I couldn't handle it. I saw Brett. I made werewolf noises. Finally, Brett shook his head and went away.

I stumbled from the dance floor. I saw Stacey back at the table, sitting all hunched over, her eyes looking at the floor. I wanted to pour ice-water over her head. I sat down, hard. A plate of prime rib, tiny little potatoes, and withered asparagus stared up at me.

"The food came," Stacey said.

I looked up at her and my eyes must have been maddened because she suddenly got up and hurried away.

At this point, we'll leave Deena in search of Phil, and pick up Kimber:

Okay, Jason. I had gone to our table for a while, holding in my fury at Lou. But there was nobody at our table since Martha and Rob were outside. Deena and Phil were holding hands and planting little kisses all over each other's face. I savagely buttered a roll and chewed it.

Lou was not there.

I let the dancing swirl around me, but it was no use. I kept seeing Martha looking despondently in through the window at the lights and laughter. Somehow, I saw her in a blinding snowstorm, wrapped in a tattered blanket, holding a baby.

"Have a good time, Kimber," she was saying as she sank into the drifts. "It's . . . your . . . (gasp) . . . Prom . . ."

I smashed my fist down on the table, making my roll jump. Deena and Phil looked at me. Deena touched my wrist. "Lighten up," she said. "There's nothing we can do."

I muttered something foul and chewed more roll. I knew Lou

226

would come back eventually, after a suitable amount of time with his buddies. They were probably smoking a joint or swigging booze, and making pornographic jokes about their girl friends, including me.

And when he came back, I'd shake him up.

Sure. I'd mumble, and I'd shrug off his slimy hands, but I'd let him get away with it. I'd let him have a glorious time while Martha froze in the snow. I'd let him know he could play with three girls in his senior year and have them all eating out of his hand.

The Prince of Westfield. And it was *his* ball, for sure.

And then I saw Greg Fratelli.

What a hunk. In his dove gray tux, he made heads turn. He led his girl friend around like a lost puppy as he accepted the greetings of his vassals. I knew his date's name was Laurie, and that she was so in love with him that she wore only the colors he liked, and wrote his term papers, and filled out his college applications, and massaged his forehead in class.

As I looked at them, I boiled over, like milk left too long on the stove. Deena and Phil got up to dance. I remembered a line from Shakespeare's *A Midsummer Night's Dream*, where a girl kind of like Laurie says to her slime:

I am your spaniel; and, Demetrius,
The more you beat me, I will fawn on you.

I remembered going "E-e-u-u-u" at the line, and agreeing with the other girls in the class that this lady was really a rag. Oh boy, did Shakespeare know what was going on!

I took the roll and flung it across the room. I don't know where it landed, but it probably started a food fight. I grabbed my handbag, stood up, and spun around. I felt like I'd felt when I found the pot in Corey's room.

I forgot that I'd taken off my shoes and left them under the table. In my stocking feet, looking pretty dwarfish I'm sure, I made my way through the waves of people. My eyes kept scanning for Lou. Out in the lobby, I looked incoherently at kids lined up for the photographer, at teachers sitting in chairs, at administrators by the window, at the abandoned table by the entrance.

I hurled myself up one of the staircases and stood on the balcony. I wondered if the guys were outside.

Then I saw him.

He came out of the checkroom area with his buddy Neil. He said something to Neil, and then headed for the rest room area.

I lost sight of him as he passed under the balcony. By this time, I was irrational. I hurtled down the stairs, twisting my foot once and nearly doing cartwheels. A teacher caught me and gave me a bizarre look. I kept going.

I ducked through the doorway to the rest room area, and squeezed past the crowds of guys and girls. I felt my perfume going rancid.

Then I was in front of the Men's Room door. I knew the slime was in there. I'd wait him out. I'd catch him as the door opened.

But that didn't last long. My poor little body got crunched and shoved and pummelled by the traffic. Each poke, each push got me crazier. I was the jerk, being abused out here while he had a luxurious cigarette. And Martha breathed her last in the snow . . .

The vision was so funny, it snapped my remaining sanity. I jabbed two guys in the ribs to get past them and I pushed open the Men's Room door with both hands. I heard voices say, "Hey! What's going on?" and stuff like that.

I was inside. The Men's Room was split into a lounge section with mirrors and sinks, and of course, the bathroom section. Lou, fortunately, was right up front. He was combing his sleek hair, bending over and glancing in the mirror. Two other guys gaped at me as I came in.

"Wrong bathroom, lady!" one of them yelled.

Lou straightened up and turned. "Kimber, are you nuts?"

Voices from the bathroom area were calling out anxiously. I looked at Lou and shuddered with all the memories. A year with a guy gets under your skin, you know?

"You're going to talk to Sachs," I said.

He leaned against the sink, water dripping from his hair. "You're out of your mind!"

"This is your girl friend?" one of the guys said.

The other guy snickered. Lou turned on him. "Something funny, asshole?"

The guy put up his hands and said, "Hey, you can stay in here with her. I'm leaving."

He threw himself out of the men's room, followed by the other guy. From the bathroom area, I heard voices yelling, "There's a girl in here!" and a lot of other things, mostly four-lettered. Toilets flushed frantically.

Lou was breathing heavy. "This is about the stupidest stunt you've ever pulled."

"I hope so," I said. "Now, are you ready to talk to Sachs?"

"Talk about *what*? You're crazy!"

"Yeah, I've *been* crazy. I know what went on in the hotel, creep. I know about your little orgy, and how you needed ice, and saw Martha, and didn't tell anyone because then they'd know you broke all the rules."

He went white. I know it's a cliché, but he literally went white. He made little choking noises, too. "Who told you that crap?"

"I don't reveal my sources," I said. "But I'll reveal you. I've been civilized until now, but Martha's out in that parking lot because of you, and I want her inside!"

There was a crash of water from sinks, and then three guys, one after the other, came running out. They glanced at me in stark terror and slammed out the door.

Lou clenched his teeth. "You're making me look bad."

"I haven't started," I said. "You let Martha twist in the wind and on top of that you hit on her? She came to you in panic and you made out! You are the lowest sludge I know!"

He pushed a hand through his hair and said, "Yeah, very impressive. You come in here saying all kinds of garbage and I'm supposed to take it. You want to have this out, fine. Not here. Not now."

He made a move to get past me, but I fell back against the door. "Don't try the righteous routine, Lou. Go to Sachs and tell him about Martha. For crying out loud, once in your life, do the right thing."

I was weakening. He exhaled and braced a hand against the sink. "Kimber, I feel bad for Martha. And I was wrong to cheat on you. Man, I'm not stupid. But I can't sacrifice myself for her. It's not my fault she got wasted and passed out by the ice machine all night. You take chances, you take the consequences."

This was his hot-oil massage voice that stroked you until you purred. I said, "You've *never* taken the consequences, Lou. Not for anything. I've taken consequences my whole life. My mom walked out, my dad's a failure, I can't pay for college. So when I needed love, I came to you, because you had it all, and I wanted a taste of that. It was pretty good being your lady, and having other girls jealous of me.

"But it wasn't worth it. Not if you can have a great time tonight while Martha loses the only chance she has left to be a kid. I don't care about your cheating. But this is real, Lou. This matters. And you really, truly don't care. And you're going to win in life, and Martha's going to lose, and it doesn't make any sense."

I was hugging myself and feeling ice cold. Lou said, "Wash your face, you look like hell."

He grabbed a paper towel and wet it. I said, "Don't come near me."

He held the dripping towel and then chucked it in the trash can. People were knocking on the door and yelling. Lou said, "Well, I'm getting out of here. You want to come with me and dance?"

I couldn't stand it anymore. "Go to hell," I said.

No. I didn't say that. I can't put down what I said. But I meant it.

I threw my shoulder against the door and it gave. I was in the corridor again, and everyone was staring at me. I shook them off and went out into the lobby. The line for the photographer still stretched across the room. I looked at all the gowns, all the tuxes, all the shining eyes, all the diamonds and gold, all the couples kissing, all the girls leaning back against their guys, smiling up at them, giggling at whispered words.

What the heck am I doing here? I thought.

Well, okay, it was a little self-pitying, but I had good reason. I saw the clock over the coat room. Nine-thirty. A long way from midnight, but I'd had it. I stalked up to the coat room and fished my ticket out of my handbag. "I'd like my coat," I said.

The coat room girl looked at the guy in there with her and gave him the raised eyebrows. I guess they'd seen a lot of fights on Prom Night. I leaned against the checkroom counter, feeling dizzy. *Don't faint*, I told myself.

I grabbed my coat and put it on. Then I walked—still without shoes!—across the lobby and out the doors. I didn't see Sachs or Jaeger or any administrator at that point. Outside, I shuddered in the sudden cool wind, and wondered what the hell to do. I couldn't take the limo, because everyone else had rented it, too.

One of the valets came up to me, a zit-faced kid with hair like straw under his cap. "What's the matter?"

"I want to go home," I said. "Can I get a cab?"

"You sure?"

"Yeah, I'm sure."

He shrugged. "Wait here."

Thank God for teenagers. No questions, no hassle, no feeble attempts to make me see reason. I wanted a cab, he'd get me a cab. I loved him.

And twenty minutes later, I was in the back seat of a cab that smelled like old liquor, rattling along Central Avenue, looking out at the blur of lights and crying my heart out. And that, my dear Author, is how Cinderella got to go to the ball with her Prince Charming!

"Kimber, do *not* tell me that's the end."

Okay, I won't tell you.

"Kimber!"

Don't get hyper. You *know* there's another chapter. Like Rob said to Martha, it ain't over till the fat lady sings.

"Who's the fat lady?"

Check out the cab driver, man!

Chapter Twenty-Two

Just kidding. The cab driver *was* built like a wrestler but she was nice. That cab ride was a major breakthrough for me. Making a scene is easy. But *getting into the cab* and riding away—that took everything I had.

Naturally, I regretted doing it, about ten minutes afterward. A voice inside me kept nudging me: *make her turn around, make her turn around.* But I said *no, I can't turn around any more.*

So I sat back and my chest filled up, and my throat burned. I'd cried so much that I couldn't even touch my cheeks. I thought about everyone at the Prom, and how they'd go to the city later and tell dirty jokes and talk to bag ladies, being kids for the last time.

Without me.

That rotten vision lasted all the way onto the Long Island Expressway. But somewhere around Exit 53, a little sense broke through. Fact was, we'd screwed *up* the chance to be kids for the last time. And when I understood that, I got pissed off. I watched the flat Long Island landscape flow past, and I decided I didn't want to go home yet. First of all, I didn't want to explain to Dad or Corey why I was home early. Second of all, I was knotted up with anger.

So I said, "I want to go to Diamond Point Beach."

The driver gave me a look through the rear view mirror. "By yourself?"

"Yes."

"That's not too bright."

"I'll be okay."

"Why don't I believe you?"

I managed a grotesque smile. "Don't worry. I'm not going to drown myself or anything."

She sighed and shook her head. "I have a daughter about your age. Never tells me anything. Just wants me to leave her alone. 'Don't lecture me, Ma,' she says. 'I gotta learn on my own.' Yeah, so who's gonna keep her from killing herself?"

She shifted her bulk as she headed down Crossland Avenue. The car dealerships and plumbing supply houses were all dark now, and the road reflected the green and red of traffic lights.

The driver yakked about her daughter for the rest of the ride. Finally, the cab rattled down Diamond Point Road, past old private houses. We were surrounded by tall beach grass. I saw the moon split by braided clouds.

The cab squealed to a stop and the driver said, "I'll wait here for you."

"I can't pay you for all that time."

"Don't worry about it. Go have your cry."

"Thanks," I said. I got out of the cab and started walking. My nostrils filled with the pungent smell of salt, dead fish, and dog poop. I know that doesn't sound appetizing, but that's the smell of the beach, and I love it.

Since I didn't have shoes on, it was no problem hiking across the hard, cool sand. It *did* hurt when I walked on coarse grass or stepped on broken shells. (I *hope* they were shells!) Moonlight flooded the black ocean, making silver fire. I listened to the waves and felt the wet wind against my face.

234

I stood on the shore for maybe an hour and I got lost in a romantic dream. I envisioned a galleon in full sail, and a boat making its way to the shore. My pirate captain stood in the prow as his trusty mates rowed. I locked eyes with him, and my bosom heaved. (Hey, it was my *fantasy*, okay?) He leaped from the boat and ran to meet me. I ran, too, my dress billowing. He swept me up and whirled me around and our lips met in a kiss of burning passion. I gazed rapturously into his eyes and I whispered, "Oh, Maxim! I thought I'd never see you again!"

He grinned through his raven beard and he said, "KIMBER! Are you out of your GOURD??"

Wait a minute. That's not right.

I blinked a few times and turned around, dizzy from the mirage. And nearly knocked over Jason.

Jason!

He was still in his tux, but his hair was blowing all over the place. "I don't believe you did this," he said. "We thought you were dead."

For a minute, I couldn't collect my thoughts. I wasn't sure if I was happy to see Jason or not. Then my heart decided I was *very* happy. I threw my arms around him and started crying again. He held onto me ferociously, not as exciting as Maxim, but very reassuring.

Finally, I stepped out of his embrace. We held hands and I kind of looked away, embarrassed. "This is pretty freaky," he said.

I laughed. "How did you find me?"

"Hot tip," he said. "Everything went bananas at the Prom, but I'll tell you about that later . . ."

"*What?*" I said. "Tell me now!"

"No," he insisted. "I've got to keep this in order. Everything went bananas, and that's when we realized you weren't around. We had every teacher and administrator searching for you."

"Yikes," I said softly. "I'm going to be in major trouble, huh?"

"Well, they ain't going to give you a plaque at graduation." He pushed back his hair and went on. "Anyway, Sachs finally found one of the parking attendants . . ."

"Right, he called a cab for me."

Jason gave me a disdainful look. "Yes, we know that *now,* Kimber. So Sachs called the cab company and they checked on all their drivers and found the one who took you, and she told them you were here, and we came after you."

"Who else is here?"

"Everyone's here. Deena and Martha and me . . ."

"Wait wait wait," I said. "Deena and Phil and Martha and Rob and Lou and I came in one limo, and you and Stacey and those other guys went in a different limo. How many limos are here?"

"Just one," Jason said. "We changed the passenger manifest."

"Huh?"

Jason said, "Come on."

He grabbed my hand and led me back. I felt giddy and terrified all at once. As we clambered over a dune, I saw the limo, parked next to the cab.

I saw a few people by the limo. First I saw the driver, who was smoking a cigarette. Then I saw Martha!

And I *yelled* "MARTHA!"

And I *ran* to Martha.

I'm amazed that I didn't finish that night covered with bruises. I nearly knocked Martha flat, which isn't easy for a pipsqueak like me! When we finished hugging I started babbling. "I told Sachs to believe you, and I told Lou to tell the truth, I swear it, Martha, I really tried . . ." and on and on. And Martha babbled back, saying, "I know, I know, shut up and let me tell you, I know, shut up, I know . . ." etc., etc.

Finally, Martha clamped a hand over my mouth.

"You're a fool," Martha said. "You made everything happen and then you ran out."

"I made *what* happen?" I said.

"Where do we start?" Martha said. Then, mischievously, she

added, "Maybe *they* should tell you. They were totally obnoxious all the way out here."

"Who?" I said stupidly. Then I followed Martha's eyes to the back of the limo. The door was open and there, arms folded, like two indicted gang bosses, sat Deena and Lou! On seeing Lou, my pulse fluttered. Instantly, I wanted to take back everything I said, drop to my knees and apologize. Amazing how it stays with you.

But—applause, please—I did not grovel. I looked at Martha and said, "Okay, now I'm *really* upset that I left. Could *someone* fill me in?"

At that point, I learned about everything that had gone on. It was all mixed up together, the story about Deena and Phil and Brett and Jason, the story about me and Lou, and all the rest. Since you already know parts of it, I'll just update you on the parts you *don't* know. And I'll leave out all the back and forth conversation. But try to imagine the bizarre scene during all of this: the limo parked on the sand, the moon-flooded sky above, and a bunch of frazzled teenagers in gowns and tuxedos. It was like one of those weird commercials for perfume.

Okay, here's the updates, told by the same people who told *me*:

DEENA AND PHIL, TOLD BY JASON

I lasted about ten minutes with Stacey and the prime rib, and then I went off to see where Deena went. Deena and Phil were *both* by the pay telephone near the coat room. He was on the phone, and she was *hanging* on him, crying. The coat room attendants were enjoying the show. I bravely hid between a potted plant and a grand piano.

Finally, Phil hung up and Deena renewed her entreaties. I mean, she was *begging*. Phil shook her loose and she went after him. He turned on her and said, "You don't know what love is, Deena. It's a kid's game for you. When you grow up, come see me."

He stopped her cold with that. He did a little pivot on his heel and stalked away. Deena stood there, crumbling. I waited until

Phil was out the door and then I sprang from my hiding place. Well, I didn't exactly spring; I sort of pushed the fronds out of my face.

I went over to Deena and said, "I'm sorry. Want to talk?"

She just stared after Phil. "No. I don't want to talk."

"You want some food?" I asked. "A brownie?"

"*No!*" she snapped. Then she sighed and said, "I know you're being nice, Jason. But it's not good enough. I love him, and he's gone. I don't know what to do."

This was not humorous. Deena had grown up, but the adult Deena had been screwed by the ditzy kid. I knew brownies and hugs wouldn't cut it anymore.

So I said, "Okay. But you can come to my table and sit down."

She stood there for a few minutes, heaving these big, deep sighs. Then she said, "Thanks, Jay. I appreciate it."

So we went back to my table and I sat with her. Stacey was gone. Later, I found out she met a guy who was there with his cousin. I stayed with Deena, and we even danced a little, but her heart and my lust weren't in it. So when Martha came running over and said you'd taken a cab to the beach, I was ready to go, and Deena had nowhere *else* to go.

MARTHA AND ROB, TOLD BY MARTHA

Well, there we were, Rob and I, making out like gangbusters in the back of the limo, drunk as skunks. I mean, the windows were *steamed*. I figured this was my Prom night, so make the most of it.

And then this *rapping* comes on the window: *rat-a-tat-tat*. We both jump up, and my heart is thumping. I'm a total wreck, my hair down and my lipstick all over my face. Rob has this idiotic grin on his face and his lips are still moving!!

"What the hell is *that?*" I whisper.

"I don't know."

Then it comes again: *rat-a-tat-tat*. And I realize: "Holy cow! Someone's knocking on the window!"

238

Rob goes the color of Elmer's glue and starts fumbling with buttons. I fluff my hair and yank at my dress. And in a moment of divine inspiration, I yell, "Who is it?"

"This is Mr. Sachs."

This is Mr. Sachs.

I had the euphoric feeling people who have had death experiences describe. You know, when you float above your body and move toward a peaceful white light? "It's Sachs!" I whispered.

"What's he doing here?"

"Checking limos for people like us."

"What do we do?"

"We have to open the door."

"We're dead."

Actually, we weren't really that panicky because we were still juiced. I wiped my mouth and, sitting up as straight and prim as I could with no brain activity, I pushed open the limo door.

Mr. Sachs stood there, with this blank expression on his face. "Sorry to disturb you," he said, "but we were looking for you and the driver said you were in the car."

"Well," I said, "you didn't let me in the *building*."

I don't know why I got so brazen, but at moments like those, you either act brazen or you freeze. Sachs gave this creepy quarter-smile and said, "Well, that's what I wanted to talk to you about."

I said, "Huh?"

"I just had an interesting discussion with Lou Ross. He backed up your story about the Senior Weekend."

I felt like I'd just reached the top of a roller coaster and started down. "What?"

"He told me he'd seen you by the ice machine and failed to get you back to your room. He confirmed that it was about two in the morning. I asked him why he was at the ice machine that long after lights out and he said he got up with a sore throat and needed ice water." Sachs gave another quarter-smile. "Needless to say, I'll be looking into *that* story. But since you apparently did not commit the act for which we denied you the Prom, you can go inside for the rest of the evening."

I stared at him. Part of me wanted to kiss him, and part of me wanted to beat him to a pulp. The creep didn't even apologize!

But we were in a pretty happy mood, Rob and I, and since we were in no position to be defiant, we said, "YEAH!" and high-fived and low-fived and said, "THANK YOU, MR. *SACHS*!" and scrambled out of the limo.

We scuffled across the parking lot, trying real hard to look steady. My head spun. We went inside and I said to Rob, "I have to use the bathroom."

I squeezed his hand once and lurched across the lobby. I just made it to the lady's room, but not quite to the bowl. I left a pretty gross mess in there. After I cleaned up, I was starving. I found Rob and we went to our table, and of course nobody was there!

I figured everyone would show up soon, and meanwhile I'd enjoy as much of the Prom as I could. We got hold of a waitress and asked for some food and we got up and danced. In the middle of the dance floor, Mrs. Vecchio came up to us and said, "You're Kimber Delaney's friend, right?"

"Yes," I said. "What happened?"

"I'm not sure," Mrs. Vecchio said. "I think she left."

Well, that wrapped it up for the Prom. I left Rob and went to find out about you. Then I got Jason, who dragged Deena along. On the way out, we checked in with Sachs and some A.P.'s. Sachs suggested we take Lou along, since the way it looked, *he* was the one who should be barred from the Prom. Lou didn't argue. He looked like he'd swallowed a toad.

I went to get Rob, and found him at a table with his buddies. I took him aside and hugged him and said that I thought he was an incredible guy and I didn't think he should miss any more of his Prom because of me and that I wouldn't mind if he called me after this weekend. He looked totally relieved and gave me a sweet kiss, and I was gone.

And here we are. And if you weren't such a jerk, we'd still be dancing our little tootsies off.

So finally, we got all our stories told, and there we stood, on the deserted beach, with our limo. We were kind of quiet for a long time, and then I said, "I'm sorry for running out. But when I thought Lou wasn't going to do anything, it just tore it."

Jason threw his arm around me. "No problem. None of us had much to do there anyway."

"Speak for yourself," Martha said. "I'd just gotten *in!*"

I felt my eyes fill again. "I feel like a turd, Martha. I wanted to do something great for you and you had five lousy minutes."

She made a face at me. "They were five great minutes, Bubba. It was getting in that mattered. Anyway, if I didn't get turned away, I'd never know that Rob is super and the Lou possesses a shred of human decency and that I love you more than I love my life."

That did it. An encore hug-and-cry.

When we finished, I said, "Hold on." I went to the cab and leaned over and said, "They're my friends."

The driver smiled. "Okay. Be careful, all right?"

She gave me a price that had to be lower than the real fare, but I gave her a nice tip. She waved, and started to sing along with the radio. I watched the cab trundle down Diamond Point Road until the taillights disappeared.

I walked back to the limo. My feet were killing me by now. Jason was holding up my shoes. "Here, Cinderella," he said. "I was hoping you'd leave a trail of underwear."

"Jerk," I said. I grabbed the shoes, but didn't put them on. No way would my swollen feet make it.

I limped to the limo and bent over. "Lou, " I said. "Thanks."

He glared at me.

"Oh, give it up," I said. "So you performed one adult action in your life. You think they're going to keep you out of graduation? It's all going under the rug, and you know it. So lighten up."

His face kind of moved around, trying to decide on an expression. But he unfolded his arms. "I did it for you," he said. "I wanted to prove myself to you."

"Get a real life," I said. "You knew you'd lost all your harem girls. So you grew up. Now you can return to Never Never Land."

I straightened up. The wind smelled like morning. Martha said, "So what do we do now?" Jason came up behind me and put his arms around my waist. I leaned back against him. He said, "We ride into the sunrise and Kimber slowly falls in love with me."

I smiled. "No way, José."

"Why not?" he said. "You're not going back to Lou *again*?"

"No," I said. "I'm not going back to Lou. And I'm not going to you."

"Who *are* you going to?" Martha asked.

"Nobody," I said. I extricated myself from Jason's grip and stood up straight. I pushed blowing hair out of my eyes. "Look at us, Martha. We're the walking wounded."

Martha laughed. "Yeah, well that's life."

"Bull! It's Prom Night, Martha, and we blew it. I spent a whole year chained to Lou because I was supposed to be in love. You almost destroyed yourself *and* Rob because you *had* to have a boyfriend. Jason sits alone because he's not a hunk. And Deena lost the first guy she really loved because of our stupid-ass rules.

"I mean, it's so dumb. Martha, look: Prom's over. It's goodbye to youth. I have to work to pay my bills. You have to de-tox and Jason has to stop chasing bimbettes with brownies."

Martha said, "What a bummer."

"Tell me about it. And we wasted all the time we had for fun, and flirting, and being kids. Man, you know the only one of us who made sense? Deena."

"Nice head!" Martha commented.

"I'm serious. That's the way it should be. One date after

another. Play around. Play with love. What the heck are we doing with commitments? What happened to the fairy tales, guys? Now we have to say good-bye to that and we never even *had* it."

I shook my head. My bones ached and I was getting a great chest cold. "Well," Martha said. "I guess we go home."

"GO *HOME*?" Jason yelled. "Are you deranged? Why, yes!" And he sang, loudly, "Let's go *HOME, HOME,* I'm *DERANGED . . .*"

"All right!" I yelled.

He spread out his arms. "I am not ready to pack it in, wenches. We're young, we're lusty, we have a limo for eight more hours! Let's not turn into pumpkins yet."

I said, "You're right, Jay! Let's hit the Big Apple!"

"I don't want to attack fruit."

We laughed. Even Lou and Deena smiled. "Where are we headed?" I asked.

Martha said, "How about a shower? I smell like a dead horse."

"Okay, group showers," Jason said. "And then body painting."

I hugged him. "See the car?" I growled. "Get in the car!"

The horizon glowed blue as we shut the limo doors. I sat in between Lou and Jason, and in a silly gesture, I threw an arm around each of them. "Gentlemen," I said. "You can have my body, but *nobody* gets my heart!"

Lou made a sour face, Martha guffawed and Deena looked at the floor. The limo pulled away and I leaned back. *Goodnight, Cinderella,* I said to myself. *Good morning, Life.*

Uh . . . I think that's the end, isn't it?

"What? Oh. Yes, Yes, I guess so."

What's wrong? Are you still ticked off about us taking over the story?

"No. I'm not ticked off at all, Kimber. It was your story; it was the way it should be."

So how come you're so down?

"Not important."

Oh, I bet I know. You like us now. You don't want to say goodbye.

"Perceptive to the end."

Don't be sad. We like you, too. But we're kind of pooped out from reliving this, and we've got to move on. So do you. Other stories, other characters, you know?

"I know. I'll miss you. A lot."

Us, too. Love ya, Babe.

"Take care . . . oops, they're really *gone*. And I can't hang around by myself. So:"

Kimber Delaney and her friends rode away from the beach in their magical black coach. They spent a wild weekend exploring Greenwich Village, playing at Great Adventure, and talking for hours in each other's houses. At the end of the weekend, everybody kissed everyone else good-bye.

And they all graduated and in time they all fell in love (nobody you know) and although nobody lives happily ever after, they all had very interesting lives.

But that's another story. And it's time for all of *you* to be in bed.